SIXKILLER, U.S. MARSHAL:
DAY OF RAGE

SIXKILLER, U.S. MARSHAL:
DAY OF RAGE

William W. Johnstone
with J. A. Johnstone

PINNACLE BOOKS
Kensington Publishing Corp.
www.kensingtonbooks.com

PINNACLE BOOKS are published by

Kensington Publishing Corp.
119 West 40th Street
New York, NY 10018

PUBLISHER'S NOTE
Following the death of William W. Johnstone, the Johnstone family
is working with a carefully selected writer to organize and complete
Mr. Johnstone's outlines and many unfinished manuscripts to create
additional novels in all of his series like The Last Gunfighter, Mountain Man, and Eagles, among others. This novel was inspired by Mr.
Johnstone's superb storytelling.

All Kensington titles, imprints, and distributed lines are available at
special quantity discounts for bulk purchases for sales promotions,
premiums, fund-raising, educational, or institutional use. Special
book excerpts or customized printings can also be created to fit specific needs. For details, write or phone the office of the Kensington
special sales manager: Kensington Publishing Corp., 119 West 40th
Street, New York, NY 10018, attn: Special Sales Department; phone
1-800-221-2647.

PINNACLE BOOKS and the Pinnacle logo are Reg. U.S. Pat. & TM
Off.
The WWJ steer head logo is a trademark of Kensington Publishing
Corp.

ISBN-13: 978-0-7860-2902-0
ISBN-10: 0-7860-2902-1

First printing: October 2012

10 9 8 7 6 5 4 3 2 1

Printed in the United States of America

Chapter One

"Sixkiller! John Henry Sixkiller, is that you?"

At the sound of that friendly voice hailing him, John Henry turned around. He was in Tahlequah, the capital of the Cherokee Nation in Indian Territory, and had quite a few friends here.

And some enemies as well, because the two men who had come up behind him weren't nearly as jovial as that shout had made them sound.

In fact, if the guns they were pointing at him were any indication, they were downright hostile.

The man on the left wore overalls, work shoes, a homespun shirt, and a battered, floppy-brimmed hat. Definitely a farmer by the looks of him. He clutched a shotgun and had the twin barrels leveled menacingly at John Henry.

His companion was better dressed, although not by much. His town suit was threadbare, and he had a derby perched on his head and a pistol in his hand.

Both men were Indians, and John Henry saw a resemblance between them. Brothers, he decided.

It wasn't unusual to see men carrying guns in Tahlequah, but the sight of weapons being pointed at somebody like that was enough to make folks yell in alarm and scurry to get off the street. That was fine with John Henry. The fewer people who were around, the less he had to worry about a stray bullet hitting an innocent bystander.

Because there *were* going to be bullets flying pretty soon, no doubt about that.

For the moment, though, John Henry put a smile on his face and asked, "What can I do for you fellas?"

"What can you do?" said the man with the derby and the pistol. He was sort of short and scrawny, but the gun in his hand meant he couldn't be taken lightly. "You can die, that's what you can do! Just like our brother Doyle done when you shot him, you . . . you damn lawman!"

John Henry lifted his left hand in a conciliatory gesture and said, "Now hold on. It's true enough I'm a lawman. Chief sheriff of the Cherokee Nation, in fact, and a deputy U.S. marshal to boot. So, in which capacity was it that I shot your brother?"

"What in blazes does that matter?" the man with the pistol yelled.

"Well, seeing as how you boys have the drop on me and it's mighty unlikely that I'm going to survive the next couple of minutes, I'd really like to know why I'm about to die. What was your brother's name?"

"Doyle Hilltop, that was his name, you no-good, badge-totin'—"

"Doyle Hilltop," John Henry repeated in a musing tone of voice. "Sure, I remember him. Held up a stagecoach and shot two people dead, as I recall." He shook his head slowly. "I surely do hate to speak ill of anybody's kin, especially after they've passed on, but your brother Doyle was not a good sort. When I went to arrest him, I told him that he had a choice. He could surrender and come back with me for trial, or I could shoot him dead. His pick. Obviously, you know what his decision was."

The Hilltop brother with the shotgun said, "Caleb, are we gonna just stand here and let him run his mouth, or are we gonna shoot him like we said we were?"

"We're gonna shoot him, of course. We said we wanted him to see it comin' and know why he was dyin', and now he does." Caleb Hilltop jabbed the pistol dramatically at John Henry. "You've run your mouth long enough. Time for you to die, lawman!"

"Now hold on, hold on," John Henry said. The street was almost clear. A teamster who'd been coming along behind the Hilltop brothers had stopped his wagon, piled off the seat, and was about to disappear inside a store. "There's just one more thing."

Caleb sneered at him.

"What is it?" he asked. "You gonna get down on your knees and beg for your life, Sixkiller?"

"No," John Henry said. "I'm going to offer you a choice. You can put those guns down and let me take you to jail peacefully, or I'll shoot you dead. Up to you."

"You son of a—"

John Henry took that for his answer.

The Colt on John Henry's hip came out of its holster with blinding speed. He went for the shotgunner first. Caleb's pistol was fairly small in caliber; the odds of surviving a hit from it were a lot higher than those of living through a shotgun blast.

John Henry triggered twice, using the revolver's recoil to help direct his shot. The first bullet went into the shotgunner's chest, the second right between his eyes. Even so, he was still able to jerk the scattergun's triggers, but he was already going over backwards and the double load of buckshot went up into the air at a sharp angle, completely missing John Henry.

Caleb rushed his shot, so John Henry didn't have to worry about whether he'd survive a wound from Caleb's gun. The Colt roared and bucked again in John Henry's hand, and Caleb was knocked halfway around by the impact of the bullet striking his skinny chest and ripping through his left lung.

For a moment, Caleb was able to stay on his feet. He struggled to raise his pistol again. He rasped, "You . . . you lousy . . ."

"Don't blame me," John Henry said as a wisp of

smoke curled from the muzzle of his gun. "I gave you boys a perfectly reasonable choice."

Blood gushed from Caleb's mouth. He dropped his gun and pitched forward on his face.

The other Hilltop brother—John Henry didn't know his name—lay on his back. John Henry checked him first, sliding a boot toe under his shoulder and rolling him onto his side enough to see the gaping hole where the bullet had blown out the back of his skull. Dead, all right, no doubt about that.

The other man was still alive when John Henry got to him, but he died without regaining consciousness, his last, blood-choked breath rattling grotesquely in his throat. John Henry looked around, didn't see any other bodies lying in the street. That was good. He punched the two empty cartridges out of the Colt's cylinder and replaced them with fresh rounds.

"John Henry!"

This time the shout wasn't meant as the prelude to an ambush. John Henry recognized the voice and holstered his gun as he turned around. He saw Captain Charles LeFlore of the Cherokee Lighthorse, the tribal police force, hurrying toward him, trailed by a couple of other policemen.

"Hello, Captain," John Henry said with a faint smile. "I reckon you heard the shooting."

"Tahlequah's not so big that the sounds of a gun battle go unnoticed," LeFlore said. "Who'd you shoot now?"

"You mean who did I *have* to shoot," John Henry said. "I gave them a choice, but they didn't give me one."

"Uh-huh." LeFlore looked past John Henry at the limp, motionless bodies. "So who are they?"

"The smaller one is Caleb Hilltop. The other one is his brother, but I don't know his name."

"Any relation to Doyle Hilltop?"

"He was their brother."

LeFlore nodded and said, "That explains why they threw down on you, then. You killed Doyle, as I recall."

"That I did. In the line of duty."

"Sure. Same as these two killings." LeFlore paused. "John Henry, how long you been in town?"

John Henry glanced at his horse Iron Heart, tied up at a hitch rack a few feet away, and said, "Oh, about five minutes, I suppose."

"That's sort of what I thought," Captain LeFlore said dryly. He motioned for the other policemen to take care of the bodies, then went on, "Were you headed to my office when these fellas interrupted your day, by any chance?"

"I was," John Henry said.

"Well, let's head on over there, then. I'll walk with you. I needed to talk to you anyway."

"About what?"

Captain LeFlore had been John Henry's boss, the one who had recruited him into the Cherokee Lighthorse in the first place so John Henry would have the legal standing to go after the murderer who had killed his father. Now, with John Henry being chief sheriff as well as a deputy U.S. marshal, the two men were of roughly equal standing. If anything, John Henry outranked his old boss, although he wouldn't have felt comfortable giving orders to Captain LeFlore.

"I got a message for you from Judge Parker," LeFlore said in answer to John Henry's question. "He wants to see you in Fort Smith."

John Henry nodded and said, "That's where I was headed when I left here."

"The judge sounded like he was sort of in a hurry to see you, John Henry. I don't think I'd linger too long in Tahlequah if I was you."

John Henry grinned and said, "Why, if I didn't know better I'd say that you were trying to get rid of me, Captain."

"Well . . . I guess it's good for the undertaker . . . but the bodies do tend to pile up a mite whenever you're around."

Chapter Two

Southwestern New Mexico Territory—several weeks earlier

The two men on the wagon kept glancing around nervously as the vehicle rolled down a fairly steep mountain trail toward the plains below, where the settlement of Purgatory was located. Four men on horseback rode with the wagon, two ahead and two behind, and they were equally wary.

They had good reason to be worried. In the back of the wagon, covered with canvas, was a cargo of gold bullion from the San Francisco Mine, named after the mountains that loomed above them and the river that ran through the valley to the east. The load was worth thousands of dollars and would be a tempting target for any outlaw or road agent.

They didn't have to be concerned about just any would-be thief who came along, though. In these parts, one group seemed to hold a monopoly on lawlessness: the gang of kill-crazy bandits led by Billy Ray Gilmore.

For months now Gilmore and his gang had been preying on the law-abiding inhabitants of this corner of New Mexico Territory. They had started out fairly small, holding up a couple of stagecoaches bound for Purgatory from Lordsburg, then robbing some freighters of the money they'd collected for some supplies they'd brought to the mining town. One of the freighters had taken exception to being robbed and tried to fight back, but he'd been gunned down without mercy before he could get off a single shot from his rifle.

As if that brutal murder had been a signal, the outlaws became even more ruthless and bloodthirsty over the succeeding weeks. They held up several gold shipments from the three big mines in the area, Jason True's San Francisco, Arnold Goodman's El Halcón, and Dan Lacey's Bonita Mine. If a driver didn't do exactly what the outlaws told him to, and quickly enough to suit them, they didn't hesitate to blast the luckless hombre. The same was true of the shotgun guards and the outriders sent with the shipments. Half a dozen men were dead as a result of the jobs that Gilmore's gang had pulled.

It had gotten to the point that not many men wanted the job of accompanying those shipments. The chore was just too blasted dangerous these days. Jason True had been forced to double the wages these men were going to collect for taking the gold to Purgatory.

Double wages wouldn't do a man any good if he was dead, though, and these guards all knew that.

Beads of sweat stood out on their faces as they headed down the trail toward Purgatory, and that didn't have anything to do with the heat.

"They always hit in the mountains," the driver, Chet Simmons, said. "If we can make it to the flats, we'll be all right."

The shotgun guard next to him, Jack Whitfield, swallowed hard and tightened his grip on the double-barreled weapon he held across his lap.

"How much longer before we're down from here?" he asked.

"Twenty minutes maybe," Simmons said. "Can't rush those mules. As steep as the trail is, if we try to go too fast the wagon'll get away from us. Wouldn't want to run over those boys ridin' ahead of us."

"Don't want to get ambushed, either," Whitfield muttered.

His eyes roved constantly over the surrounding terrain. A steep, almost sheer mountainside rose to the left of them, while to the right the ground fell away in an almost equally steep slope dotted with boulders and clumps of hardy brush.

The trail itself, though, was nice and wide and there weren't any hairpin turns. Whitfield could see for several miles ahead of them. In fact, in this clear, dry air, he thought he could make out the settlement down in the valley, which was still a good seven or eight miles away.

Up higher, they'd had to travel through several passes that were prime sites for an ambush, and Whitfield's heart had been in his throat the whole way. Nothing had happened, and once they were past those places he'd begun to breathe a little easier. He was far from convinced, though, that they were out of danger.

Something made him turn his head and look up to the left. The slope in that direction ran upward for maybe a hundred feet before it leveled off into a narrow shoulder. A few pretty good-sized boulders perched on the edge of that shoulder.

As Whitfield watched, one of those boulders moved, rocking back and forth for a second and then overbalancing, toppling forward to roll down the mountainside. It started to bounce, the *whump! whump! whump!* of the impacts sounding like a giant stomping toward them.

"Look out, Chet!" Whitfield yelled.

There weren't enough loose rocks for the falling boulder to start an avalanche, but it was a danger in itself. The two outriders in front of the wagon jerked back on their reins and wheeled their mounts, which was a mistake. One of the men barely had time to scream before the big rock hit him and his horse and carried both of them over the brink on the other side of the trail.

More rocks were already crashing down toward the wagon and the men accompanying it. The racket was terrifying and disorienting. Simmons brought the wagon to a halt, and Whitfield flung the shotgun to his shoulder.

But there was nothing to shoot at. Buckshot wouldn't stop a five-hundred-pound boulder. One of the falling rocks landed on the wagon team, crushing two of the mules to bloody pulp. Another was headed straight for the driver's seat. Simmons and Whitfield dived off the vehicle just in time to avoid being smashed as well. They landed on the hard-packed ground to the left of the wagon, which now sat at an angle because the weight of the boulder striking it had snapped the front axle.

One of the outriders behind the wagon suffered the same fate as his comrade up front. A boulder struck him and knocked him over the edge of the trail. More than likely he was killed by the impact, but if he wasn't, the fall would kill him.

Shots sounded from up the trail. Whitfield looked in that direction and saw half a dozen riders charging down at them with guns blazing. The remaining outrider behind the wagon was driven from his saddle by outlaw lead. Whitfield lifted the shotgun and Simmons clawed his revolver from its holster, but both men knew they were probably doomed.

Still, they were Western men, and they weren't going to give up without a fight.

It didn't last long. Whitfield felt the fiery lance of a bullet piercing his shoulder and dropped the shotgun. He went to his knees and scrambled to pick it up despite the pain in his arm and shoulder. Beside him, Chet Simmons grunted and rocked back as slugs punched into him. Simmons collapsed, blood welling from his mouth and from three wounds in his chest.

Whitfield heard rapid hoofbeats from the other direction and glanced over his shoulder as he fumbled with the shotgun. The lone surviving outrider was lighting a shuck, galloping away down the trail as fast as his horse would carry him. Whitfield felt a surge of anger at the man for abandoning them like that, then realized that he might very well have done the same thing if he'd been in that position.

He couldn't seem to pick up the shotgun. His muscles just wouldn't work well enough. Then dust swirled around him as the outlaws rode up. One of them dismounted, gun in hand, and strode over to where Whitfeild knelt beside the gold wagon. He put a booted foot on the shotgun's barrels just to make sure Whitfield couldn't use it.

Gasping for breath, sweating, bleeding from his wounded shoulder, Whitfield looked up at the outlaw, who smiled down at him and said, "Looks like you're out of luck, amigo." The man wasn't very big, but he gave off such an air of menace that he seemed larger than he really was. Whitfield recognized him.

Billy Ray Gilmore. Wanted in several states and territories for murder, robbery, rape, and other crimes, all heinous, before he'd brought his gang and his particular brand of villainy to New Mexico Territory. Just to look at him, he didn't seem like a monster.

But Whitfield knew that he was, and Gilmore confirmed that by saying, "So long," and thumbing back the hammer of his gun.

Whitfield heard the roar of the shot that sent a bullet smashing through his brain, but that was all.

"Billy Ray, this is too damn much like work," Duke Rudd said as he and the other men loaded bullion into pouches slung over the backs of the pack mules they had brought down the trail. "First, some of us have to sweat like field hands leverin' those boulders off the rim up there, and now we got to tote all this heavy gold. If the team hadn't got squashed, we could've just turned the wagon around and hauled the loot away in it."

"Unfortunately, you can't really aim a boulder too well," Gilmore said as he sat on the wagon's lowered tailgate, supervising the operation. Flies had started to buzz around the bodies of the dead men and mules, and they were getting on his nerves. He went on, "We knew we'd probably have to pack the bullion out. That's why we were ready."

"I know, I know," Rudd said. "And I reckon I shouldn't complain about havin' to tote gold." A familiar cocky grin creased his face. "It's just that we're outlaws. The idea is, we take what we want from other folks so we don't have to work for it ourselves."

Gilmore chuckled instead of letting himself get annoyed with Rudd.

"That's true, but there's one thing you've got to remember, Duke," he said. "Nothin's free in this world. You may think you've had a fortune fall right in your lap and it's all due to good luck, but somehow, sometime, you've still got to pay a price for it. We're payin' that price today, by havin' to load up this gold."

"Well . . . some of us are payin' it," Rudd said. His grin took any sting out of the words.

"My part of the payin' was comin' up with the idea in the first place," Gilmore bantered back at him.

"How much you reckon this bullion's worth?" Sam Logan, another of the outlaws, asked as he took off his hat and mopped his forehead with his bandanna.

"Plenty," Gilmore answered. "It was worth the lives of five men, I know that much." He squinted up at the peaks of the San Francisco range, where the mines were located. "And here's the best part . . . there's more where that came from."

Chapter Three

The Barrymore House was the best hotel in Purgatory. It was also the only real hotel, since the other places in town that rented rooms were attached to saloons and the men who stayed there were just as interested in whiskey and whores as they were in a place to sleep.

Jason True had a home in Santa Fe, but he kept a suite in the hotel in Purgatory, too, because he was here quite a bit of the time tending to the business of the San Francisco Mining Company, of which he was the president and chief stockholder. Sometimes when people heard the name, they assumed that his mine must be in California, and he had to explain that San Francisco was also the name of the mountain range that ran just east of the border between New Mexico and Arizona Territories.

This evening, his hand shook a little as he poured brandy from a crystal decanter into three heavy tumblers. True was a man with a stiff-backed stance—a

holdover from his days as a colonel in the army—
iron-gray hair, and a neatly clipped mustache.

Back home in Santa Fe, if he was going to serve
brandy to his guests his wife, Laurinda, would insist
that he use the expensive snifters, he thought. In a
rough mining town like Purgatory, nobody really
cared what a man drank his booze out of. They just
held out their glasses or cups or canteens for more.

He handed one of the tumblers to Arnold Goodman, another to Dan Lacey, and kept the third one
for himself. As he raised the drink, he said, "I'd say
cheers, but there's nothing to celebrate tonight.
Absolutely nothing."

"You're right about that," Goodman said.

He was short and wide, built like a tree stump,
and his face was about as blunt and hard as a stump,
too. He was from back East someplace, True didn't
know exactly where, and a few years earlier he had
bought the struggling El Halcón Mine from the
Mexican ranchero who'd originally owned it as part
of a land grant legacy.

The gamble had paid off for Goodman, not so
much for the ranchero. A couple of months later,
workers in El Halcón had come across a previously
undiscovered vein of ore that had made the mine
quite successful.

"Do you know how much you lost, Jason?" Lacey
asked. Like True, he was originally from the Mid-
west, a wiry, balding man who ran the Bonita Mining
Corporation with an iron fist despite his mild ap-
pearance.

True shook his head and said, "The bullion hadn't been weighed and assayed yet, of course. Eight thousand dollars, perhaps. A significant amount, certainly."

"But not as much as you stood to lose if you'd sent down all the bullion you have on hand," Goodman pointed out.

"That's right. But the bullion doesn't do me a damned bit of good sitting up there at my mine, either."

The three men had gathered here in the sitting room of True's suite at the Barrymore House. True had sent for his fellow mine owners as soon as he received word of the attack on his gold wagon that afternoon. The surviving outrider had reached town and reported the holdup to the local lawman, Marshal Henry Hinkle, who had made noises about getting a posse together, but in the end hadn't done anything about going after the outlaws . . . as usual.

Today's violence had Jason True at the end of his patience. He was about to do something he didn't particularly want to do, but he didn't see that he had any choice.

"I think it's time we go ahead with what we talked about before," he continued. "The three of us have always been rivals, but we're going to have to put that aside."

"We've been rivals," Lacey said, "but not enemies. There's a big difference. I'm perfectly willing to work together on this matter."

Goodman frowned but didn't say anything. After a moment, True said, "How about it, Arnold? What do you think?"

"It goes against the grain to help the competition," Goodman said. "That's not the way I've done business all these years. But it's obvious none of us can handle this by ourselves. Maybe if we throw in together we can stop those damned outlaws from bankrupting us!"

Lacey smiled and lifted his glass.

"Maybe that's worth saying cheers to," he suggested. "Arnold Goodman actually being reasonable."

Goodman didn't seem to take offense at the words. In fact, a curt bark of laughter came from him. He threw back the rest of his drink.

"All right," True said as he placed his empty glass next to the decanter on the sideboard. "We each have approximately $25,000 worth of gold bullion at our mines in the mountains. If the three of us go in together, we can hire enough guards to transport that bullion safely down here to Purgatory, one mine at a time."

"Where it'll have to sit and wait until the gold from the other mines is brought down," Goodman said. "I don't like that part of it very much."

Lacey said, "That worries me a little, too, Jason."

"The bullion will be locked up securely in the bank," True said. "It'll be guarded around the clock. Gilmore won't try for it right here in the middle of town."

"Are you sure about that?" Goodman asked. "He

and his men don't seem to mind coming into town and running roughshod over the citizens any time they want." His tone became even more scornful as he added, "You can be sure that Hinkle's not going to do anything about it. How did a man like that ever become marshal, anyway? He's nothing but a blasted coward!"

"Nobody else wanted the job," Lacey said. His mining operation had been here in Purgatory longer than the other two. "Gilmore and his bunch hadn't shown up yet to make our lives miserable, of course, but Purgatory was still a pretty wild place. How do you think it got its name? The respectable citizens insisted that the town had to have a marshal, but they couldn't find anybody who'd take the badge until Henry Hinkle did it."

"Not exactly a town tamer, is he?" True said.

"Maybe not, but things *did* improve a little. My personal feeling is that all the folks who'd been raising hell looked at Hinkle and realized they'd be embarrassed to shoot down such a . . . well, such a craven coward. I sometimes think that's all that's kept Hinkle alive."

True shook his head in disgust.

"And that's what we have to rely on for law and order around here. No wonder it's become clear that we're going to have to take things into our own hands. It's agreed, then, gentlemen? We pool our resources, do whatever is necessary to get our gold down here, and then ship it out at the same time with Wells Fargo?"

"Agreed," Lacey said. Goodman just jerked his blocky head in a nod.

"All right," True said. He reached for the brandy again. "I think we ought to have another drink on that."

What he didn't mention to either of the others as he poured the brandy into their tumblers was that he had another idea to go along with the one he had just proposed and they had agreed to. True didn't know if it would work out or not, but after losing another gold shipment today he was willing to try anything.

Nor was he going to reveal his plan to his new allies. They might be working together for the moment, but sooner or later they would all be rivals again.

And when that day arrived, Jason True intended to be the one who came out on top.

Billy Ray Gilmore downed the shot of whiskey, set the empty glass on the hardwood in front of him, and patted the shapely rump of the bar girl called Della, who was leaning close beside him, trying to convince him to take her upstairs.

"I'm afraid I don't have the time right now, darlin'," he told her. "I got to see a man about a horse."

Della pouted prettily. She was a honey blonde about twenty years old, and she'd been working in saloons for a short enough time that she still had her looks. Her fresh-faced beauty made her popular and, normally, Gilmore would have been glad to go upstairs with her, but he was in Purgatory tonight on business.

"I'm disappointed, Billy Ray," she said. "I had my heart set on spending some time with you tonight."

"No need to feel like that," he told her. "You know there's a dozen men in here who'd fall all over their boots for a chance to take you upstairs."

"Yeah, but none of them is Billy Ray Gilmore."

He grinned and said, "I am a notorious individual, aren't I?"

It was an odd situation. The first few jobs Gilmore and his gang had pulled in this part of the territory, they had always worn masks. People had a pretty good idea who was responsible for those holdups, but nobody could stand up in court and testify beyond a doubt that Billy Ray and his boys were the culprits.

They weren't as careful about concealing their identities these days, but they didn't leave many witnesses alive, either. And by now folks were too *scared* to identify them, afraid that would mean a bullet in the back some dark night, or a house burned down around them.

So the county sheriff, Elmer Stone, had no real evidence to go on, and Purgatory's marshal, Henry Hinkle . . . well, Hinkle was worthless no matter how you looked at it. Anyway, Gilmore and his men hadn't committed any serious crimes inside the town limits.

So for now they came and went as they pleased, enjoying the comforts and entertainment the town had to offer, such as the Silver Spur Saloon where Gilmore was at the moment. He told Della that maybe he would see her later and sauntered out of the place.

"I'll probably be busy!" she called after him as he pushed though the bat wings. That drew a chuckle from him. He didn't doubt that she would be busy, but if he wanted the pleasure of her company, whoever she was with wouldn't waste any time lighting a shuck and leaving her to him.

Gilmore walked a block or so and then turned down a dark alley. He followed it to the rear of a building and stood there waiting until a door opened somewhere nearby and let a shaft of light spill out. Whoever was inside blew out the lamp in the room. Gilmore heard the puff of air.

Then a moment later a man's voice asked softly, "Are you out there?"

"I'm here," Gilmore said. "Everything go as planned?"

"Exactly as planned. Give it a few weeks and we're both going to be very rich men, my friend."

"I like the sound of that."

Not the part about being friends, Gilmore thought. He wasn't this man's friend and never would be.

But the part about being very rich . . .

That was sweet, sweet music to Billy Ray Gilmore's ears.

Chapter Four

Fort Smith, Arkansas

The town of Fort Smith perched on a bluff over-looking the winding course of the Arkansas River. It was the gateway to Indian Territory, which to some people meant that it was the last outpost of civilization.

Those people were somewhat ignorant, because the Indians who made their homes over there in the Territory weren't called the Five Civilized Tribes for no reason. In many ways, the Cherokee, Choctaw, Chickasaw, Creek, and Seminole were just as civilized as their white brethren. They had schools, churches, businesses, farms, and ranches. They had their own written language and their own newspaper. They lived in towns and dressed much like the white man dressed.

And in some ways, John Henry Sixkiller mused as he rode into Fort Smith, the tribes were more civilized than the whites. After all, they had never forced their peaceful neighbors to pick up and move for no good reason, never driven an entire people into a pilgrimage over a route that took so many lives it came to be known as the Trail of Tears, as the whites had done with their Indian Removal Act.

John Henry felt no personal animosity toward white people because of that history. For one thing, he was half white himself. His father James Sixkiller had met his mother, Elizabeth, during the trip west and married her after the two of them fell in love. John Henry had been born in Indian Territory. It was the only real home he had ever known. And while he knew from listening to the old-timers that Indian Territory was considerably different from the lush forests of the East, it turned out to be pretty good land that would support people if they were willing to work.

And Indians, despite the reputation they had with some as lazy, were always willing to work hard when it came to taking care of their families, John Henry knew.

He rode straight to the big, redbrick federal courthouse where Judge Isaac C. Parker had his office. As a member of the Cherokee Lighthorse, John Henry's jurisdiction had been restricted to Indian Territory, and he wasn't allowed to arrest white criminals or even to interfere with them, a rule he had bent from time to time when the situation made it necessary.

When Judge Parker had offered to appoint him

as a deputy United States marshal, John Henry had accepted with no hesitation. For one thing, that appointment had saved him from being tried for murder in the deaths of two white outlaws he'd been forced to shoot. For another, with the power of the federal government behind him, he could go after the desperadoes who plagued the frontier, whether they were red, white, black, or brown, and stay on their trail no matter where they went. That sort of freedom was very important to someone like John Henry, who was determined to bring law and order to the West.

He tied Iron Heart at the hitch rack in front of the courthouse and glanced toward the gallows that sat off to the side of the big building. It was a permanent structure and quite impressive in its grim way, because it was big enough that six men could be hanged at once there. During the years since Isaac Parker's appointment to the bench, enough badmen had dropped through those trapdoors that Parker was starting to be called the Hanging Judge.

John Henry walked past two men who were leaving the courthouse and talking to each other in the soft, drawling accents of Texans. He climbed the steps and went inside, heading straight for Parker's office. He took off his hat, knocked on the door, and opened it when the judge called, "Come in."

Parker was behind his big desk. He got to his feet. He was a compact man with a neatly trimmed beard. Wearing his habitually solemn expression, he extended a hand to his visitor.

"Marshal Sixkiller," Parker said. "Good to see you. Did you just get here?"

"That's right," John Henry said.

Parker grunted and motioned him into a leather chair in front of the desk.

"Then you missed all the excitement. We had some prisoners try to escape."

"I'm sorry I wasn't here to lend a hand," John Henry said as he balanced his hat on his knee.

"Oh, that's all right. A couple of Texans pitched in and helped us round them up." Parker began looking through some of the papers on his desk. "I wanted to see you on an entirely different matter. That's why I sent a note to Captain LeFlore asking him to send you directly here if he saw you."

"Yes, sir," John Henry said. "I came as soon as I heard. What can I do for you?"

"Ah, here it is." Parker picked up one of the pieces of paper. "This is a letter from an old friend of mine. His name is Jason True. Have you heard of him?"

John Henry shook his head and said, "No, sir, I don't think so."

"Well, no reason you should have. He owns a gold mine in New Mexico Territory, near the Arizona border. Rugged country, from what I hear, and virtually lawless."

"I imagine so," John Henry said, although he had no real knowledge of the area. In his lifetime he had only been to Indian Territory, Arkansas, and Kansas.

Parker went on, "It seems that Jason and the other mine owners in the area have been having trouble with a gang of outlaws stealing their gold shipments. They bring the gold down from the mountains where the mines are located to a settlement called Purgatory."

"That doesn't sound promising," John Henry said with a slight smile.

"The town is well named, from what I know of it," Parker agreed. "From Purgatory, the gold is taken to Lordsburg and shipped out by rail with Wells Fargo. Ultimately, of course, it winds up at the mint in Denver. Therefore, any interference with that gold falls under federal jurisdiction."

John Henry wasn't sure why the judge was telling him all this. As a deputy appointed to Judge Parker's court, he served in the Western Federal District of Arkansas, which meant Indian Territory and part of Kansas.

He was about to ask Parker what this had to do with him when the judge continued, "In approximately one week's time, Jason and the other two large mine owners, men named Goodman and Lacey, are going to pool their resources and assemble a massive shipment of gold in Purgatory. Wells Fargo has agreed to take responsibility for it there."

John Henry frowned and said, "That sounds a

little risky. Like the old saying about putting all your eggs in one basket."

"They believe that the gold will be safe there, if they can get it to town. All the holdups so far have taken place between the mines and Purgatory. Instead of each mine owner hiring guards to bring down their gold, they're going in together to hire a large enough force to keep it safe. It seems like a plan with a reasonable chance of success."

"Maybe," John Henry said. "You can't ever predict what some bandit's going to do, though."

Parker shook his head and said, "No, of course not. But there's a risk in anything."

"And I'd still be worried about having that much gold in one place. How much did you say it's going to amount to, Judge?"

"I didn't," Parker said dryly. "But Jason estimates that the total will be around $75,000."

John Henry couldn't help it. He let out a low whistle.

"That's a mighty big pile of gold, Your Honor. If it belonged to me . . . if even a third of it belonged to me . . . I'd be more than worried. I'd be downright scared."

Parker tapped the letter he had laid back down on the desk.

"That's why Jason wrote to me. Since any attempt to steal that gold would be a federal crime, he asked if I could send him a deputy marshal to help protect it."

"New Mexico Territory's sort of out of our baili-wick, isn't it?" John Henry asked.

"Normally, yes. Jason should have sent his re-quest to the chief marshal in Denver. But as I said, Jason is an old friend, so he turned to me instead. There's another angle to consider, too. Whoever is sent to Purgatory to look after that gold might be able to do so more effectively if it's not widely known that he's a federal officer. That way if the outlaws do make a play for it, he can take them by surprise."

"Begging your pardon, Judge," John Henry said, "but I think I can see the trail you're laying down here. You want me to go to New Mexico and make sure that gold gets where it's supposed to go."

"That's the idea, yes," Parker said with a nod. "Your record speaks for itself, Deputy Sixkiller. De-spite your relative youth, you're an experienced lawman, and you've found yourself in a number of tight spots. The fact that you're still here says something about your abilities."

"And nobody in New Mexico is liable to recog-nize me as a deputy marshal, that's for sure."

"Exactly. Because of my friendship with Jason, I consider this to be a personal matter, at least to an extent, so I'm loathe to make it an order. . . ."

John Henry smiled and said, "No need to worry about that, Your Honor. A federal lawman has jurisdiction anywhere in the country, right?"

"That's right. Your badge means just as much in New Mexico as it does here."

Picking up his hat from his knee, John Henry leaned forward. He said, "There's one problem, though. Iron Heart's pretty fast, but I don't think he can get all the way from here to the other side of New Mexico in a week."

"We'll put you on the train. You can be in Lordsburg in a couple of days." Parker smiled and added, "Jason can reimburse the federal government for that expense. There's a stagecoach from Lordsburg to Purgatory."

"That sounds pretty good." John Henry paused. "But I was wondering . . . Is there any chance you could put Iron Heart on the train, too, and I could ride him to Purgatory? I can make almost as good time that way as traveling by stagecoach."

Parker gave him a severe look, and John Henry figured he had pushed things too far. Then the judge abruptly let out a laugh and said, "Jason can pay the freight on that horse of yours, too, if that's the way you want it. What do you say, Deputy?"

"I say I'm on my way to New Mexico," John Henry replied with a smile.

Chapter Five

In Purgatory, Duke Rudd and Sam Logan were bored. Both men had been outlaws since they were in their teens, and when they weren't busy robbing and killing, sometimes they found that they didn't know what to do with themselves. And Billy Ray just kept telling them to be patient, claiming that there was a big job coming up but the time wasn't right for it yet.

So here they sat at a table in the Silver Spur, nursing beers. Logan was playing a game of solitaire with a deck of greasy, dog-eared cards. Rudd wasn't interested in cards. He just scowled as he looked around the room.

"Might as well be in a damn cemetery," he muttered. "It's sure enough dead in here."

"It's early," Logan said without looking up from his cards. "Place'll get busier later on."

"Well, what if I don't want to wait for later on? What if I want some excitement right now?"

"Then I guess you'll have to manufacture your own. Why don't you take one of the gals upstairs?"

"Because the only one down here right now is that damned Linda Sue," Rudd snapped. "I swear, my horse is better lookin' than her."

"Then why don't you—"

Logan must have sensed the look Rudd was giving him, because he didn't finish that sentence. Instead, he frowned at his cards and moved some of them around so he could continue playing. That was cheating, sure, but he didn't figure it really mattered since he wasn't likely to shoot himself over it.

"Anyway, I'm a mite low on funds," Rudd went on.

"I know. Billy Ray don't give us enough spendin' money. As much loot as we've got stashed at the hideout, seems like we ought to be flush all the time."

"He says he wants to save it up and not do the divvy until we're ready to rattle our hocks and shake the dust of New Mexico off our boots. Well, how long is that gonna be, I ask you? How much is enough?"

"Money's like sweet lovin' from a gal," Logan said with a grin. "Ain't no such thing as enough."

"Maybe so, but I'm gettin' tired of just sittin' around and waitin'— All right."

Logan glanced up.

"All right what? What's goin' on?"

Rudd nodded toward the staircase at the side of the big barroom.

"Look who's woke up and comin' downstairs," he said.

The pretty blonde called Della was descending the stairs. As Rudd and Logan watched her, she stifled a yawn. Her hair had been brushed but was still a little tousled from sleep. She paused halfway down, grasped the low neckline of her dress, and gave it a tug to adjust it over her breasts.

"Lordy," Rudd breathed. "You ever had her, Sam?"

Logan shook his head.

"She charges more than the other gals, and she can get away with it, too, lookin' like she does. Besides, I, uh, think that she's kinda sweet on Billy Ray. She's always hangin' all over him when he's in here."

"Yeah, but he ain't sweet on her, is he?" Rudd asked. "I mean, she don't mean nothin' special to him. I never knew Billy Ray to get moony-eyed over any gal in particular. So he hadn't ought to mind if I was to spend some time in Miss Della's company."

"I thought you said you didn't have any money," Logan said.

"I've been savin' some back for somethin' special." Rudd licked his lips as Della reached the bottom of the stairs. "And if that ain't special, I never seen anything that is."

Logan shook his head and said, "Go ahead. Don't be too surprised if she laughs in your face, though."

"Why in the hell would she do that?" Rudd asked with a puzzled frown.

"Because you're about the ugliest peckerwood south of the Picket Wire!" Logan said.

Rudd glared and said, "I reckon I'll shoot you for sayin' that, Sam. One of these days I will, you just wait and see. But not today." He downed the rest of the beer in his mug, stood up, and hitched his trousers a little higher. "Today I got more important business to take care of."

"You do that," Logan said, apparently unconcerned about Rudd's death threat. He rearranged the cards again in his solitaire game.

Rudd cocked his hat at a jaunty angle and crossed the room to the bar. Three men were drinking there, none of them paying any attention to the others. Della was near the end of the bar, talking to Linda Sue and the bartender, a consumptive-looking gent named Meade.

As he came up to them, Rudd ignored Linda Sue and Meade and said, "Good day to you, Miss Della. Remember me? Duke Rudd? We've spoke before."

"Why, of course I remember you, Duke," Della replied with a smile. "How are you?"

Rudd thought it was likely Della would have claimed to remember any man who spoke to her, whether she really did or not. Whores were that way. But he didn't care. He said, "I'm doin' fine, I reckon. But I'd be even finer if you'd go upstairs with me and allow me the pleasure of your company for a spell."

"Oh," she said. "Oh, Duke. I'm flattered. But it's

early in the day and I really haven't been awake that long."

"It's after noon," Rudd pointed out.

"Well, that's early for me, honey." Della paused. "Besides, I sort of doubt that you'd be able to afford me."

"How much?" Rudd asked.

Linda Sue laughed and said, "Boy, he comes right out with it, don't he?"

"I'm willin' to pay," Rudd went on. "Just tell me how much."

Della glanced at the bartender. Rudd thought she might have been appealing to Meade to get rid of him, but the man pointedly looked away and started wiping the bar with a rag, each movement taking him a little farther away. The message was clear: He wasn't going to interfere with one of Billy Ray Gilmore's men.

Looking a little annoyed by Meade's desertion, Della said curtly, "Ten dollars."

That brought another laugh from Linda Sue. She said, "Lord, who do you think you're talkin' to, Della, the president of these here United States? Nobody's gonna pay ten dollars for a poke."

"Not if you're the one they're pokin'," Rudd said.

Linda Sue drew back and frowned. She said, "Well, that's rude."

"No, it's Rudd. Duke Rudd." He reached into his pocket and brought out a ten-dollar gold piece. He slapped the eagle on the bar and said to Della, "There you go."

She looked surprised that he had actually met her price. Called her bluff, as it were. And now there was nothing she could do about it.

"Fine," she said, not sounding happy about it. Her hand moved over the eagle and swooped down on it like the coin's namesake. "Let's go."

She turned and led the way toward the stairs. Rudd divided his time between watching the appealing sway of her rear end in the tight dress and smirking in triumph at Logan, who sat there openmouthed.

As she started up the stairs, Della looked over her shoulder at Rudd and said, "You don't get anything special for that price, so don't even think about it."

"Just bein' with you is special enough for me, darlin'," Rudd assured her.

She took him along the balcony to her room on the second floor, which was spartanly furnished with a narrow bed, an old wardrobe with the doors taken off of it, a ladderback chair, and a small table that had one leg shorter than the others. The only remotely feminine touch was a gauzy yellow curtain over the single window.

Della put the gold piece on the table next to a basin of water. With her back turned to Rudd, she said, "Unbutton my dress for me."

"Oh, I'd be glad to," he said.

His blunt fingers weren't really meant for delicate work, though, and in his eagerness he fumbled even more than he might have otherwise. Della sighed in impatient exasperation.

"Hang on, hang on," he told her. "I'm gettin' it."

"I sure hope you're better at other things than you are at this, Duke," she said.

For some reason that really rubbed him the wrong way. Ever since he'd walked up to her at the bar, she'd been talking to him like she looked down on him. Her, a whore, doing that. It just wasn't right.

So without thinking much about what he was doing, he grasped her dress where he had already gotten a couple of the buttons unfastened and wrenched the fabric in opposite directions. Buttons popped and cloth tore, and Della exclaimed, "Hey! What the hell—"

Rudd ripped the dress all the way down the back, exposing the short, thin shift she wore under it. She opened her mouth to scream, but Rudd gave her a hard shove that sent her sprawling facedown on the bed. He threw himself on top of her and planted a hand on the back of her head, shoving her face into the bedding to muffle any cries.

"I don't let no damn whore talk to me that way," he said in a low voice as he leaned down close to her ear. His other hand tore the shift from her.

Her right hand slid under the pillow and came out with a straight razor that she opened with a practiced flick of her wrist. She swiped back with it and he felt the blade's fiery bite on his thigh where it sliced through his jeans and into his flesh. He yelled and jumped back.

She rolled over on the bed, moving fast, and

slashed at him again, but this time he was able to grab her wrist. A brutal twist made her hand open. The razor fell to the mattress. Rudd swept it off onto the floor.

Then in an extension of the same motion, he backhanded Della across the face. The blow landed with a sharp crack and jerked her head to the side. Curses and even worse filth spewed from Rudd's mouth as he hit her again. She was still conscious, but she went limp, all the fight going out of her.

"You're gonna pay for what you done," he threatened as he loomed over her. "I might even take my ten dollars back. You're gonna have to work mighty hard to convince me I shouldn't cut you, too, like you did to me. I could fix it so no man'd ever want you again, missy."

"I . . . I'm sorry," Della panted. "You just . . . took me by surprise. I'll make it up to you, I swear."

"Well, now, that's more like it. What're you gonna do to make it up to me? Show me."

She did, and while she was at it he couldn't see her eyes anymore. If he'd been able to, he might have been worried.

Because in their green depths lurked the promise that someday he was going to pay for what he'd done, sure enough, and not with money, either.

Chapter Six

The railroad linking southwestern New Mexico Territory with the rest of the country had been completed not that many years previously, and getting from Fort Smith to Lordsburg by rail still wasn't what anybody would call a simple task. You had to either go north to Missouri on the Santa Fe, and then circle back through Kansas and Colorado before turning south through New Mexico to El Paso, and *then* finally turn west to Lordsburg; or else travel south through Texas to Houston and switch to the Southern Pacific, which roughly followed the old Butterfield Stage route through Texas to El Paso. The last stretch of the trip from El Paso to Lordsburg was the same either way. It was about the same distance out of the way no matter which route you chose, too.

John Henry took the Texas route, which cut across the corner of Indian Territory. He'd had a little to do with that rail line being completed, so he thought it was fitting he put it to use now.

Northern Texas, he discovered when the train crossed the Red River, looked a lot like southern Indian Territory. It stayed that way for several hundred miles before growing more wooded.

Houston was the biggest town John Henry had ever seen. He and Iron Heart switched to a Southern Pacific train there. San Antonio was the next stop. John Henry wouldn't have minded doing some looking around in that historic old city, but he didn't have the time. He wasn't traveling for pleasure. He had to reach Purgatory well before Jason True and the other mine owners brought their gold down, so he'd have a chance to get the lay of the land and sniff out any trouble.

After San Antonio the terrain changed. The train rolled through a band of rugged hills, then hit a stretch of flat, semi-arid plains. This was drier country than John Henry had ever seen, and it seemed to get more dry the farther west he traveled. Here and there, rough-looking buttes thrust up from the tableland, and trees became scarce. Low brush and clumps of ugly-looking grass covered the ground, interspersed with cactus and areas of bare rock. Settlements were few and far between, too. Often when the train had to stop for water, there was nothing to be seen but the water tank itself, sitting up on stilts, and the telegraph line that ran alongside the railroad tracks.

John Henry wasn't sure why anybody would want

to live out here in the middle of nowhere. Some people did, though. He'd been told that there were vast ranches out here in western Texas. He believed it, because country like this sure wasn't good for anything else.

He slept sitting up, since he had the frontiersman's ability to doze off just about anywhere, under any conditions. A cheap carpetbag containing his belongings was under the seat. When he reached Lordsburg, he would switch his things over to his saddlebags and leave the carpetbag at the depot for safekeeping until he returned.

When he awoke, mountains had replaced the desert. He bought an apple for breakfast from a boy who came through the car selling them and looked out the window to the south as he munched on the fruit.

Someone sat down on the bench seat beside him. He looked over and saw a thickly built, middle-aged man with curly, graying hair under a pushed-back derby. The man wore a dusty town suit. He said, "Mexico."

"What?" John Henry said.

"Mexico," the man repeated. "That's what you're looking at. Those mountains over there are on the other side of the border. You can't see it from here, but the Rio Grande runs between us and them."

"All right," John Henry said. "They look just like the mountains on this side of the border, don't they?"

The stranger chuckled and said, "Yeah, I guess they do." He put out a pudgy hand. "Mitchum's the name, Thaddeus Mitchum. Most folks call me Doc."

"Because you're a doctor?" John Henry asked as they shook.

"Oh, shoot, no. In my younger days I was a traveling man, sold elixirs and patent medicines."

"Snake oil, in other words," John Henry said.

Mitchum laughed.

"You're a plain-spoken young man, aren't you?"

"I try to be. I mean no offense by it, though."

"Oh, none taken, none taken," Mitchum said with a wave of his hand. "I've been called much worse than a snake oil salesman in my time. But, as a point of fact, the nostrums I sold actually did bring some relief to people who bought them."

"Mix enough alcohol and opium in something, and that'll do it."

"Indeed. I don't believe I caught your name, friend."

John Henry had done some thinking about that very thing. Judge Parker had suggested, and he agreed, that it might make his job easier if he didn't go around announcing the fact that he was a federal marshal. So the question was, should he use a false name?

In Indian Territory, quite a few people had heard of him; he was chief sheriff of the Cherokee Nation, after all, in addition to his duties as a deputy U.S. marshal. He was somewhat well-known in certain parts of Arkansas and Kansas, too.

But it was hard for him to believe that out here, with the vast reaches of Texas between him and home, that anybody would have ever heard of John Henry Sixkiller. So it just seemed simpler to use his real name.

"It's John Henry Sixkiller," he said in reply to Mitchum.

"Sixkiller," the man repeated. "You're an Indian?"

John Henry knew that his dark hair and blue eyes made him look more like his mother's Scotch-Irish ancestors than the Cherokee on his father's side. He said, "Half." He didn't go into detail since it was none of Mitchum's business.

"Oh. Well, that's fine. You may run into some people out here who are bothered by that, but I'm not one of 'em. I've studied history enough to know that most people are mongrels of one sort or another. I mean nothing derogatory by the word."

John Henry nodded. He didn't have anything against Mitchum, but he didn't particularly want to encourage a long conversation with the man, either. He found his eyes drawn back to those mountains that Mitchum had told him were in Mexico. This was the first time he had seen a foreign country, and he found it fascinating, even though it didn't really look any different from Texas. This trip was awakening a wanderlust inside John Henry that he hadn't known was part of his personality. He found himself wondering what it would be like to see an ocean, or a city like San Francisco, or even the great capitals of Europe.

Not that he was ever likely to travel that far. But as long as he was a U.S. marshal, there was a chance he'd be sent to more places that he'd never been before, like this journey to New Mexico Territory.

"Where is it you're bound, if you don't mind my asking?" Mitchum said.

John Henry did mind, but he'd been raised to be polite. His mother, Elizabeth, wouldn't have had it any other way. He said, "A little town in New Mexico Territory called Purgatory."

"Yes, I've heard of it," Mitchum said. "Never been there, though. It's a mining town, isn't it?"

"I think so." John Henry kept his answer deliberately vague.

"Going there on business? You didn't mention what line of work you're in."

"No, I didn't," John Henry said. He left it at that. He figured he'd been polite enough, long enough, and he didn't want to encourage this busybody any more than he already had.

Mitchum seemed to take the hint. He didn't ask any more questions, and after a few inconsequential comments about the landscape, he stood up and said, "Perhaps I'll see you again later. Good luck on your journey, Mr. Sixkiller."

"You, too," John Henry said.

Mitchum moved off along the aisle that ran through the center of the car. John Henry leaned back against the hard seat and closed his eyes, tipping his hat down over them. Even though he hadn't been awake all that long, the sleep he had gotten sitting up hadn't really been all that restful, either. Besides, the gently rocking motion of the train and the monotonous clicking of the joints in the rails combined to make him drowsy. A nap wouldn't hurt anything, he told himself.

He dozed off and didn't dream. He expected he might sleep all the way to El Paso.

That turned out not to be the case. He didn't know how long he had been asleep when he sensed someone else sitting down beside him. He opened his right eye only the tiniest slit, trying to get a glimpse of his fellow passenger. If Doc Mitchum was back, John Henry intended to go right on sleeping, or at least pretending to do so. He didn't want to have to entertain the old medicine show conman.

To his surprise, the person sitting beside him seemed to be wearing a dress. Some sort of bottle-green traveling outfit, to be precise. Still slumped against the seat with the hat partially shielding his face, John Henry opened his eye a little more and let his gaze trail up the woman's body. He could see the curve of her bosom and above it her chin, and a fine chin it was, too, with a hint of firmness and determination about it.

He couldn't see the rest of her face, though, unless he lifted his head and revealed that he was awake. He was debating whether or not he wanted to do that when he felt the soft pressure of her shoulder against his. She was leaning toward him, and a second later he felt the warmth of her breath touch his cheek as she whispered, "Please, sir, you have to help me, I beg of you!"

Chapter Seven

Under those circumstances, John Henry didn't see how he could pretend to go on sleeping. He sat up straighter, opened his eyes all the way, and lifted a hand to thumb his hat back into its normal position. He turned his head to look at the woman sitting close beside him. Improperly close, some people would have said.

She was very attractive. Probably around twenty-three years old, he would have guessed, although like most men he was far from an expert at guessing a woman's age. Lustrous brown hair was pulled back and up to form an elaborate arrangement of curls upon which sat a stylish hat that matched her traveling dress. Her eyes were a rich, warm shade of brown, too. Her face had a small beauty mark just to the right of her mouth that only added to her striking looks.

"Can you help me?" she said again. Her voice had a breathy, throaty quality about it, so that even if she hadn't been whispering, the words would have sounded intimate.

"Help you to do what?" John Henry asked.

"There's a man. . . . He's bothering me."

John Henry smiled. He might not be a sophisticated man of the world, but he had *some* experience. Any time a man was approached by a beautiful woman he didn't know who claimed that she was being bothered by someone, it tended not to end well for the fella being approached. The mark, John Henry believed he was called.

But the train had emerged from the mountains, he saw as he glanced out the window, and while he could still see some peaks to the south, across the Rio Grande, the scenery back to the north was downright boring again.

"How long will it be before we get to El Paso?" he asked.

The question seemed to take her by surprise. She frowned—which didn't make her any less pretty, he noted—and said, "What? How long to El Paso? I . . . I don't know. Another hour or two, maybe."

"I'm sorry," he said. Figuring out exactly what sort of trick she was trying to pull on him would help pass the time. "I just got distracted for a second. What were you saying about needing my help?"

She looked relieved.

"There's a man who's been watching me ever since we left San Antonio," she said. "He's very bold about it, and he makes me uncomfortable. I moved from the car where I was sitting originally, but he followed me. And then he *spoke* to me."

"I'm speaking to you," John Henry pointed out. "It doesn't seem so bad."

"Yes, but he wanted to know if I was stopping in El Paso. He suggested that he and I . . . well, I don't want to repeat what he suggested, but I found it very offensive!"

John Henry was sitting toward the front of the car, with only a couple of rows of seats between him and the vestibule. He turned his head to look behind him at the other passengers.

"Is he in this car?"

"I don't know . . . I think he followed me. . . ." The young woman looked, too, then jerked her head around so she was facing forward again. "Yes! He's back there. He's a big man, with . . . with a large nose and a black mustache."

John Henry looked again. There was an hombre several rows back who matched that description, all right, but he didn't seem to be paying any attention to them.

Maybe that was just an act. Maybe he really had been harassing this young woman. John Henry didn't think it was likely, but it was possible. He was enough of a gentleman that he thought he ought to give her the benefit of the doubt, despite his suspicions of her.

"Do you want me to go talk to him and ask him to leave you alone?" he asked.

She put a hand on his arm and squeezed gently.

"Could you?" she said, her voice again with that breathless quality.

"Of course. First, though, I'd like for you to tell me your name."

"Is . . . is that really necessary?"

"I think it is," John Henry said.

"Very well. My name is Sophie. Sophie Clearwater."

Clearwater sounded a little like an Indian name. John Henry knew it could just as easily be a white person's name, though. She didn't look the least bit Indian.

"All right, Miss Clearwater . . . it is *Miss* Clearwater, isn't it?"

"That's right. I'm not married."

"All right, I'll go have a word with the gentleman."

A little shudder ran through her.

"He's not a gentleman," she said. "He's a brute."

"I'll talk to him nonetheless," John Henry said as he got to his feet. "Why don't you just scoot on over there by the window? Easier for me to get out that way." She did as he suggested. He touched a finger to the brim of his hat and added, "I'll be right back."

He felt the motion of the train under his boots as he walked along the aisle. The man Sophie Clearwater claimed to be afraid of sat by himself on one of the benches, looking out the window. John Henry stopped beside him and said, "Excuse me, sir?"

The man looked around and said, "Yeah? What do you want?"

"I was wondering if I could have a word with you?"

"What about? I don't know you, do I?"

"No, but it's important." John Henry gestured at the seat. "If I could . . . ?"

The man grimaced and slid over with obvious reluctance. He made it plain he didn't want any company.

"Now, here's the situation," John Henry said quietly when he had taken off his hat and sat down. "There's a young woman up there . . . you see her, brown hair, green hat? She's not looking this way."

"Yeah, I see her. What about it?"

"Are you acquainted with her?"

"Not that I know of. I can't see her face, so I'm not sure. But as far as I know I'm not acquainted with anybody on this train." He added pointedly, "That includes you, mister."

"I neglected to introduce myself. My name's John Henry Sixkiller, and yes, before you ask, I'm part Indian."

"I don't give a hoot about that. Get to the point, before I call the conductor."

"Well, you see, that young woman claims that you've been bothering her. That you looked boldly at her, made improper suggestions, and followed her from another car to this one. Is there any truth to those charges?"

The man's face had begun to flush with anger as John Henry spoke, and by the time he was finished the man looked like he was about to explode. He opened his mouth to say something, but John Henry held up a hand and said, "Quietly now. We don't want to cause an unnecessary scene."

"You've already done that," the man grated out, "by coming back here and leveling these ridiculous accusations at me. I'd never bother any woman like that, and I don't appreciate her saying that I did!"

"Is there any way you can prove that?" John Henry asked.

"I don't have to prove anything!"

"Maybe not, but it would help me out if you did."

The man continued to fume for several seconds, then said, "All right. My name is Harlan Phillips. I'm the pastor of a Baptist church in El Paso. I'm on my way back from San Antonio, where I attended a denominational meeting where I was cited for my work in the service of the Lord. I'm happily married and have five children. Is that enough *proof* for you, mister?"

"Am I supposed to take your word for it that you're this Pastor Phillips?"

The man reached under his coat, and John Henry tensed. If that hand came out with a gun in it, he was going to throw a punch before the man could bring the weapon to bear.

Instead, Phillips, if that was his name, was holding an envelope. He showed it to John Henry, who saw that it was addressed to Harlan Phillips, Grace Baptist Church, El Paso, Texas.

"Just because you've got a letter addressed to this Pastor Phillips doesn't mean you're him."

"Maybe not. Why don't you bring the young woman back here and I'll address her accusations directly."

"I don't believe that'll be necessary," John Henry said. "I'll accept that you're who you say you are, Brother Harlan, if you'll do me a favor."

"What sort of favor?"

"Don't argue with me when I say what I'm about to say."

Phillips looked confused. He started to say, "What—" but John Henry got to his feet, pointed his hat at him, and said in a loud voice, "And don't you forget it!"

Then he clapped his hat on his head, gave Phillips a curt nod, and turned to stride back up the aisle to his seat.

A few of the other passengers had looked at him oddly when he spoke that last bit to Phillips, but most ignored him. Not Sophie Clearwater, though. She turned to watch him approach, and she started to move as if she intended to slide off the bench and let him reclaim his seat by the window.

John Henry moved too fast for her to do that. He sat down beside her instead and let his long legs extend casually in front of him, as much as they would in the space between benches. Sophie couldn't get out now unless he let her out, short of climbing over the back of the bench.

"You don't have anything else to worry about," he told her as he glanced down and saw the corner of his carpetbag sticking out from under the seat. It hadn't been like that when he left. "I gave the man a good talking to, and he won't bother you anymore."

"Thank you," she said. "You're a true gentleman. Now, I shouldn't take up any more of your time—"

"I don't have anything *but* time until we get to El Paso," John Henry said, "and I'd be honored if you'd spend it talking with me, Miss Clearwater."

She looked uncomfortable, sort of like a deer that wanted to bolt. She forced a smile and said, "Well, I suppose—"

"And the first thing we can talk about," John Henry said, "is why you lied to me and told me that a fine, upstanding Baptist preacher with a wife and five children was making improper advances toward you."

Chapter Eight

Her brown eyes widened in surprise, and her lips compressed into a thin, taut line.

"Just because a man's a preacher doesn't mean that he can't sin," she said.

"Anybody can sin," John Henry said. "Some people do it like breathing. I've even heard it said that preachers are good at sinning because they've studied it so much. That doesn't answer my question."

"You think that he's telling the truth and I'm lying?" she snapped.

"I do, yes. I also think that you went through my carpetbag while I was talking to the good pastor. Find anything interesting?"

He knew she hadn't, unless she was interested in a few spare shirts, socks, changes of underwear, and a couple of boxes of .44 ammunition. His wallet and the leather folder containing his deputy marshal's badge and bona fides were resting snugly in his inside coat pockets.

"Are you accusing me of being a thief?" she asked, still tight-lipped.

"Well, a would-be thief, anyway. I doubt if you took anything, since I don't really have anything worth stealing."

"Please let me out of this seat right now."

John Henry shook his head and said, "Not until you tell me the truth."

"I'll scream. The conductor will come."

"Go ahead. I wouldn't mind having a word with him myself."

She sighed and her hand moved slightly. He saw the twin barrels of an over-and-under derringer peeking out at him from her fingers.

"I don't want to shoot you—"

"And I don't want to be shot," he said. Moving so quickly she couldn't stop him, his hand clamped over hers and forced it down so if she pulled the trigger, the bullet would go into the bench between them. He reached across his body with the other hand, tightened his grip enough so that she gasped softly in pain, and plucked the derringer from her grasp. As she glared at him, he let go of her, broke the little gun open, removed the shells, and handed it back to her.

"I don't like people pointing guns at me," he said. "Not even beautiful women."

She said, "You son of a—"

"Now, that's not very ladylike," he broke in. "But if you want to start calling names, I reckon I could come up with a few to apply to you, as well."

"All right! Yes, I looked through your bag. But I didn't take anything."

"And Brother Harlan back there hasn't been bothering you, has he?"

"He's really a preacher?"

"Seems to be," John Henry said.

Sophie sighed, shook her head, and said, "I just picked the meanest-looking man I could find. And he turns out to be a blasted sky pilot!"

"That *was* an unfortunate turn of events for you," John Henry said with a smile.

Sophie surprised him a little by returning the smile. She didn't seem to be playing up to him, either. She appeared to be genuinely amused by the irony. Of course, she was good at lying, John Henry reminded himself.

"Are you going to turn me over to the law?" she asked.

He didn't tell her that he was a lawman himself. Instead, he said, "What for? You didn't take anything. And if you could get in trouble with the law for lying to a man, all the women in the world would be behind bars, wouldn't they?"

"That's a rather cynical attitude, isn't it?"

"Not really, because if the reverse was true, all the men would be locked up."

"So you have no faith in humanity at all, is that it?"

"Let's just say that my belief in the goodness of humankind has its limits."

She was silent for a moment, then asked, "If

you're not going to have me arrested, you can let me out of this seat."

"So you can find some other poor unsuspecting gent to rob between here and El Paso?" John Henry shook his head. "No, I think we'll just continue our conversation, as I suggested earlier. For starters, is your name really Sophie Clearwater?"

"As a matter of fact, it is," she said.

"My name is John Henry Sixkiller. Now that we've been properly introduced, tell me . . . do you do this sort of thing often?"

"That's none of your business."

"No, I suppose not. But you can't blame me for being curious."

She sighed and said, "You wouldn't believe what a woman has to do sometimes to get along in this world. Believe me, Mr. Sixkiller, there are worse ways than lifting an occasional wallet or watch."

"I'm sure that's true. That's a fairly expensive traveling outfit you're wearing, though. You must not be completely broke."

"I never said that I was. But . . . at this particular moment I don't own much more than the clothes on my back."

"I'm sorry to hear that."

"Sorry enough to perhaps help me out?" No sooner had she asked that then she shook her head and smiled. "No, forget I said that. Force of habit. And you wouldn't fall for it anyway."

"No, I would not," John Henry agreed. "Where are you from?"

"North Carolina, originally. A little town you've never heard of."

"Probably not, since I doubt that I could name a single town in North Carolina."

"What about you?" She studied him with a degree of intentness. "There's something unusual about you."

"I'm half Cherokee. Born and raised in Indian Territory."

"You don't look like any Indian I've ever seen."

"We don't all wear feathers and war paint," John Henry said dryly. "My father's people are one of the so-called Civilized Tribes. We live in houses, not buffalo hide lodges."

"I should have guessed, with a name like Six-killer."

"I thought you might be part Indian, as well, with a descriptive name like Clearwater."

She smiled and shook her head.

"No, my ancestors were English."

"Ah, dukes and earls."

"More like indentured servants and criminals. So you see, I come by it honestly."

"Just because your ancestors were one thing doesn't mean you have to be, too. That's one of the good things about this country."

"I suppose not, but there's an old saying about the apple not falling far from the tree."

She was charming, John Henry had to give her that, but he wasn't taken in by it. He was well aware that in her line of work, charm was one of the tools of her dishonest trade.

What she did wasn't a federal crime, though, and he had a job of his own to worry about. When the train reached El Paso it was likely they would be parting ways, since he doubted if she was going on to Lordsburg. A bigger town like El Paso would present more opportunities for her.

They spent the next hour talking, John Henry telling her some about his life but leaving out the parts about his being a member of the Cherokee Lighthorse, chief sheriff, and finally a deputy United States marshal. For her part, Sophie skillfully turned aside any questions that delved too deeply into her own past, although she said enough that John Henry got the idea she had gone through some tough times.

That didn't excuse her turning to crime, of course. John Henry was a firm believer in the law. There were plenty of opportunities in Indian Territory for a man to stray from the honest path, but he had never taken them. Well, not other than bending the rules a little now and then when he had to in order to bring in a wanted fugitive.

The conductor walked through the car to announce that they were approaching El Paso and that the train would be stopped there for half an hour before it rolled out heading west again. Since it was the middle of the day, John Henry said to Sophie, "Maybe you'd like to have some lunch with me while we're stopped?"

"Thank you, but no," she said. "I'm meeting some-one in El Paso."

He smiled and said, "Ah, well, my loss."

"You can say that even though I tried to rob you?"

"But you didn't rob me, and that's the whole point."

She laughed.

"Not for lack of trying."

"If everybody was condemned for what they tried to do but failed—"

"I know, the whole world would be locked up," she said with a smile.

"Half of it, anyway."

When the train came to a stop at the station in downtown El Paso, John Henry stood up to let Sophie out. She started to move past him, then paused so that she was standing right in front of him, only inches away, her head tilted back slightly so she could look up into his face.

"Thank you," she said. "You've been a real gen-tleman about this whole thing."

"Would it do any good to ask you to stop doing things like this?"

"What do you think, Mr. Sixkiller?"

"I think . . . I wish you the best, Miss Clearwater."

"And the same to you," she said. Then she moved past him, merged into the stream of passengers getting off the train here in El Paso, and was gone. John Henry looked through the window, trying to spot her on the platform, but he didn't see her anywhere.

He supposed he would never see her again.

That was all right. He had a job to do, and he knew that by the time he reached Purgatory, he would have forgotten all about Sophie Clearwater.

Chapter Nine

Once the train left El Paso, the terrain got flat, empty, and monotonous again. Occasionally, some mountains were visible in the distance to the north or south, but the railroad always skirted around them.

At one point the conductor came through the car and announced that they had just crossed the Continental Divide. Wasn't that something, John Henry thought. This trip was just chock-full of new experiences for him.

It was late in the afternoon when the train reached Lordsburg. John Henry took his carpetbag and went to the stable car where Iron Heart was being unloaded. His saddle and rifle were there, too, and he put the clean clothes and ammunition in the saddlebags, then handed the carpetbag and a dollar to a porter and said, "Can you see that this is kept here for me?"

"Of course, sir," the man said. "When do you expect to be back to get it?"

John Henry smiled and said, "Well, now, that's a good question. I'd say it'll be a week, maybe more."

"That's fine," the porter assured him. "It'll be here waiting for you."

And if he wound up dead, John Henry thought, as was always a possibility in his business, eventually somebody who worked here at the depot would claim the bag. At least that way somebody would get some use out of it.

He propped his saddle on his shoulder, tucked the Winchester under his arm, and led Iron Heart to the nearest stable. It was too late in the day to start for Purgatory. That would have to wait for morning. He made arrangements with a Mexican hostler to care for the horse and saddle overnight, then asked for directions to a decent hotel.

"I don't know how decent it is, *señor*," the stable-man said with a grin, "but the Lordsburg House is just up the block."

"I'll give it a try," John Henry said. "*Muchas gracias.*" He didn't know much Spanish, but he had picked up a few phrases here and there.

The Lordsburg House appeared to be a fairly clean and respectable establishment. John Henry rented a room. The clerk looked a little warily at the rifle in his hand and said, "I hope you're not expecting trouble, sir."

"I'm not expecting it," John Henry said, "but I

wouldn't want to be downright shocked if it showed up, now would I?"

The night passed peacefully, and John Henry slept well. He ate breakfast in the hotel dining room the next morning, settled his bill, then went to the stable to pick up Iron Heart.

The same friendly hostler was working again this morning. John Henry asked him, "Are you familiar with a settlement called Purgatory?"

"Oh, sure, *señor*. It's about seventy miles north of here, in the San Francisco Valley. Never been there, but I've heard about it."

"Was what you heard good or bad?"

The hostler shrugged.

"Well, you know, *señor*, there's usually a reason people name a place Purgatory."

John Henry grinned and asked, "There a good road between here and there?"

The stableman shrugged his shoulders.

"There's a road, *señor*," he said. "I couldn't tell you how good it is. The stagecoach uses it, though, so it must be not too bad."

John Henry gave the man an extra half-dollar, despite his habit of giving noncommittal answers to questions, then swung up into the saddle and set out on the last leg of the journey.

A low ridge paralleled the road, running a mile or so west of it. By noon, the ridge had petered out, but John Henry could see some mountains in the distance to the east. Where he was, though, the land was flat, brown, and dusty. The vegetation consisted of greasewood bushes, bunch grass, cactus, and the occasional scrubby mesquite tree. Everything seemed bigger and vaster out here than back home . . . but not necessarily better.

At least the road was good, fairly wide and packed hard by the wheels of the stagecoaches and freight wagons that made regular trips to Purgatory.

He had stopped at a store in Lordsburg on his way out of town and picked up a few supplies for the trip. At midday, he made do with some jerky for lunch, washed down with water from his canteen. He had taken off his coat and rolled up his shirt sleeves because the sun was hot. He was glad for the shade that the broad brim of his hat provided.

While he was letting Iron Heart rest, he spotted a cloud of dust approaching from the south. As the cloud came closer, the dark shape at its base resolved itself into a stagecoach being pulled by a fast-moving team of horses. John Henry took hold of Iron Heart's reins and led the horse off to the side of the road so they wouldn't be in the coach's way.

It rattled past, bouncing on its broad leather thoroughbraces. The canvas curtains were pulled over the windows to keep out some of the dust. John Henry took off his hat and swiped at that same dust in an attempt to clear some of it away from his face.

As he did so, one of the passengers inside the coach pulled back the curtain and looked out at him. Because the dust was making his eyes water and the coach was moving fast, John Henry caught only a glimpse of the man. That glimpse was enough to make him frown, though.

He would have sworn the man who looked out at him from the stagecoach was Doc Mitchum, the old snake oil salesman.

That was certainly possible, John Henry thought. He had told Mitchum that he was on his way to Purgatory, but Mitchum hadn't revealed his destination. He could be headed there, too, although such a coincidence seemed a little fishy to John Henry. Wouldn't Mitchum have said something on the train if that was the case?

But for the life of him, John Henry couldn't see any reason why Mitchum would try to beat him to Purgatory. He'd never met the man until the previous day, and then they had only spoken for a short time.

John Henry wasn't the sort to waste time pondering matters he couldn't do anything about. He put the question of Mitchum's motive out of his mind. He would deal with that later if it became necessary.

Anyway, it was always possible he'd been mistaken about the identity of the man in the stagecoach. It wasn't like he'd gotten a real good look at the fellow.

That evening he reached some mountains with a broad, shallow stream flowing at their base. Iron Heart's hooves splashed in the water as John Henry crossed the river. The mountains were covered with pine trees that came all the way down to the stream. After all the brown and tan and gray in the landscape, it was good to see some greenery again, John Henry thought. He made camp in a clump of pines, building a fire to boil a pot of coffee and fry up some of the bacon he had brought from Lordsburg.

After supper, when it was dark, he let the fire die down and then led Iron Heart to another spot about a quarter of a mile away before he unsaddled the horse and spread his bedroll. There was no reason to think that anybody out here in New Mexico Territory would want to ambush him, but his time as a lawman had taught him that it never hurt to be careful.

After another good night's sleep and some more coffee and bacon for breakfast, John Henry headed north again, still following the stagecoach road. The coach had probably reached Purgatory by now, but he would get there later today, still well ahead of the time when Jason True, Arnold Goodman, and Dan Lacey were scheduled to bring their gold down and deposit it in the bank to wait for Wells Fargo. If he had taken the coach, he probably would have had to rent a horse when he got to Purgatory, and he would rather have his regular mount with him. As the horse's name indicated, he knew he could depend on Iron Heart.

The road followed the valleys between the rugged peaks. He came to another stream, this one flowing north and south instead of east and west, and its valley gradually broadened until there were two distinct mountain ranges flanking it. This had to be the San Francisco River, John Henry thought, which made the mountains to the east the Mogollons and the western range the San Franciscos. That was where the mines were.

Purgatory was located on the river, so with both the stream and the stagecoach road to follow, John Henry knew he wouldn't have any trouble finding the settlement. Sure enough, about four o'clock that afternoon he spotted smoke rising from chimneys up ahead, and a few minutes later he began to be able to make out some of the buildings in the distance.

Purgatory was on the western side of the river, the road on the east, so John Henry had to turn and cross a sturdy-looking log bridge to reach the settlement. Purgatory itself was a decent-sized town with a main street lined with businesses that stretched for three blocks and a couple of side streets where the residences were located. Most of the buildings were made of logs or lumber, but John Henry saw a few constructed out of brick, including an impressive edifice that had to be the bank, along with some made from adobe or chunks of native stone mortared together. One of those stone buildings, a squat, squarish structure, had a sign on it that read MARSHAL'S OFFICE AND JAIL. A smaller sign underneath it proclaimed HENRY HINKLE, MARSHAL.

John Henry wondered if he ought to introduce himself and reveal his true identity to the local lawman. Judge Parker hadn't said anything about this fellow Hinkle, so John Henry didn't know what sort of man he was. If he'd been in Hinkle's place, though, he knew he wouldn't appreciate it if a federal officer came into his bailiwick on an assignment without him knowing about it.

This would require some scouting around, he decided. He would try to find out more about Henry Hinkle before spilling the truth to the man.

He rode past the impressive brick building he had taken for the bank, and fancy gilt lettering on one of the front windows confirmed that the establishment was the First Territorial Bank of Purgatory. Not only the first but also the only bank in town, as far as he could see, John Henry mused. He took note of several other businesses, including an assay office, several mercantiles, a couple of stores that sold hardware and mining equipment, a blacksmith, a pair of stables, a newspaper office, two cafés, a nicer-looking restaurant, a hotel called the Barrymore House, and at least half a dozen saloons, the biggest and fanciest of which appeared to be the Silver Spur.

John Henry was easing Iron Heart along the street at a walk and debating what to do next when the decision was made for him.

Somewhere behind him, possibly in the vicinity of the bank, shots suddenly blasted out, shattering the late afternoon calm.

Chapter Ten

Duke Rudd was still as bored as he'd been the day he forced himself on that saloon girl Della. Showing her what a mean, tough hombre he was had made things better for a while, but it hadn't taken long for the feeling to wear off. Rudd leaned his skinny frame against a hitch rack and idly considered going over to the Silver Spur to see if Della was around. He hadn't been there since that day, thinking that maybe it would be a good idea to stay away for a spell and let her get over being mad at him. She might've complained about him to Royal Bouchard, who owned the place.

Rudd wasn't worried about Meade, the bartender, but Bouchard was a different story. Rudd wasn't exactly scared of Bouchard—he wasn't scared of anybody except Billy Ray Gilmore, and only a damned fool wouldn't get nervous sometimes around Billy Ray—but he was wary of the saloon keeper. Most folks in Purgatory wouldn't meet your eyes when you looked at them. Bouchard would, and although he had never given the members of the gang any trouble, there was always the sense that he might be willing to if he was pushed into a corner.

Sam Logan was sitting on the edge of the boardwalk behind Rudd, a barlow knife in his hand as he whittled on a piece of wood. Logan always had to be doing something with his hands: whittling, playing cards, cleaning his gun, or just fidgeting until Rudd sometimes wanted to yell at him to just stop it. Usually it was little fellas like Rudd who were nervous and fidgety, but not always. Big, bulky Sam Logan was proof of that.

"I think maybe I'll go over to the Silver Spur," Rudd said.

Without looking up from the piece of wood he was trying to fashion into a whistle, Logan said, "I thought you said we oughta lie low for a while, Duke. That whore might still be on the prod after what you done to her."

"I didn't do nothin' that ain't been done to her hundreds of times before," Rudd insisted. "Maybe thousands."

"I wouldn't want to have to do the cipherin' to count it up," Logan said.

"Maybe I'll tell her I'm sorry," Rudd mused. "I ain't, really, of course. But I could tell her that."

"You think she'd go upstairs with you again?"

"She might."

"But you don't have ten dollars."

"I got three," Rudd said. "How about you, Sam? You be willin' to spot me seven until the next time Billy Ray gives us some dinero?"

"I don't know," Logan said. "Seems like I've spotted you a few bucks in the past that you never paid back."

"I'll get even with you, don't you worry about that. Come on, Sam—" Rudd stopped short. He was still looking out into the street, and he had just seen a rider go by whom he didn't recognize. "Who's that?"

"Who's who?" Logan asked.

"That fella there on the gray horse," Rudd said, nodding toward the stranger.

Logan closed his knife and slipped it and the partially completed whistle into his pocket as he stood up. He stepped over to the hitch rail and stood beside Rudd.

"Him?"

"Yeah."

The man was average sized, but there was something about him that made him seem a little bigger. Maybe it was the powerful shoulders. He wore jeans, a gray shirt with the sleeves rolled back a couple of turns, and a broad-brimmed, cream-colored hat thumbed back slightly on dark hair. The butt of a Winchester jutted up from a sheath strapped to his saddle. From where Rudd and Logan stood, they couldn't see the man's handgun, but they could see the shell belt strapped around the man's hips so they knew he was packing a revolver.

"Must be new in town," Logan said. "I never seen him before, and he don't look like the sort of hombre you usually find in Purgatory."

"No, he don't," Rudd said. "He looks like trouble."

"But not for us, because we ain't got nothin' to do with him." Logan nudged his friend in the ribs with his elbow. "Hey, there's Cravens. Why don't you go ask him for the loan of seven bucks so you can maybe play slap and tickle with Miss Della?"

Rudd looked around and saw a stout, middle-aged man in a town suit and narrow-brimmed hat crossing the street near them. He appeared to be heading for the bank, which was no surprise since Joseph Cravens was not only the mayor of Purgatory, he also owned the First Territorial Bank.

"Oh, sure," Rudd said. "I'm gonna ask the town banker to loan me whore money."

"Can't ever tell," Logan said with a grin. "He might say yes."

Rudd doubted that very seriously . . . but hell, it was something to do, he thought, and it might be good for a laugh just seeing the look on Cravens's face.

"Fine," he said. "Let's go."

With Logan trailing him, he moved quickly to intercept Cravens before the banker reached the boardwalk. Rudd lifted his hand, put a friendly grin on his face, and said, "Howdy, there, Mr. Cravens. Talk to you for a minute?"

Cravens stopped and frowned worriedly. He recognized Rudd and Logan, of course. Just about everybody in Purgatory knew who the members of Billy Ray Gilmore's gang were, even though the law didn't seem to be able to do anything about them.

"What is it you men want?" Cravens asked in a curt voice.

"Well, that's no way to talk to a potential customer," Rudd said. "I want to discuss a business transaction with you."

That seemed to surprise Cravens. He said, "Really?"

"Sure 'nough. I'd like to see about gettin' a loan from your bank."

"A loan? Really?" Cravens still seemed wary, but the instincts ingrained in him by years in the banking business made him ask the question. "What sort of loan? How much money are we talking about?"

"I need ten dollars for a whore," Rudd declared. Might as well let Logan keep his three bucks and get the whole shooting match from the bank if he could, he thought.

"Ten d-dollars," Cravens said, starting to sputter a little. His face turned red, either from anger or embarrassment, or both. "For a . . . a prositute!"

"Whore, prostitute, soiled dove, call her whatever you want," Rudd said. "You should know, though, Mr. Cravens, that she ain't your run-of-the-mill whore. She's special. In fact, if you was to loan me twenty dollars, there ain't no tellin' what I might be able to talk her into doin."

Cravens moved to the side, as if to try to get around them.

"You'll have to excuse me," he said. "I have business to tend to."

Rudd put a hand on the banker's chest to stop him.

"Now, I've made you a fair business proposition," he said. "You gonna approve my loan or deny it, Mr. Banker Man?"

"I . . . I can't. . . . Please, let me by—"

Rudd stepped back. He wasn't getting out of the way to let Cravens pass, though. Instead, he reached down to his hip and closed his hand around the butt of his gun.

"I guess if you ain't gonna loan me that money, the least you can do is dance a mite to entertain us."

He drew his gun and pulled the trigger, sending a bullet smashing into the ground about three inches from Cravens's left foot.

Cravens let out a startled, frightened yelp and jumped instinctively away from where the bullet had kicked up dust. Logan laughed at that, shrugged, and pulled his gun as well. Both weapons roared, spraying lead around Cravens's feet and making him hop frantically as Rudd cackled and said, "Dance, Banker Man, dance!"

Then Logan yelled, "Oh, hell, Duke, look out!"

When John Henry heard the shots coming from the vicinity of the bank, he figured somebody was holding up the establishment.

Instead, as he wheeled Iron Heart around, he saw two men standing at the edge of the street firing their revolvers at the feet of a third man, who was leaping around desperately trying to stay out of the way of the slugs.

The sight of it made John Henry mad. Just downright mad.

He heeled Iron Heart into motion, sending the big horse galloping toward the three men.

The two gunnies heard the thundering hoof-beats just in time. One of them let out a warning yell, and they leaped in opposite directions, barely avoiding being trampled. One of the gunmen was a little, rabbity-looking man. The other hombre was big and stolid, slower to move. Iron Heart's shoulder almost clipped him.

John Henry reined in and turned his mount again. The smaller man yelped, "What the hell are you doin'? We was just makin' him dance!"

John Henry's Colt flickered out of its holster and roared, sending a bullet smashing through the smaller man's left foot. The man screeched in pain, flung his arms in the air, and went over backwards. His gun slipped from his fingers, flew up about ten feet, then fell and thudded into the dust of the street.

John Henry twisted in the saddle. The bigger man was trying to draw a bead on him. John Henry fired first, targeting the man's right foot. He yelled and started hopping around. He hung on to his gun, so John Henry sent Iron Heart lunging past the man and swung his Colt so that the barrel cracked across the wrist of the man's gun hand. The man dropped the weapon, sobbed, and tried to cradle his injured wrist against his body. His wounded foot wouldn't support his weight, though, so he fell into a heap on the ground.

"Sorry, boys," John Henry said. "I just meant to make you dance. Reckon I'm not as good a shot as you fellas are."

The man in the town suit stared wide-eyed at John Henry as if struggling to comprehend the sudden violence that had broken out in front of him. He said, "You . . . you shot them!"

"If there's one thing I hate, it's seeing somebody being picked on," John Henry said. Actually, there were plenty of examples of injustice that he hated, but that was one of them.

"You don't understand!" the townsman said. "Those men are part of Billy Ray Gilmore's gang!"

Chapter Eleven

Well, that was interesting, John Henry thought. He didn't know exactly who Billy Ray Gilmore was, but from the sound of it, the man was a notorious desperado and the leader of a gang of bandits.

Probably just the man John Henry was looking for.

The smaller of the two gunnies was rolling around on the ground, clutching his wounded foot as blood leaked through the hole in the top of his boot. He yelled a curse at John Henry and added, "You'll pay for this, mister! By God, you'll pay!"

John Henry ignored him and said to the townsman, "Should I be worried about this fella Gilmore?"

The man swallowed hard and said, "I . . . I prefer not to talk about him."

That response jibed with John Henry's initial hunch. Gilmore was the man who had this town buffaloed, all right. That meant he was the one Jason True and the other miners were afraid of.

"Well, if he has a bone to pick with me, he ought to be able to find me. My name's John Henry Six-killer, and I aim to be around for a while."

That laid it out simple enough and amounted to throwing down a gauntlet. John Henry liked to know what sort of odds he was facing. He hadn't intended to announce his presence in Purgatory quite so dramatically, but he might as well try to take advantage of the situation, he thought.

He looked at the townsman, who appeared prosperous enough, and waited for the man to return the favor and introduce himself. After a moment, the man said, "I'm Joseph Cravens. I own the bank here, and I'm the mayor of Purgatory, as well."

"It's good to meet you, Mayor," John Henry said with a nod. He looked at the two men lying in the street. Both gunmen were whimpering in pain, but they had stopped writhing around. "What about these two?"

"Their friends will come along and tend to them, I suppose," Cravens said. "I don't see any of them on the street right now, but some of them are bound to be around and someone will tell them what happened." A disapproving note came into Cravens's voice. "There are people in Purgatory who are eager to curry favor with Gilmore and his ilk."

"All right." John Henry looked around. There were quite a few people standing around on the boardwalks, and more were looking on from the doors and windows of the buildings. "I'm surprised the local law hasn't shown up to see what all the commotion was about."

"Marshal Hinkle?" The mayor's dismissive tone made it clear he didn't think that was likely to happen. "He'll poke his nose out later, when the trouble is all over."

"I see. So you don't think he'll arrest me for shooting these two?"

"I don't think you have to worry about that," Cravens said. "But I can't say the same about Gilmore."

"Like I said, he can look me up if he wants to talk about it." John Henry started to turn Iron Heart away, but he stopped and said to the two men he had wounded, "You fellas remember my name, too. John Henry Sixkiller."

"We'll remember you, all right," the smaller one snarled. "And we'll see you again . . . over the barrel of a gun!"

"Looking forward to it," John Henry responded dryly. He lifted his reins and heeled Iron Heart into a walk.

He didn't think either of the outlaws would make another try for him right now, but he listened closely for any sounds that might warn him they were scrambling after their guns. He didn't hear anything except the soft thuds of the horse's hooves in the dust.

John Henry rode to the Silver Spur Saloon and dismounted. After most of two days on the trail, he was thirsty, and a cold beer sure sounded appealing right now. Back home, people sometimes looked at him a mite odd when he went into a saloon, because it was well known that Indians could not handle "firewater" very well. He always had to explain to them that it was the white half of him drinking, not the Indian half.

As he looped Iron Heart's reins around a hitch rail and stepped up onto the boardwalk, he spotted a young woman watching him through one of the windows. She was a nice-looking honey blonde. Their eyes met for a second before she abruptly turned away.

He wasn't totally unaccustomed to having women look at him. Back in Indian Territory, there was a beautiful young lady named Sasha Quiet Stream who had been friends with John Henry since they were both little more than kids. He had risked his life to save her from a vicious killer, and there was a chance that in time their friendship might grow into something more.

Right now, however, John Henry's work kept him on the move nearly all the time, so it was difficult to even consider anything serious where the future was concerned. For him, the future had to be about doing the job he had set out to do.

Which meant that if an attractive woman wanted to smile at him, he certainly wasn't opposed to the idea, and he wasn't going to feel guilty for not being opposed to it, either.

He pushed the bat wings aside and stepped into the saloon. Instantly, he felt the eyes of a number of people on him. That wasn't surprising, since he'd just been involved in a shooting. The fact that the other two hombres involved in that shooting were members of the local outlaw gang just made him even more notorious.

He pretended not to notice the scrutiny and strolled toward the long mahogany bar that ran down the right side of the big room. The hardwood gleamed in the light from a number of chandeliers. Tables were scattered to the left. About half of them were occupied by drinkers. The bar was busy, too, but not packed. The rear portion of the room was devoted to gambling, with several poker tables, a roulette wheel that wasn't being used at the moment, and a faro layout where men could take their chances on bucking the tiger.

A staircase to the left led up to a second-floor balcony that went around two sides of the room. Judging by the number of women in short, spangled dresses in evidence, there would be rooms on the second floor where fellas could try their luck at another kind of bucking, John Henry thought with a wry smile.

The blonde John Henry had seen in the window was wearing one of those eye-catching dresses, he noted as he spotted her standing at the bar talking to a man in a suit with a fancy vest and a gold watch chain draped across it. The man looked like a gambler, but John Henry thought there was a good chance he owned this place.

The bartender was already moving to meet him

as he stepped up to the bar. John Henry nodded and said, "I could sure do with a cold glass of beer, friend."

"Coming right up," the aproned man replied. He drew the beer and set it in front of John Henry, then glanced to his right and added, "It's on the house."

"First one's free, eh? Is that the policy?"

"Well . . . not always. But this is sort of a special occasion."

"It is?" John Henry said. "Some holiday I don't know about?"

The well-dressed man who'd been talking to the blonde moved alongside him in time to hear that question.

"It's a local holiday," he said. "I just declared it."

John Henry lifted the glass in his left hand and took a swallow of the beer. It wasn't ice cold, but it was cool and tasted mighty good going down his throat.

"What are we celebrating?" he asked.

"It's not every day that somebody stands up to a couple of Billy Ray Gilmore's gun-wolves," the man said. "That makes it a holiday as far as I'm concerned, and since I own the Silver Spur, I think I can declare one." He raised his voice and addressed the bartender. "I'm buying the next round for the house, Meade."

"Yes, sir, Mr. Bouchard," the bartender said as customers began to crowd up to claim their free drinks.

The man extended his hand to John Henry and introduced himself.

"Royal Bouchard. This is my place."

John Henry gripped his hand and said, "John Henry Sixkiller. I'm drinking in your place."

"It's a pleasure to meet you, Mr. Sixkiller. You're new to Purgatory, aren't you?"

"Just rode in about fifteen minutes ago."

"And rode right into trouble, from what I hear."

"You didn't see it?"

"I was upstairs when I heard the shooting," Bouchard said. "By the time I got down here, it was all over. But one of the girls who works for me told me all about it. She said Duke Rudd and Sam Logan were shooting at our esteemed mayor, and you came along and shot them."

John Henry nodded and said, "That's about the size of it."

"In the foot."

"Seemed appropriate, since their bullets were kicking up dust around your mayor's feet."

"Maybe, but it would have been all right with me if you'd put your slugs in their gizzards, instead. They're dangerous men, and they won't take kindly to being wounded."

"Since I'm the one who shot them, seems like I might be a little dangerous myself."

Bouchard chuckled and nodded.

"Point taken, Mr. Sixkiller," he said. "Is that an Indian name?"

"It might be," John Henry allowed.

"None of my business, of course," Bouchard went on smoothly. "I'll venture to ask something else that's none of my business: What brings you to Purgatory?"

"I'm just passing through," John Henry said. "I have to admit, though, I like the looks of the country around here, and Purgatory seems like a nice enough town . . . if you don't mind a few vermin like Rudd and Logan. Wasn't that their names? Anyway, I might stay awhile."

"You'll be welcomed, at least by some of us. Gilmore and his men are tolerated around here, but they're certainly not liked."

"This Billy Ray Gilmore, he's the big skookum he-wolf in these parts?"

Bouchard glanced toward the entrance, stiffened, and said, "You can ask him yourself. Here he comes now."

Chapter Twelve

Without getting in a hurry about it, John Henry took another sip of his beer, then set the glass on the bar and turned to look at the man coming toward him. Billy Ray Gilmore wasn't a big man. In fact, he was a couple of inches below medium height, and he was slender.

But there was something about him that drew the eye and compelled men to be careful around him. He moved with a lithe, catlike grace that said if he decided to strike, it would be swift and deadly.

Because of that, the men who'd crowded around the bar moved away in a hurry, putting some distance between themselves and the predator they'd suddenly found in their midst.

Bouchard didn't run, though. He stood his ground next to John Henry as Gilmore came up to them.

"Hello, Bouchard," Gilmore said as he nodded

to the saloon keeper. He was surprisingly soft spoken.

"Gilmore," Bouchard said.

"And you must be the hombre who shot my friends Duke and Sam," Gilmore went on as he turned to John Henry. "They said the man was a stranger, and I don't recall seeing you in Purgatory before."

"Just got here," John Henry confirmed. He stood casually at the bar, but underneath that negligent pose he was ready to draw if Gilmore reached for his gun. He went on, "I can't say as I care much for your taste in friends."

"Well, life has a way of bringing folks together who might not be, otherwise. Look at us. Without that bit of gunplay, we might never have met, Mister . . . ?"

"Sixkiller." John Henry smiled faintly. "Are you saying that you and I are going to be friends?"

"Why not?"

"For one thing, I shot those fellas in the foot."

Gilmore nodded and said, "Yes, and I'm afraid poor Duke's going to lose a toe. He'll live, though, and so will Sam, and I have a hunch that if you'd wanted to, you could have killed both of them. So, in one way of looking at it, you saved their lives."

John Henry had to laugh.

"I suppose you could look at it that way, if you wanted to," he said.

"That's what I'd prefer." Gilmore held out his hand. "No hard feelings?"

John Henry had been watching the room to make sure none of Gilmore's men snuck in and tried to get the drop on him. As far as he could tell, Gilmore wasn't trying to tie up his gun hand so somebody else could ventilate him, so he shook with the man and said, "None on my part."

"Good. Since you just got here, I wouldn't want you to, ah . . ."

"Get off on the wrong foot?" John Henry suggested.

"Exactly."

"So you'll see to it that Duke and Sam don't hold a grudge? I'd hate to have them throw down on me from an alley some night."

"That won't happen," Gilmore said. "I'll see to it."

"All right." John Henry nodded. "I appreciate that."

"Enjoy your stay in Purgatory," Gilmore said. He turned and headed for the bat wings. Some of the men had drifted back up to the bar. They made sure to stay well out of his way.

"He seemed like a reasonable enough fella," John Henry said to Bouchard once Gilmore was gone.

"Don't believe a word he says," the saloon keeper advised. "He's a vicious outlaw. The rest of his bunch is bad enough, but he's the worst and everybody around here knows it."

"But nobody does anything about it."

Bouchard shrugged.

"Our marshal can break up a fight if a couple of miners get too rowdy. That's about all he's good for. Besides, he has his sights set on bigger things. He wants to be sheriff of the whole county."

"What about the sheriff?"

"He stays up at the county seat, doesn't get down this way very often."

"So you're sort of on your own when it comes to the law."

"Unfortunately, yes," Bouchard agreed. "Don't get me wrong. I run a saloon. I don't want some heavy-handed star packer coming in here and trying to clean up the town. But that doesn't mean I like the way Gilmore and his men think they can do what-ever they want and get away with it, either. Why, not that long ago, those two you tangled with today—" Bouchard stopped and shook his head. "Never mind. There's no point in going into that. Let's just say I won't shed any tears over you plugging the both of them."

"You just wish it had been in the gizzard," John Henry said.

Bouchard grinned and gestured toward John Henry's glass.

"Meade, fill that up again. For today, your money's no good in here, Mr. Sixkiller."

"I'm much obliged for that," John Henry said. "I'll try not to take advantage of your generosity." He paused. "Does this mean any time I want a free drink, all I have to do is shoot one of Gilmore's men?"

"Shoot Gilmore. You'll drink for free from now on."

"Hmmm," John Henry said.

Bouchard was called over to one of the poker tables to settle a minor dispute. John Henry picked his newly refilled glass of beer and went to one of the empty tables to sit down. He made sure his back was turned toward a blank wall and that no one could get behind him without his noticing. Like just about everybody else in the country, he had heard about how the famous pistoleer Wild Bill Hickok had been killed up in Dakota Territory when he sat in on a poker game with his back to the door.

He hadn't been sitting there long when one of the saloon girls started toward him. She had taken only a couple of steps in his direction, though, when another woman moved in front of her, cutting her off. They exchanged icy stares in a stalemate that lasted only a moment before the first woman shrugged and turned away.

The second one came toward the table where John Henry sat. He wasn't surprised to see that she was the honey blonde who'd been watching him through the window.

"Mind if I sit down?" she asked as she came to a stop on the other side of the table.

"Not at all," John Henry said. He stood up. He had already taken off his hat and placed it on the table next to his glass, or else he would have tipped it to her. As it was, he stepped around the table to hold the chair for her.

"My goodness, I don't encounter such gentlemanly behavior very often in a place like this," she said.

"My mother raised me to always be courteous, no matter what my surroundings," he told her as he resumed his seat.

"You weren't very courteous when you shot Rudd and Logan."

"The way I see it, I gave them all the courtesy they deserved."

"No, you gave them more than they deserved. If those two got what they deserved, they'd both be dead, especially that weaselly little Rudd."

"He did seem a mite weaselly," John Henry agreed. "Would you like a drink?"

She surprised him by saying, "No, that's all right. There wouldn't be any real booze in anything Meade sent over for me, anyway."

"That's one of the points of your occupation here, isn't it?"

"One of them," she admitted. "My name's Della. Della Turner."

"John Henry Sixkiller."

"That's a very impressive name. Almost as impressive as the way you handle your gun. I just wish your aim was a little better."

"Beg pardon?"

"You should've hit those two a few feet higher."

"Your boss said about the same thing to me a few

minutes ago." John Henry leaned back in his chair and smiled. "I'm starting to get the idea that Purgatory's a bloodthirsty place."

"If you had to put up with Billy Ray Gilmore and his bunch, you'd be bloodthirsty, too. Everybody in town is scared of them."

"I got the feeling that Bouchard isn't."

Della thought about that for a second and nodded.

"Royal isn't scared for himself, but he worries about what would happen if they went on a rampage. A lot of innocent people might get hurt. And that would be bad for business."

"I get the impression that you're not particularly scared of them, either," John Henry said.

"You're wrong. I may hate them. . . . I do hate them . . . but they scare me, too. About the only ones around here who aren't frightened of them are the men who own those gold mines up in the mountains."

"Mines?" John Henry repeated with a bland, innocent smile.

"Yes, there are several pretty good mines up there. If there weren't, Purgatory probably wouldn't be here. Most of the businesses are supported by the mines and the men who work there."

"That's interesting. I'd heard there was gold and silver in these parts."

"You're not a prospector, are you?"

"Me?" John Henry laughed. "No, that's too much

work for me. There are easier ways to make a living than with a shovel and pickax."

"Like with a gun?" Della said.

John Henry didn't respond right away. He hadn't made any firm plans about how he was going to proceed once he got here, but fate seemed to have stepped in and mapped a course for him. Della clearly thought he was a drifting gunman, and Bouchard had seemed to be of the same opinion. Pretty much the whole town had either witnessed or heard about that ruckus with Rudd and Logan, two members of the outlaw gang that was responsible for his being here. So even though he had been in Purgatory only a short time, he already had a dangerous reputation whether he wanted one or not.

He might as well take advantage of that if he could, he decided. He was here to stop Gilmore from stealing that massive gold shipment, and the best way to do that might be from the inside.

So he just smiled and said in reply to Della's question, "A gun's a lot lighter than a shovel or a pickax. You don't have to swing it all day to make a living, either."

She could take that however she wanted to, he told himself.

"That's what I thought," she said. "I've got another question for you." She leaned forward, giving him a nice view of the creamy valley between her breasts. "Would you like to go upstairs with me, Mr. Sixkiller?"

Chapter Thirteen

That was certainly plain enough, he thought. To buy himself a little time, he said, "You should call me John Henry."

"The question's still the same, John Henry," Della said. "Would you like to go upstairs with me?"

"The invitation has a definite appeal," John Henry allowed. "But just because I'd like to do something doesn't mean it would be the right thing."

"You don't make it easy to get a straight answer, do you?"

"Life's questions are often quite complex."

Della rolled her eyes.

"All right, forget it," she said. "You must have a girl back where you came from."

As a matter of fact, John Henry was very fond of Sasha Quiet Stream. But neither of them had committed to the other just yet, and it might help his cause here in Purgatory to have Della on his side. . . .

No, he was just trying to talk himself into something, he realized. He said, "I'm sorry. Don't take it personal."

"When a girl offers to take you upstairs and you turn her down, there's no other way to take it but personal." She shrugged, making the neckline of her dress do interesting things. "But it's your loss, cowboy."

John Henry nodded slowly and said, "That's what I figure. And I may regret it later on."

"Oh, you will," she said. "I can guarantee that."

The words could have been taken as a threat, but she was smiling so he didn't think she meant them that way. If she did, that was just something he would have to deal with.

"Tell me more about that fella Gilmore," he said. "Can I trust him to keep his dogs called off, like he said he would?"

"I don't know. He's never said anything to me that I was sure was an outright lie, but that doesn't mean he's not capable of it."

"What about Rudd and Logan? Would they come after me even if Gilmore told them not to?"

"I don't think Duke Rudd would stop at anything," Della said sharply, and once again John Henry got the feeling that there was some bad blood between her and Rudd. "And Sam Logan just goes along with whatever Duke tells him to do. I'm not sure if he's dumb or just too lazy to do his own thinking. So if I was you, John Henry . . . I'd sure keep an eye out behind me. Unless you're thinking of leaving Purgatory right away, while they're still laid up."

John Henry sipped his beer and then shook his head.

"Nope," he said. "I'm going to be around here for a while."

Henry Hinkle was filing the latest batch of wanted posters he'd received. Some lawmen just crammed those reward dodgers in a desk drawer and left them there, but Hinkle believed that organization was important. He sorted them out according to the crimes with which the miscreants were charged, then put them in alphabetical order by the outlaws' last names. That way he could find anything he wanted in a hurry.

Not that he'd ever really needed to do that. He didn't particularly want to know that a wanted desperado was in his town. If he did, he might have to do something about it.

Hinkle was a stocky man in his thirties with slightly wavy dark hair. His face had the heavy look of a man who enjoyed good food and drink maybe a little too much. He usually wore a white shirt and black vest and had a string tie around his neck in an attempt to look dapper. The nickel-plated revolver in his holster had ivory grips, and Hinkle liked the way it looked. He rode out of town once a month and shot a few rounds with it, to make sure that it stayed in good working order, even though he had never used it otherwise and had no plans to do so.

He was big enough that his size, along with the badge pinned to his vest, intimidated most drunks and petty criminals, and he wasn't going to deal with anything worse than that. The marshal's job didn't pay much, but his needs were simple and few, at least for the moment.

Henry Hinkle wasn't completely unambitious, though. He had his sights set on Sheriff Elmer Stone's job. The wages were better, and he would have plenty of deputies to take care of the actual work. Mayor Cravens and the town council wouldn't let him hire any deputies here in Purgatory. They claimed the town didn't have enough money for that.

As much gold as passed through here, it seemed like the town ought to be rich, Hinkle had thought on more than one occasion.

He picked up a stack of the reward posters he'd been sorting and tapped it against the desk to straighten the edges. As he was doing that, the door of the marshal's office opened. Hinkle looked up and saw Billy Ray Gilmore lounging in the doorway with a shoulder propped against the jamb. At the sight of the outlaw, Hinkle's heart slugged in alarm inside his chest.

"Marshal," Gilmore said in that soft, scary voice of his. "How you doin'?"

"I . . . I'm fine," Hinkle replied, wishing that his voice hadn't caught that way and revealed how nervous he was. "What can I do for you, Mr. Gilmore?"

"I suppose you know there was some trouble earlier?"

Hinkle swallowed and said, "I heard something about that."

"You didn't hear the gunshots?"

"I . . . might have," Hinkle admitted. "But by the time I had a chance to check on it, everything was all over."

"That's a shame. You might have been able to arrest the troublemaker on the spot. He shot two of my friends."

"I heard a rumor. . . . I've been meaning to check it out. . . ."

"Let me save you the trouble," Gilmore said. "Duke Rudd and Sam Logan were both shot. In the foot."

"In the foot," Hinkle repeated. "Then they're not . . . dead?"

"No, but they're in a heap of pain. One of Duke's toes was shot half off, and the doc says he's gonna lose what's left of it. It doesn't seem right that a fella should get away with doing that."

"I'm afraid I don't know the details," Hinkle said. "I'll have to investigate the case—"

"Again, I'll save you the trouble, Marshal. My pards weren't doin' anything, just havin' a little sport with the mayor, you know, just some good clean fun, when this stranger gallops up, nearly tramples them, and then up and shoots 'em both with no warning. It's just not right, Marshal. Something's got to be done about it."

"What . . . what do you want me to do?"

Gilmore ignored that question for the moment. He said, "I went and talked to the man myself. His name's Sixkiller, John Henry Sixkiller. Might be an Injun, I ain't sure about that. But he's unrepentant. Threatened poor ol' Duke and Sam again, in fact. I assured him they wouldn't come after him seekin' revenge, but he pretty much came right out and said that if he sees 'em again, he intends to kill them. I think you need to step in and keep the peace here, Marshal."

"You . . . you want me to . . ."

"Arrest this varmint Sixkiller," Gilmore said. "I promised that me and my friends wouldn't bother him, but I didn't say anything about the law catchin' up to him for his misdeeds."

Hinkle felt beads of sweat forming on his forehead. One of them trickled down into his left eye, making him blink and grimace. He swiped a hand across his forehead and said, "I'm not sure I can do that, Mr. Gilmore. Like I said, I didn't see the incident take place myself—"

"There are plenty of witnesses," Gilmore cut in. "They'll tell you what I just told you. Now, you need to go do your duty, Marshal."

"Maybe this man Sixkiller will ride on out of town—"

"That's exactly what I don't want. Man like that needs to be behind bars." Gilmore smiled. "Don't you think so, Marshal?"

Hinkle fought down the feeling of panic that

tried to well up inside him. He said, "I'll look into it. You have my word on that."

"When?"

Hinkle wished that Gilmore hadn't asked that quite so insistently.

"First thing in the morning—" he began.

"That might be too late. Sixkiller's over in the Silver Spur right now. If you'll go and arrest him, Duke and Sam will press charges against him. I'm sure of it."

"Do you think . . . do you think he'd come along peacefully?"

"Why, I don't know," Gilmore said. "But that doesn't matter, does it? It's your job to take him into custody either way."

"Yeah."

A feeling of fatalistic gloom settled over Hinkle. He wasn't sure why Gilmore was doing this. Normally, if anybody stood up to the outlaws, they got slapped down hard, sometimes even fatally. When that happened, Hinkle would make noises about investigating, but nothing ever got done. It was a good system.

"You want to come with me?" he asked.

"I wouldn't think of interferin' with the workings of the law," Gilmore said. "You can handle this, Marshal. I'm sure of it. Fact of the matter is, when you talk to Sixkiller just leave my name out of it. Say you had reports about him from concerned citizens."

The only thing Hinkle was sure of was that he didn't want to leave this office. But it was obvious that Gilmore was going to keep prodding him until Hinkle did what he wanted.

And when you came right down to it the stranger, that John Henry Sixkiller, was an unknown quantity. Hinkle didn't know what he would do.

Gilmore, on the other hand, was a devil. Even though he hadn't voiced a single word in a threatening manner during this visit, Hinkle knew perfectly well what the outlaw was capable of. He had no choice but to go along with what Gilmore told him to do.

"All right," he said as he put his hands flat on the desk and pushed himself to his feet. He felt like he weighed a thousand pounds, that was how badly he didn't want to leave his chair right now. But he stood up and reached for his flat-crowned black hat, which hung on a peg on the wall behind the desk. "I'll go over to the saloon and arrest this man Sixkiller."

"I'm glad to hear it," Gilmore said. "Duke and Sam can rest easier now, knowin' that the varmint who caused them such misery is gonna be behind bars where he belongs."

"Yeah," Hinkle said as he came out from behind the desk. "You tell them justice will be done."

A big grin broke across Gilmore's face when he heard that, and Hinkle knew what the outlaw was thinking.

There was no justice in Purgatory these days . . . and there wouldn't be as long as Billy Ray Gilmore was around.

Chapter Fourteen

Despite some of the thoughts in his head, John Henry enjoyed talking to Della, so he was a bit disappointed when she stood up and told him that she had to leave. It wasn't surprising, though; she was a working girl, and she wasn't making any money sitting there and chewing the fat with him.

Royal Bouchard came over a few minutes later and sat down when John Henry waved a hand at the empty chair on the other side of the table.

"It looked like you and Della were getting along well," Bouchard commented as he took a cigar out of his vest pocket. "Smoke?"

"Thanks," John Henry said, taking the cigar. "Don't mind if I do."

Bouchard got out another cigar for himself, then scraped a match to life and lit both of them. After puffing on his, John Henry went on, "I don't think Della and I got along quite as well as she'd hoped."

"She's a lovely girl," Bouchard said with a smile.

"You either have a lot of willpower, or your tastes run in other directions."

"They run in Della's direction, you can be sure of that," John Henry said. "But there's another girl . . ."

"Ah, a gentleman." Bouchard chuckled. "I haven't run into too many of those in my life. You're a rare breed."

John Henry shrugged.

"What can I say? Loyalty's important to me."

"It's a fine quality. Also rare."

They smoked in companionable silence for a few moments. Then Bouchard glanced toward the door as the bat wings swung open, and his eyes narrowed. John Henry saw the reaction and looked toward the entrance, too. The man who stepped into the Silver Spur wasn't very impressive. Medium height, thickly built, with dark hair under a flat-crowned black hat. The string tie he wore and the ivory-handled gun on his hip made him look a little like a dude.

"Who's that?" John Henry asked quietly.

"Our esteemed marshal," Bouchard answered, with scorn evident in his voice. "Henry Hinkle."

"Does he come in here often?"

"Not if he can help it. He seems to be looking for someone." Bouchard paused as Hinkle looked at them and then started across the room toward the table where they sat. "And that someone appears to be you."

"Or maybe you," John Henry suggested.

Bouchard shook his head.

"Not likely. He has his sights set on you."

John Henry sighed. Here he was, faced with a dilemma again. It went against the grain for him to conceal his identity from a fellow lawman, yet doing so for the time being might help him accomplish the job that had brought him here. Like it or not, he was going to play the hand the way fate had dealt it to him.

Marshal Hinkle came to a stop beside the table, between the two men who were sitting there, and nodded to the saloon keeper.

"Evening, Mr. Bouchard," he said.

"Marshal." Bouchard's tone was civil, but nothing more. "What brings you here?"

"I'm looking for this gentleman here. Is your name Sixkiller, mister?"

"It is," John Henry said. "What can I do for you, Marshal?"

Hinkle drew in a deep breath. He squared his shoulders, hooked his thumbs in his gun belt so that his right hand was close to the butt of his revolver, and drew himself up to his full height, which wasn't anything special. Clearly, he was gathering his strength and girding his loins for battle, and John Henry might have been impressed if he hadn't been able to see the panic lurking in the marshal's eyes.

Hinkle said, "You're—" then had to stop as his breath caught in his throat. He cleared it and started again. "You're under arrest," he got out this time.

"Is that so?" John Henry asked calmly. "What are the charges?"

"Attempted murder."

John Henry frowned and said, "Honestly, I don't recall trying to murder anyone since I rode into town, Marshal. Refresh my memory for me."

"You shot Duke Rudd and Sam Logan. I've had reports about it from, uh, concerned citizens. We don't like violence in the streets of Purgatory."

"Well, I can't blame you or the citizens for that," John Henry said, "but I didn't try to murder those two gents. I shot 'em in the foot. If I wanted them dead, they'd be dead now."

"Maybe you were aiming to kill them and . . . and just missed."

John Henry shook his head and said, "No, I don't think so. I generally hit what I aim at."

Hinkle looked like he wanted to bolt, but he made himself stay where he was. He glanced around as if searching for someone to tell him what to do next, then said, "But that's still, uh . . . assault. You can't just go around shooting people, even if it's just in the foot."

"I might agree with you, except I had a good reason for shooting those two boys. They'd been shooting at your mayor just before I came up. They were making him dance, just like two-bit despera-does in some dime novel. I figured I'd better make them stop before somebody got seriously hurt, and that seemed like the quickest way."

The corners of Bouchard's mouth twitched a little. John Henry could tell that he was struggling to keep from laughing. He hoped Bouchard would be able to keep the impulse under control. Marshal Hinkle didn't seem like much of a threat, but if a man felt humiliated enough, he might snap and do something foolhardy.

After a moment, Hinkle said, "I didn't know that about Mayor Cravens."

"There are plenty of witnesses who saw it, Marshal," Bouchard said. "Some of them are still here in the saloon. You can ask around if you want. You'll find somebody to back up Mr. Sixkiller's story."

Hinkle swallowed and nodded.

"I'll do that," he said. "I'll conduct a full investigation. In the meantime, Mister, uh, Sixkiller, I'd appreciate it if you didn't leave town."

"Wasn't planning to," John Henry said with a smile.

"All right." Hinkle jerked his head in a curt nod. "Fine."

He turned and tried to stalk out of the saloon with some of his dignity intact. He didn't succeed very well, because by the time he reached the bat wings he was hurrying so much he was almost running.

"And that's our noble defender of law and order," Bouchard drawled. "You can see now why Gilmore and his men do pretty much whatever they want around these parts."

"Who do you reckon put him up to that?" John

Henry asked. "Or is trying to arrest me something he would have come up with on his own?"

Bouchard snorted and shook his head.

"Not likely," he said. "Maybe Gilmore, just to see what you'd do? He said he wouldn't let Rudd and Logan come after you, but he didn't say anything about not going to the marshal."

John Henry nodded and said, "That's what I wondered, too. Kind of risky, though. What if Marshal Hinkle had gone for his gun and I killed him?"

"Hinkle was never going to slap leather against you, Sixkiller. Might as well ask what if he flapped his arms and flew like a bird."

"That would be a sight to see, wouldn't it?" John Henry said with a grin.

He finished his beer and spent some more time chatting with Royal Bouchard. Della had vanished from the saloon. John Henry assumed she was upstairs with a customer. For some reason he felt a little bad about that, even though he knew he shouldn't. He supposed it was just that he felt no woman should have to make her living that way. Della didn't appear to mind all that much, though. He supposed she had come to terms with it, as much as anybody could, anyway.

And he wasn't here to right the wrongs of the world, he reminded himself. He was here to make sure that $75,000 in gold bullion didn't get stolen.

It was getting on toward evening, so he excused

himself and said he was going to find a stable for Iron Heart, a hotel room for himself, and a good place to eat supper.

"Patterson's Stable and Wagonyard is the best place for your horse," Bouchard told him. "You should be able to get a room at the Barrymore House. There are cheaper places, but it's the cleanest. They have a decent dining room there, too, or you can eat at the Red Top Café. It's not fancy, but the food's good."

"I'm obliged for the advice," John Henry said with a nod.

"And if you want, stop back by later this evening," Bouchard added. "I meant what I said about your money not being any good here today. Might as well drink for free while you can."

"A man'd be a fool not to," John Henry replied with a grin.

He left Iron Heart with a gruff, ginger-bearded hostler at the stable. The man handled the big gray with a firm but gentle touch, and John Henry knew his trail partner would be well cared for. He left his saddle there, too, but took his rifle and saddlebags with him as he walked to the hotel.

On the way he passed the café Bouchard had mentioned. It was a squat building made of blocks of red sandstone with a tile roof that was an even darker shade of red. A number of horses and wagons were tied up outside, so he suspected Bouchard was right about the food being good.

The clerk at the desk in the Barrymore House took his money and gave him a room key.

"Number Six," the man said. "Top of the stairs and turn right. It's on the front. Noise from the street shouldn't bother you too much, though, since it's not the weekend, or payday at the mines."

"Gets a little rowdy at those times, does it?" John Henry asked.

"You know how miners are."

Actually, John Henry didn't, not that well, anyway. Mining wasn't a major activity in Indian Territory. There were some coal mines in the mountains in the northeastern part of the territory, but John Henry had never spent much time up there.

He let the clerk's statement pass without comment, nodded his thanks to the man, and went upstairs. The room was comfortably furnished with a good bed, a rug on the floor, a dressing table and a couple of chairs, a washstand, and a wardrobe. There was an oil lamp on the table for later, when it got dark.

John Henry went to the window and pushed back the curtain. He had a good view of the street, all right. And there was none other than Marshal Hinkle, striding along the opposite boardwalk and nervously hitching up his gun belt after every few steps. Hinkle looked worried. John Henry had a feeling that was common. A man who was a coward was always worried. That was one of the worst things about it.

John Henry let the curtain fall closed. He would deal with Hinkle later, if he had to. For now it was enough to know that if Gilmore's gang did make a try for the gold, he wouldn't be able to count on the local lawman for any help.

Chapter Fifteen

Marshal Hinkle was almost back at his office when a figure stepped out of the gathering shadows at the mouth of an alley. He stopped short. Most Westerners, if confronted by that situation, would have reached instinctively for a gun. Henry Hinkle's first instinct, which he controlled with an effort, was to turn and run.

"Marshal," Billy Ray Gilmore said as he materialized out of the gloom. "I thought you were going to lock up that fella Sixkiller."

"I . . . I spoke to him," Hinkle said. "He claimed that your friends Rudd and Logan started the trouble by shooting at the mayor's feet and making him dance."

"Did you believe him?"

"Well, I don't know. Evidently there are witnesses to the incident who'll back up Sixkiller's story. I told him I'd have to conduct an investigation and . . . and warned him not to leave town."

"Well, I guess that's about all you can do, then," Gilmore said. "Meanwhile, poor Duke and Sam are laid up with those bullet wounds in their feet. It's a real shame. But I did what I could to get justice for 'em, I reckon. I went to the marshal and lodged a complaint, just like law-abidin' folks are supposed to do."

Despite his fear, Hinkle was angry again. He knew Gilmore was mocking him. He and the rest of those outlaws did what they wanted to do, whenever they wanted to do it, and never worried for a second about the law. Everybody in Purgatory knew that. All Gilmore was doing now was rubbing Hinkle's nose in how powerless he really was.

Hinkle ducked his head and started to move past Gilmore. He muttered, "I hope your friends get better."

Gilmore put out a hand to stop him. With an effort, Hinkle didn't flinch from the touch on his sleeve.

"You'll let me know how that investigation of yours turns out, won't you, Marshal?" he asked.

"Sure." Hinkle swallowed. "Sure, I will."

"Fine. Good evenin' to you."

Gilmore sauntered away along the boardwalk without looking back. Hinkle turned to watch him go. The marshal sleeved sweat from his forehead despite the fact that it wasn't a particularly warm evening.

Maybe it was time for him to leave Purgatory behind, he thought. He probably would have before now if it weren't for certain arrangements he'd made. Because of that, he was sort of stuck here. He had to wait and see what was going to happen.

And hope that he didn't wind up dead first.

The Silver Spur wasn't the only saloon in Purgatory, just the biggest and best. But there were several other places where a man could find a drink, a game of cards, or a woman, depending on what he wanted at the time. One of them was called Red Mike's, after the Irishman who owned it. Smaller and more squalid than the Silver Spur, nonetheless it was still popular among the settlement's more unsavory element.

The Gilmore gang certainly fit into that category.

Billy Ray Gilmore saw half a dozen of his men in the room when he came into Red Mike's. Two of them were at a table playing dominoes, while the other four leaned on the bar, nursing mugs of beer. The man closest to the door noticed Gilmore and nudged his neighbor, who looked around and then passed on the news that the boss was here. When all four men were looking at him, Gilmore silently inclined his head toward the rear table where the other two outlaws sat.

They drifted back to the table, carrying their drinks with them. Gilmore joined them. The table was big enough for all seven men, but just barely.

Gilmore had to swipe a chair from a vacant table. He turned it around and straddled it as he sat down.

"How are Duke and Sam doin'?" Junior Clemons asked. Junior was a big, jovial man who looked like somebody's friendly cousin. He'd killed his first man at the age of twelve. Cut his throat while the unlucky gent was sleeping.

"They'll be all right, I expect," Gilmore replied. "I'm pretty sure Duke will limp the rest of his life, and Sam may, too. But at least they'll still be able to get around some."

"What about the marshal?" Jack Bayne asked. "Did he arrest the fella who shot 'em, like you talked about, Billy Ray?"

Gilmore smiled ruefully and shook his head.

"The marshal claims he's gonna conduct a full investigation." Gilmore waved a hand. "I never expected him to do anything about it. Mainly, I just wanted to see the look on his face when I asked him to, and I have to tell you, it *was* pretty amusing."

Another of the outlaws, Ben Morton, spoke up.

"So what do we do now, Billy Ray? You talked to that bastard Sixkiller. What's he like?"

"Cool," Gilmore said. "So cool butter wouldn't melt in his mouth. And a good hand with a gun, too, although we already knew that. Sam's feet are pretty good-sized, but as a target for a gunshot, they're on the small side. Duke's are even smaller. Sixkiller didn't hit 'em where he did by accident, though."

"We can't let him get away with what he done,"

Junior declared. "If he does, folks won't be a-scared of us no more. Not scared enough, anyway."

"What do you suggest, then, Junior?" Gilmore wanted to know.

"Let me kill him. I'll take care of the son of a bitch."

"I want in on it, too," Bayne said. "And when he's dead, we'll hang his body up by its feet from that tree down by the well and leave it to rot. If folks have to see that every time they go to get water, they'll damn sure know they better not step out of line with us."

Gilmore thought about it for a moment and then nodded.

"You boys think you'll need any help?" he asked.

"Hell, no," Junior said. "We can take care of him, can't we, Jack?"

"Count on it," Bayne said.

Gilmore said, "Go to it."

It would be interesting to see how this turned out, too.

John Henry decided to eat in the hotel dining room. By doing that he could find out right away if the food was any good. Since he was going to be here in Purgatory for several days, maybe as long as a week, it wouldn't hurt to settle on several places to eat.

An attractive young woman with red hair came to his table to take his order. She wore a blue dress and a crisply starched white apron and gave him a friendly smile as she asked, "What can I get for you, sir?"

"What's the best thing you have on the menu?" John Henry asked.

"The roast beef and potatoes, I'd say."

He nodded and told her, "That's what I'll have, then. And coffee."

"I'll see to it right away."

She brought the coffee first, then a basket of rolls, then a plate full of thick slices of roast beef, along with chunks of potatoes and carrots swimming in gravy. John Henry dug in eagerly. It had been a long day on the trail, and he had an appetite.

The food was as good as he'd hoped it would be, but not all of his attention was focused on it. Without being too obvious about it, he had a look at his fellow diners, too. Most of them were hotel guests, he suspected, although some might be townspeople who had chosen to dine here. The ones who interested him the most were three middle-aged men who sat at a table in the rear of the room, talking among themselves as they ate.

Back in Fort Smith, Judge Parker had given him the names of the three men who owned the big mines in the area. John Henry wondered now if he was looking at Jason True, Arnold Goodman, and Dan Lacey. True was the only one of the three Judge Parker knew personally; the man with the iron-gray hair and neatly clipped mustache might be him, John Henry reflected. But there could be a dozen men in Purgatory who would match that same general description, so he couldn't be sure.

His instincts told him he was right, though. All three men were well-dressed, and when the stocky one with a face like a bulldog spoke to the waitress, he had the curt tone of someone used to giving orders. They just looked like captains of industry, John Henry thought dryly.

He could stand up right now, walk over there, make sure who they were, and introduce himself. That would certainly be the simplest course of action.

But would it be the most effective? Or should he remain unknown to them for the time being, unknown to everyone in Purgatory except as the man who had ridden into town and plugged two of Billy Ray Gilmore's henchmen?

He would play things along a little further and see what happened, he decided.

After he finished eating, he complimented the redheaded waitress on the food. She smiled a little more warmly than was absolutely necessary and said, "You come on back any time you want to, sir."

"I'll do that," John Henry said. He picked up his hat from the table, settled it on his head, and strolled out of the hotel.

Royal Bouchard had invited him to return to the Silver Spur and have a few more drinks. That sounded like a decent way to pass the evening. Besides, the saloon was probably the busiest place in town once the sun went down. By spending more time there, John Henry might be able to get an even better feel for what the situation was in Purgatory. He started in that direction.

His route took him beside a parked wagon with an arching canvas cover over its back, a Conestoga wagon like immigrants used to travel west. He had just walked past the apparently empty vehicle when the smell of recently-smoked tobacco drifted to his nose. There was nothing unusual in that—somebody could have walked along here a minute earlier puffing on a quirly—but John Henry's keen mind asked what if somebody sitting inside that wagon had been smoking instead? Why would somebody just sit there inside a darkened wagon?

There could be a number of different reasons, but at least one of them wasn't good. Following his instincts, John Henry started to turn around. His hand moved toward the butt of his Colt.

Muzzle flame lanced through the darkness and split the night as shots roared from inside the wagon.

Chapter Sixteen

John Henry kept turning, twisting out of the way as slugs sizzled through the air near his head. His gun came up and he triggered a pair of return shots at the wagon, then left his feet in a dive that carried him behind a water trough. He heard bullets thudding into the trough's thick wooden side.

His hat had flown off when he hit the dirt, but it had landed within reach. John Henry snaked his left arm out and snagged it. He waited for a brief lull in the firing, then popped up long enough to send the hat sailing through the air toward the arched opening at the rear of the Conestoga.

The gunmen inside the vehicle reacted instinctively, as John Henry expected they would. They started shooting at the hat, which was just a vague, light-colored shape as it spun through the darkness. At the same time, John Henry surged to his feet and ran alongside the wagon, firing three more shots through its canvas cover. He heard a man scream in pain.

Those shots emptied John Henry's revolver, because he always carried the hammer on an empty chamber. He bounded to his right, onto the boardwalk, and as he did, he heard another shot from the wagon. The hot breath of the bullet fanned his cheek. He darted into an alcove where the entrance of a store that was closed down for the night was located. That gave him a little cover.

He knew he had scored at least one hit; the scream from inside the wagon told him that much. But at least one of the bushwhackers was still in the fight. Lead-chewed splinters from the building wall near John Henry's head as he thumbed fresh cartridges from his shell belt into the Colt. Under the circumstances, he filled all six chambers this time.

Along the street, people were yelling, wanting to know what all the shooting was about, but everybody who had been outside had scurried for cover when the bullets began to fly and they weren't venturing back out into the street. That much was good, anyway, John Henry thought. He didn't have to worry as much about hitting an innocent bystander.

He went down on one knee, thrust the barrel of his gun around the corner of the alcove, and fired two shots at the wagon. That canvas cover was full of holes by now. The wagon's thick sideboards would probably stop most bullets, but the canvas might as well not have been there.

A dark shape leaped down from the rear of the

wagon. One of the bushwhackers was fleeing. John Henry snapped a shot at him, but the man broke into a run and didn't slow down.

Maybe that was a trick. Maybe the second ambusher, even though wounded, was waiting in the shadows inside the wagon for John Henry to step out and give chase.

Or maybe the second bushwhacker was dead, and the other one was just cutting his losses and trying to get away before he caught a bullet, too.

John Henry didn't believe in being foolhardy, but he wasn't the sort to sit back and wait when somebody tried to kill him, either. He left the cover of the alcove in a rolling dive that carried him into the street. As he used his momentum to come back up on his feet, he swung the Colt toward the wagon.

No shots came from the vehicle. John Henry's gut told him there was no longer a threat lurking inside it.

He set off in pursuit of the other bushwhacker, his long legs carrying him swiftly along the street.

He caught a glimpse of the man ducking around a corner and pounded after him. As John Henry approached the corner he slowed, knowing that the bushwhacker might have doubled back in an attempt to take him by surprise. He turned into the cross street moving low and fast, but no shots rang out. John Henry pressed himself against the building wall to his left and listened intently.

Shuffling footsteps and the rasp of someone breathing hard sounded ahead of him. The gunman was still on the move, even though John Henry couldn't see him. He moved along the boardwalk, moving now with the lethal grace of a big cat stalking its prey.

Every few steps, John Henry stopped to listen again. When he didn't hear the unsteady footsteps and the labored breathing anymore, two possibilities occurred to him. One was that the man he sought was wounded and had succumbed to his injuries, either passing out or dying.

The other was that the would-be killer was waiting for him.

As John Henry paused to consider his next move, thoughts raced through his head. He was convinced that the men who'd come after him were members of Billy Ray Gilmore's gang. Gilmore had set the marshal on him, and when that hadn't done any good, he had allowed a couple of his men to seek revenge for what had happened to Rudd and Logan.

The two bushwhackers weren't Rudd and Logan themselves, though. With bullet holes in their feet, neither of them would have been able to move as spryly as the man John Henry had seen jump down from the wagon and run off along the street.

None of that really mattered right now, John Henry told himself. The only important thing was that somewhere in the darkness lurked a man who wanted to kill him. John Henry supposed he could turn and walk away, but it wasn't like him to leave such a threat on his back trail.

He stepped out to the edge of the boardwalk where he'd be nice and visible and advanced steadily, well aware he might as well have painted a target on his chest. That was the quickest way to draw out the second bushwhacker. His every sense was on highest alert.

He heard the rustle of cloth at the same instant he spotted a flicker of movement in the shadows along the wall about a dozen feet in front of him. He threw himself forward onto his belly as a pair of muzzle flashes lit up the night. The gun in John Henry's hand roared and bucked as he thrust it in front of him. In the flickering glare from its explosions, he caught a glimpse of a man standing behind a barrel that sat next to the wall. The bushwhacker rocked back against the boards as John Henry's slugs smashed into his chest.

The man's gun clattered on the planks. He rebounded from the wall and pitched forward to lie sprawled across the boardwalk, one hand hanging limply over the edge.

Two rounds were left in John Henry's gun. He kept it trained on the fallen man as he climbed to his feet. He approached the man carefully and used his left hand to fish a match from his pocket. He snapped the lucifer to life with his thumbnail and held it high so the flickering glow from its flame washed over the boardwalk.

The man lay facedown in a spreading pool of blood. John Henry kicked the dropped gun into the street, then got a boot toe under the man's shoulder and rolled him onto his back. Just before the match flickered out, he saw the lifeless eyes staring up at him.

John Henry dropped the match and started reloading his gun again, this time leaving one of the chambers empty as he usually did. This fight seemed to be over. He hoped so, anyway.

A door creaked open behind him. An old man's voice asked nervously, "Who's there? Don't move, mister! I got a greener pointed right at you!"

"Take it easy, old-timer," John Henry said. "I'm not looking for any trouble with you."

"Gents go to shootin' holes in each other right outside my door, I'd say it's trouble, all right," the man replied. "Is it over?"

"It is," John Henry confirmed. "Is this your store?"

"My shop," the old-timer said. "Leather goods. Saddles, bridles, holsters. I got a room in the back where I sleep. Which is mighty danged hard to do when all hell's breakin' loose right outside!"

"I'm sorry," John Henry said. "The other fella started it, though. He and a partner opened fire on me, around the corner on Main Street."

"And you done for both of 'em?" The old-timer sounded like he had a hard time believing that."

"Evidently," John Henry said. "I'm not sure about the other one, but this hombre is dead."

"That's pretty good shootin'."

"Good enough to keep me alive, anyway. Do you have an undertaker in this town?"

The old man snorted.

"Of course, we got a undertaker. What sort o' uncivilized place do you take us for?"

"How about going and fetching him for this varmint while I check on the other one?"

The old man stepped closer. John Henry could see him now, skinny, bald, with a drooping white mustache, a long nightshirt flapping around his spindly shanks. The shotgun he carried appeared to weigh almost as much as he did. He had the weapon's twin muzzles pointed down now.

"Reckon I can do that," he said. "You sure you don't need help with the other rapscallion?"

"I don't think so," John Henry told him.

Keeping his gun in his hand instead of holstering it, he walked back to the corner and turned onto Main Street. He saw that several people were gathered around the wagon where the bushwhackers had hidden, and one of them was holding up a lantern.

Several of the townsmen drew back skittishly as John Henry walked up.

"It's all right, fellas," he said. "No need to worry, my problem's not with you."

"You're the one who shot the fella in the wagon?" one of the men asked.

"I am. Is he dead?"

"Dead as can be," another man replied. "Got a bullet hole in his shoulder, but that's not what killed him."

"No, it was the slug that blew half his head away did that," the first man said. "It left enough for us to recognize him, though. Just barely. Mister, you killed Junior Clemons."

"And who would that be?" John Henry asked.

"You don't know? Hell, he's one of Billy Ray Gilmore's men!" The man squinted at John Henry in the lantern light. "Son of a— You're the man who shot Rudd and Logan in the foot, too!"

The townsmen began backing away, as if they were afraid to get too close to the stranger who had ridden into Purgatory and started attracting bullets right off the bat.

John Henry couldn't say as he blamed them for feeling that way.

Chapter Seventeen

More people came along, giving in to their curiosity now that the shooting seemed to be over. One of them was Royal Bouchard, who smiled and said, "When I heard guns going off, I had a hunch you might be in the vicinity, Sixkiller. It looks like Gilmore didn't keep his promise about not coming after you."

"He said he wouldn't let Rudd and Logan come after me," John Henry pointed out. "Setting a couple of his other dogs on me isn't exactly the same thing."

"I suppose not. Come on back to the Silver Spur with me," Bouchard suggested. "After all the excitement, I'm sure you could use a drink."

"You don't think I should wait for the marshal to show up and look into this shooting?"

"I suppose you can if you want to stay out here all night," Bouchard said. "I wouldn't expect Hinkle to get around to it before morning, if then."

"You have a point," John Henry agreed. "If he wants to talk to me, I shouldn't be that hard to find."

John Henry asked a couple of the townsmen to let the undertaker know he had another customer in the wagon. He retrieved his hat, which had landed near the back of the wagon after he threw it in the air as a distraction. Luckily, the shots fired at it by the bushwhackers had missed, so there were no bullet holes in it. Then John Henry and Bouchard walked toward the saloon.

"You killed the other bushwhacker, too, I assume," Bouchard said.

"Seemed like the thing to do at the time."

"Get a look at him?"

"Not a good one. But since that hombre Clemons was one of Gilmore's men, I think it's a pretty safe bet his partner was, too."

"Yeah, I'd say so. You just keep making enemies, don't you? On the other hand, you've done a good job of whittling down the opposition."

John Henry laughed and said, "I suppose you could look at it that way. They're not really my opposition, though. I'm willing to leave them alone as long as they leave me alone."

"It may be too late for that now," Bouchard said solemnly. "You've done more than spill a little blood. Two of Gilmore's men are dead. He's going to have to square accounts for them, or he'll lose the respect of his gang."

"Well, if it comes down to that, I'll deal with it."

"By yourself?"

"Who else can I count on for help around here?"

"You might be surprised," Bouchard said. "There are plenty of folks in Purgatory who are sick and tired of being pushed around by outlaws."

"I'll keep that in mind," John Henry said as they reached the Silver Spur and went into the saloon.

Della was standing at the bar talking to Meade, the bartender. When she saw John Henry and Bouchard come in, she hurried over to meet them.

"You're all right?" she asked John Henry.

"You don't see me leaking blood, do you?" he replied with a smile.

"No, you look to be reasonably intact."

"What makes you think I was even mixed up in that shooting?"

She gave him an exasperated look and said, "Who else would it be? You ride into town and hell starts to pop. Is it that way everywhere you go?"

"All too often, yes," John Henry admitted. That was because of his job as a lawman, he thought, but he wasn't ready to reveal that secret just yet.

"Meade, send a bottle of brandy over to my private table," Bouchard told the bartender.

"I'll bring it myself," Della said.

Bouchard led John Henry to a different table from the one where they had been sitting earlier. This one was tucked away in a rear corner of the room where there was at least an illusion of privacy, and the chairs around it were padded and more comfortable. They sat down, and Bouchard again offered John Henry a cigar. He turned it down this time, saying, "One a day is about my limit."

Bouchard smiled and said, "There are no limits on fine cigars. But suit yourself."

Della arrived with the bottle of brandy and two crystal tumblers on a tray. She poured the drinks, then Bouchard said, "Why don't you stay, Della? It's obvious you want to."

"You're sure, Mr. Bouchard?"

The saloon keeper waved toward an empty chair. John Henry started to get up and hold it for her, but she said, "Just keep your seat. You don't have to treat me like a lady. I'm about the farthest thing from being one of those that you can imagine."

"I was raised to treat every woman like a lady," John Henry said.

"That's sweet of you to say, but it's not necessary. In case you hadn't noticed, I'm not exactly a shrinking violet."

John Henry shrugged. He wasn't going to argue with her. That wouldn't be the gentlemanly thing to do, either.

After they had sipped their brandy for a couple of minutes, Bouchard said to John Henry, "We've seen two demonstrations that you're mighty handy with a six-gun. Tell me the truth . . . is that how you make your living?"

"Most of the time," John Henry said. That wasn't exactly a lie, he thought. As a deputy marshal, most of the work he did involved at least a little gunplay.

"You're an outlaw?"

"There's no paper out on me."

That was true, as well. Bouchard and Della seemed to take it as a vague, noncommittal answer, though, which was exactly what John Henry intended.

"Are you in Purgatory for a reason, or did you happen to just drift in?"

John Henry took another sip of the smooth, fiery liquor and said, "You're sort of full of questions this evening, aren't you, Bouchard?"

"I've got a good reason to be asking questions," the saloon keeper said. "I've got a proposition for you."

John Henry's eyebrows rose in surprise. He said, "Is that so?"

"I've talked to some of the other businessmen in town," Bouchard said. "Gilmore and his men don't show any signs of leaving, and people are getting more and more frightened of them. To be blunt, they're bad for business. If you're interested, we'd like to hire you to deal with that situation."

John Henry certainly hadn't expected the turn this conversation had just taken. He asked, "You want to hire me to kill Billy Ray Gilmore?"

"And as many of his men as you can," Bouchard said with a solemn nod. "We'll make it worth your while, too."

John Henry leaned back in his seat and shook his head.

"I'm not a hired murderer," he said.

"You've already killed two of Gilmore's men and

put two more out of commission," Bouchard argued. "He's going to come after you anyway. You might as well get paid for taking on him and his gang."

John Henry considered the idea, but only briefly. He couldn't see how it would help him complete his assignment.

"Sorry," he said. "Not interested."

"I was afraid you'd say that. So we have an alternate suggestion. Take the marshal's job. The pay's not as good, but you'd have the backing of the law."

"You mean you'd fire Hinkle?"

"The town council is prepared to do so, yes. It wouldn't be any great loss to the town, I assure you."

There wasn't much brandy left in John Henry's glass. He tossed it back and then said, "Just like I'm not a hired killer, I'm not going to pin on the marshal's badge, either. You can tell the town council that I pass."

Bouchard sighed and nodded.

"All right, if that's the way you want it." His eyes narrowed. "I'm a pretty good judge of character, Sixkiller. I think you're up to something, but damned if I know what it is. If you want to keep on playing a lone hand, though, I can't stop you."

"That's the way it has to be," John Henry said.

Bouchard reached for the bottle.

"But you don't mind drinking my brandy, do you?"

"As long as there are no strings attached to it."

"None at all." Bouchard splashed the amber liquid into the tumblers and then raised his. "To your good health."

Della said, "That's not going to last very long, the way things are going around here."

Bouchard would have been happy to sit and kill the whole bottle with John Henry, and Della dropped several hints that showed she hadn't forgotten about wanting to go upstairs with him. John Henry didn't take up either of those offers. After he finished his second drink, he said, "I believe I'll head back to the hotel. I was on the trail for a lot of hours today, and I could use some shut-eye."

"Be careful," Bouchard cautioned him. "Gilmore almost surely knows by now that the men he sent after you are dead. They could have half a dozen ambushes laid for you between here and the Barrymore House."

"I'm in the habit of keeping my eyes open." John Henry turned toward the honey blonde. "Good night, Miss Della."

"There you go, treating me like a lady again," she said. "Sooner or later I'll break you of that habit."

"We'll see," John Henry told her with a grin. He put his hat on and left the saloon.

He knew that Bouchard was right: There was every chance in the world that more of Gilmore's men, maybe even the boss outlaw himself, were out there waiting for him. He remembered his mother reading Bible stories to him when he was a boy, and one of them was about Daniel in the lion's den.

That was a little bit like the way he felt tonight, like he was walking right into a den full of hungry lions.

Nothing happened during the short walk to the Barrymore House, though. The undertaker must have come and gone already, taking the bodies of the dead bushwhackers with him. The street was quiet and almost empty again.

John Henry nodded to the clerk as he went through the hotel lobby. The man looked away and didn't meet his eyes. John Henry wondered a little about that, and it made him even more cautious as he climbed the stairs and approached the door of his room. If Gilmore or some of the other outlaws had come to the hotel and demanded to know which room was his, the clerk probably would have been too scared not to tell them.

It was possible they were waiting in there for him now, ready to blast him through the door as soon as they heard his key in the lock.

Because of that, John Henry drew his gun as he catfooted along the hall. When he got closer to the door, he froze. A tiny gap was visible along the edge of the door, just enough to tell him that someone had opened it, gone inside, and pushed it back up so that it was almost closed, but not quite.

Somebody out to kill him wouldn't do that, John Henry thought as a frown creased his forehead. He couldn't have failed to notice that the door was open, so he wouldn't just waltz into the trap waiting for him.

No, leaving the door cracked that way was more like something a thief would do, so that he could hear anybody approaching the room.

However, the thief, if that's what he was, hadn't counted on John Henry's ability to move in complete silence. John Henry eased closer, and as he did, he saw the faint glow of a light in the room. A match burning, maybe. He reached the door, rested his left hand against it, and lifted the Colt in his right.

Then he shoved the door open, stuck the gun out in front of him, and snapped, "Don't move!"

The figure beside the bed didn't follow that order. John Henry heard a startled gasp as the intruder whirled around. The match fell and went out, but not before John Henry caught a glimpse of the face of the person waiting in his room.

It was a woman, but not either of the ones he might have expected, blond Della or the pretty redheaded waitress from the hotel dining room. This woman had hair that was a rich dark brown, along with a lovely heart-shaped face with a tiny beauty mark near her mouth to accentuate her attractiveness. John Henry needed only a second to recall her name.

Sophie Clearwater, the young woman who had tried to rob him on the train the other side of El Paso.

Chapter Eighteen

With the match out, shadows suddenly cloaked the room. Some light penetrated from the hallway, but the wall sconce containing an oil lamp was all the way down at the other end of the corridor. John Henry saw a flash of movement to his right as the woman darted in that direction.

Surely she didn't think she could get past him with his blocking the door the way he was. As he twisted to intercept her, though, he saw that she had fooled him. Just as he had thrown his hat to draw the fire of the bushwhackers in the wagon, she had tossed something to distract him, too. As it slapped across his arm, he realized it was his saddlebags.

The next instant something slammed into his left shoulder and shattered with a crash. The chamber pot from under the bed, he thought. He was glad he hadn't used it earlier.

The impact from the heavy ceramic pot staggered him a little and made him take a step back. She barreled into him a split-second later and knocked him even more off balance. She couldn't weigh much, but she was moving fast. To his amazement, John Henry realized that she was about to slip past him.

His left hand shot out and grabbed the collar of her traveling dress. Despite his upbringing, he wasn't inclined to worry too much about being gentle with an intruder in his room, male or female. She let out a soft cry of alarm as he pulled her back and heaved her toward the bed. He put enough strength into it that her feet completely left the floor. She landed on her back, lying across the mattress, and bounced a little.

John Henry stepped into the room, heeled the door closed behind him, and pulled out a match of his own. He squinted against the glare as he snapped it to life.

Sophie Clearwater lay there on his bed, her breasts made more prominent by the way she was lying on her back and breathing heavily. She started to roll to the side, but John Henry pointed the Colt at her and said, "Nope."

She settled back, propped up on her elbows, and glared at him.

"You wouldn't shoot an innocent woman," she said.

"No, I probably wouldn't," he agreed. "Know where I can find one around here?"

"I didn't do anything!"

"Except break into my room."

"I didn't break into anything," she insisted. "The clerk let me in."

"Why would he do that?"

"Because I told him I was your wife!"

"In that case, you're in the right place, lying in my bed like that, I suppose," John Henry said. "You're a little overdressed for the setting, though."

When he took a step toward her, she gasped and said, "You wouldn't dare!"

"Wouldn't dare claim my husbandly privileges, you mean?" he said. "I wouldn't be so sure of that, Mrs. Sixkiller."

"It's Miss Clearwater!"

"Not if you're my wife, it's not."

"Fine, damn it," she said. "So I lied. I never claimed I didn't."

"And I have a feeling you were searching my saddlebags when I came in," he went on. "That's why you had them in your hand and were able to throw them at me. You must have been disappointed when you didn't find anything except the same stuff that was in my carpetbag on the train. Why in blazes are you so determined to rob me, anyway?"

She sniffed in disdain and said, "I wasn't trying to rob you. I have better things to do than that."

"Then what *are* you after, and what are you doing here in Purgatory? Did you follow me here?"

"Don't flatter yourself," she snapped.

John Henry's brain worked swiftly. He said, "If you're not trying to rob me, and if you didn't follow me here, which means you were already on your way to Purgatory when we met on the train, that leaves only one answer: You're trying to find out who I am and what *I'm* doing here. Am I right?"

He saw by the sudden flash of reaction in her eyes that he had reasoned it out correctly. But why would she be interested in his identity and his reasons for coming to Purgatory?

"I don't have to talk to you," she said. "Call the law on me if you want. I don't care. I haven't done anything wrong."

John Henry thought about what a waste of time it would be to turn her over to Marshal Henry Hinkle. Besides, he wanted answers, and if he turned her in, he wouldn't get any.

"Go ahead and sit up," he told her. "Just don't try anything."

"What would you do, throw me across the room again?"

"The way you landed on the bed, you didn't hurt anything," he pointed out.

"Did you know for sure that was how I was going to land?"

As a matter of fact, he hadn't. He'd just been trying to stop her from getting away. It was luck that made her fall harmlessly across the bed.

He didn't admit that. As she sat up, he said, "Just tell me why you're so determined to search my gear, and maybe I'll let you go."

She sighed and said, "Look, I'm a thief, all right? I might as well admit it. I use my good looks to distract men, and I sneak around and steal. But I haven't stolen anything from *you*, so you've got to let me go."

John Henry waggled the gun in his hand.

"I don't think I *have* to do anything right now."

"Well, if you're going to force yourself on me, go ahead and get it over with."

"Nobody said anything about that." John Henry was still thinking fast, considering everything he knew about the situation here in Purgatory, and he decided to take what might turn out to be a blind shot. "Just like nobody said anything about $75,000 in gold bullion, either, but I think we both know about it."

Maybe she was just one hell of an actress, but from the way Sophie's jaw dropped, John Henry thought he had taken her completely by surprise. Despite the gun he still had pointed at her, she came to her feet.

"How did you . . . You *know* about the gold?"

"Of course, I do, and so do you."

Now they were getting somewhere, he thought.

Sophie stubbornly shook her head, though, and said, "I don't know what you're talking about."

"You just admitted that you did."

"I did no such thing. This is mining country. Of course, there's gold around here." She laughed. "But $75,000 worth of bullion. That's ridiculous. Nobody would ever put that much gold in one place. That's just asking for it to be stolen."

"But if you could put together a shipment of that

size and get it safely into the hands of Wells Fargo's, that would be better than losing a lot of smaller shipments, wouldn't it? Bigger risk, bigger reward."

She looked like she was about to argue with him some more, but abruptly she changed her mind.

"Fine," she snapped. "You know about the gold. But that doesn't mean you can horn in on it."

"You've got your sights set on it?" John Henry asked.

"Of course! If I could get my hands on that bullion it would be the biggest haul of my life! No more lifting wallets or . . . or the other things I've had to do to get by."

"So why get me involved?" he said. "Why were you so determined to find out who I am?"

"Because I thought you might be after the same thing. And I was right! You wouldn't even know about the gold if you weren't planning to steal it."

There was another way he'd know about it, he thought: if he'd been sent here to protect it. But he wasn't going to admit that to Sophie.

"That doesn't explain why you thought I might be after the gold," he said.

"Look. I have my sources on the railroad. When I heard about the gold, I was able to find out who had tickets for Lordsburg, since that's the closest stop to Purgatory. I figured it would be a good idea to find out as much as I could about them. I don't need the competition. You were the only one I wasn't able to pin down and peg as harmless. And then when you actually showed up here in Purgatory, I knew I was right to be suspicious of you."

"How'd you find out about the gold in the first place?"

"I have sources in other places besides the railroad," she said, being deliberately mysterious about it.

According to what Jason True had told Judge Parker in his letter, the only ones who knew about the planned massive gold shipment were the three mine owners and officials of the Wells Fargo Express Company. The mine owners were here in Purgatory, so that meant Sophie must have learned about the shipment from somebody who worked for Wells Fargo. It would be a good idea for the company to ferret out that indiscreet employee . . . but that could be dealt with after the gold was safely on its way to the mint in Denver.

"Look, I'm the only one who's giving away any information here," Sophie went on. "You still haven't told me who you are and exactly what you're planning, or how you found out about the gold, for that matter. Don't you think turnabout is fair play?"

"Not as long as I'm holding the gun, I don't," John Henry said. He was busy trying to figure out what to do about this adventuress and would-be gold thief. Her presence was something he hadn't expected, and it was a complication he didn't really need, since he already had a gang of bloodthirsty outlaws to deal with.

He could reveal who he really was and arrest her,

but then what would he do with her? There was a jail here in Purgatory where he could lock her up, but he didn't really trust Marshal Hinkle to keep her behind bars. Besides, what would there be to stop her from telling anybody who would listen that he was a deputy United States marshal? That was something he was trying to avoid for the time being.

An idea occurred to him. It was risky, but it was really the only thing he could do.

"I don't believe in telling anybody my plans unless I'm sure I can trust them," he went on. "And there's only one way I know I can trust you, Sophie."

"Fine," she said. She reached for the top button on her traveling outfit.

"That's not what I meant," John Henry said quickly.

She lowered her hands and said, "Oh." John Henry thought she sounded a little disappointed. "What did you mean, then?"

"I was suggesting that you and I should throw in together. There's a whole gang besides us after that gold, you know."

"The Gilmore gang," she said. "I've heard about them. And I've also heard that you've tangled with them a couple of times already."

John Henry shrugged.

"We're going to have to swipe it out from under their noses. We'll have a better chance of doing that if we're working together, rather than against each other, as well. And a two-way split would be better than getting nothing at all."

"Who said it would be a two-way split?" Sophie asked.

John Henry frowned and asked, "What do you mean?"

The door opened behind him, and a familiar voice said, "The lady means she already has a partner. Don't move, mister, or I'll blow your head off."

Chapter Nineteen

"Well, well," John Henry said. "Doc Mitchum. Fancy meeting you here."

"I meant what I said," the old snake oil salesman warned. "Don't try anything or I'll shoot."

"Not fast enough to stop me from pulling the trigger and killing your partner here," John Henry said. "The two of you *are* partners, aren't you? I should have figured that out from how nosy you were on the train, Doc. You were trying to find out who I was, too, and when you weren't able to get anything except my name, Sophie moved in."

Sophie looked past John Henry and said, "Don't shoot him, Doc. He wants to work together with us."

Mitchum snorted.

"I heard that while I was listening through the door. And of course he says he wants to work together. But why should we trust him, and more importantly, why do we need him?"

"Maybe because I've already knocked out four

members of the competition?" John Henry suggested.

"It's true," Sophie said with a nod. "He's killed two of Gilmore's men and wounded a couple of others."

Doc Mitchum closed the door, then moved into the room and circled widely around John Henry, giving him plenty of room and not coming within reach. John Henry watched the man from the corner of his eye and saw that Mitchum had a dubious frown on his face and a small-caliber pistol in his hand.

"I heard about that," Mitchum admitted. "It still doesn't mean we should let him in on the deal."

"You wouldn't be letting me in on anything," John Henry pointed out. "I already know about the gold."

"Could we please just stop pointing guns at each other?" Sophie asked. "It's starting to make me nervous."

Still frowning, Mitchum said, "I'll put my gun away if you will, Sixkiller."

"How about we just lower them instead?" John Henry said. "I'm not sure I'd feel comfortable holstering my iron just yet."

"Fine." Mitchum lowered the small pistol he held.

John Henry pointed his Colt at the floor and asked Sophie, "Better now?"

"Much," she said fervently. "Listen, Doc, we knew

we'd have to recruit somebody here in Purgatory to help us. We can't pull off a heist like this by ourselves."

"Yeah, but whoever we hired wasn't going to know what we were after until it was too late to double-cross us." Mitchum nodded toward John Henry. "He already knows about it."

"All the more reason to considering joining forces. Otherwise, it's going to be a three-way scramble for that gold."

"At least three ways," John Henry put in. "We can't be sure that nobody else in town knows about it and is planning to make a try for it."

"He's right," Sophie said.

"I don't trust him," Mitchum said stubbornly.

"You think I do? I'm just trying to make the best of a bad situation, that's all."

He looked at her with narrowed eyes.

"You sure it's not more than that? You sure you haven't let this fella's looks take you in?"

"He's not exactly what I'd call good-looking," Sophie said in a scornful voice. "Look at him. He's been in too many fights in his life. And think about it, Doc . . . Have you *ever* known me to let my judgment be compromised by a man?"

"Well, come to think of it, no," Mitchum admitted. "You've always had a pretty level head on your shoulders."

"Thank you. I'm glad you haven't forgotten that."

John Henry said, "I sort of feel like a piece of

livestock, the way you two are talking about me like I'm not here, or too dumb to understand what you're saying, anyway."

Mitchum ignored him and went on, "There's something else I'm worried about. What if we agree to work with him, and then he goes to the law and tells them we're after the gold? That'd be a good way for him to get rid of us."

"Then we'd turn right around and accuse him of the same thing," Sophie said. "He can't risk it. Anyway, the law in this town . . ."

She made a face to show in how much disdain she held Marshal Henry Hinkle.

"She's right about that, Doc," John Henry said. "The law's not something we need to worry about. The guards hired by those mine owners, on the other hand . . . they could pose a problem. If the three of them have thrown in together, they can afford to hire plenty of guns."

"How do you know they're working together?" Mitchum asked suspiciously.

"How else are they going to come up with that much gold unless they plan to combine their shipments?"

"That agrees with what we've been told," Sophie said, ignoring Mitchum's warning frown. "That's why we're not going after the gold on its way down from the mountains. The two of us can't fight a war against a bunch of hired guards. But there'll be some time between when the gold gets to Purgatory and Wells Fargo picks it up to take it to Lordsburg and the railroad."

"That's when you're going after it?" John Henry asked. "While it's stashed in the bank here?"

Sophie nodded and said, "That's the idea."

"And it might work," John Henry told her, "but there's one big thing wrong with it."

"Oh?" Mitchum said with the suggestion of a sneer on his face. "What's that?"

"You really think Billy Ray Gilmore is going to let the gold get to town in the first place?"

Sophie and Mitchum glanced at each other. John Henry could tell that they were concerned about the very thing he'd just suggested.

He pounded the point home by saying, "All the planning in the world isn't going to do you any good if Gilmore gets the gold while it's on its way down from the mountains."

"So what are you suggesting?" Mitchum demanded. "That we wipe out Gilmore and his gang?" He snorted. "That'd be a pretty big job, don't you think?"

"I don't know," Sophie said slowly. "Sixkiller's already made a start on it."

John Henry shook his head.

"That's probably asking a mite too much, even for me," he said.

"Don't be so modest," Sophie told him with a sneer. "You're obviously quite a gunman."

"This is ridiculous," Mitchum snapped. "He can't help us."

"Sure I can," John Henry said.

"How?"

"By working against Gilmore from the inside."

It was an audacious idea that had come to John Henry while he was talking. The easiest way to find out Gilmore's plans would be if Gilmore told him. But the only way that would happen was if he was part of Gilmore's gang.

"If you mean what I think you do, you're loco," Mitchum muttered. "You'll just get yourself killed." He brightened. "So go right ahead with it, I suppose. That'll simplify matters for us."

"Hold on," Sophie said. "How in the world do you think you're going to get into Gilmore's gang when you've already killed two of his men and wounded two more?"

"Well, under the circumstances wouldn't you say that I'm worth at least as much as those four men?" John Henry asked. "If Gilmore's really interested in stealing that gold, he's going to want the best men he can get for the job, right?"

Sophie looked at him for a long moment, then said, "You may be on to something there. It would be a big risk for you, though. He might just say the hell with it and kill you, or have his men do it for him."

"They could try. But there's at least a chance he'd see my point and agree to the deal. Besides, I'd approach him with the idea while we were in a public place."

Mitchum snorted and said, "You think that'd stop Gilmore from plugging you if he wanted to? You don't have to be here in Purgatory very long to know that he does whatever he damned well pleases most of the time."

"It's up to you. I just made the suggestion."

"There's another thing to consider, Sophie," Mitchum went on. "Maybe Sixkiller wouldn't betray us to the law, but he might tip off Gilmore that we're after the gold, too. That might be how he convinces Gilmore to let him join the gang."

"I'd have to be a pretty big fool to do that," John Henry said. "If I work with you, I'm looking at twenty-five grand. If I were to throw in with Gilmore for real, my slice of the pie would be a lot smaller than that."

Sophie nodded and said, "He's right. And I have a hunch he's smart enough to go after the biggest possible payoff."

"There you go again, talking about me like I'm not here," John Henry drawled, smiling.

"We can talk this around and around in circles until we're blue in the face," Mitchum said. "We need to decide, Sophie. Is he in or out?"

"If we say he's out, what do we do with him?"

Mitchum frowned and said, "I wish now I hadn't lowered my gun."

"We should let the lady leave the room first if it's going to come down to that," John Henry suggested.

"I'm not going anywhere, damn it!" Sophie snapped. "You men are always too blasted eager to start shooting at each other." She nodded curtly as she reached a decision. "I say Sixkiller is in on the job with us."

"And I vote yes, too," John Henry said.

Mitchum glared at him and said, "You don't get a vote, at least not until I say you do." He sighed. "But I reckon that'd be the easiest thing to do. If I get even the littlest hint, though, that you're trying to double-cross us or sell us out to Gilmore . . ."

"The same goes for me," John Henry promised. "We have to trust each other, and that goes both ways."

"That leaves us with the question of how you're going to convince Gilmore to accept you as part of the gang," Mitchum said.

"I have an idea about that," John Henry said, "but it involves the two of you."

"Before we get to that . . ." Sophie moved closer to him, within arm's reach. She proved that by putting her arms around his neck and lifting her face to his for an urgent, passionate kiss. John Henry was surprised, but he didn't pull away from the warm sweetness of her lips.

When she stepped back after a moment, she went on, "There. That ought to seal the deal."

"For God's sake, Sophie!" Mitchum burst out.

"No need for you to get jealous, Doc. You and I are just business partners, that's all. Besides, you're old enough to be my father."

"But I'm not your father, and you don't need to start alley-cattin' around with our new *business partner*."

Sophie smiled at John Henry and shrugged.

"I suppose he's right," she said. "Now, what were you saying about a way for you to get into Gilmore's gang . . . ?"

Chapter Twenty

Despite everything that had happened, John Henry slept well his first night in Purgatory, after Sophie Clearwater and Doc Mitchum left his room. He didn't really trust them, and he wasn't sure that teaming up with them wouldn't backfire on him, but there was nothing else he could do about it right this minute, so he might as well sleep. That attitude had always worked out well for him in the past and he didn't see any reason to change it now.

In the morning, he went to the hotel dining room for breakfast. The pretty redheaded waitress was there, and when she came to his table, John Henry smiled and asked her, "Do you do anything besides work here?"

"Oh, I do a lot of things, Mr. Sixkiller," she replied as she returned his smile.

"You know who I am?"

"I figure 'most everybody in Purgatory knows

you after yesterday. It doesn't take you long to make an impression on people."

John Henry chuckled and said, "Thanks . . . I think."

She brought him flapjacks and a plate filled with fried eggs and thick slices of ham. John Henry nearly always had a good appetite and this morning wasn't any different. He washed the food down with several cups of strong black coffee and felt pretty good when he left the hotel.

It wasn't too far-fetched to think that more of Gilmore's men might come after him in retaliation for the events of the previous day, and he agreed with Doc Mitchum that the fact of it being broad daylight in the center of town probably wouldn't stop them if they wanted to kill him.

But he thought it was unlikely that any of them were stirring this early. Outlaws tended to prefer late hours, whiskey, women, and cards, and Gilmore and his men were probably sleeping off binges or dozing in some whore's crib at this hour.

John Henry was alert anyway as he walked along the street. He never wanted to underestimate anybody who might want to put a bullet through him.

He was strolling aimlessly when he heard someone call his name. He turned to look and saw Mayor Joe Cravens hurrying toward him.

"Mr. Sixkiller, I thought that was you," Cravens said. "I never got a chance to thank you properly for your help yesterday."

"You thanked me, Mr. Mayor," John Henry said.

"Didn't really do it for you, though. No offense meant by that. I just don't like to see varmints like those two getting away with what they consider fun."

Cravens frowned in concern.

"I heard this morning that there was an attempt on your life last night," he said. "That had to be related to your efforts on my behalf."

"The two men were friends of Rudd and Logan, all right," John Henry admitted. "But they weren't successful, so that's all that really matters, isn't it?"

Cravens didn't answer that question. Instead, he suggested, "Why don't you come over to the bank with me? I'd like to talk to you about something."

Remembering the offer that Royal Bouchard had extended to him on behalf of the town council, John Henry said, "If this is about the marshal's job, or that other business—"

Cravens shook his head.

"Bouchard already told me you turned those proposals down. I was sorry to hear it. This is about something else."

John Henry didn't really have anything else to do right now, so he said, "I suppose I could hear you out."

Cravens smiled and nodded, obviously pleased.

John Henry had wanted to get a good look at the setup in the bank. What better way than to have the banker himself show him around, he thought with a faint smile as he walked with Cravens toward the redbrick building.

The tellers all said good morning to Cravens

when he and John Henry came into the bank, as did several of the customers. Purgatory might be a fairly small settlement, but its bank could have been in a bigger town. There was a lot of gleaming marble and polished wood in evidence, and fancy chandeliers hung from the ceiling.

To one side of the room was a set of thick doors that stood open at the moment. Beyond those doors, in a small, square room, stood a massive safe, painted dark green with gilt trim. It was quite impressive, John Henry thought, and appeared utterly impregnable. He wondered if all $75,000 worth of bullion would fit into it, or if some of the gold would have to be stored elsewhere. There were shelves along one side of the room containing the safe, so he supposed some of the bars could be stacked there.

He took that in with a quick glance, not wanting it to seem like he was paying an undue amount of attention to the safe.

Cravens led John Henry into his private office, which was comfortably furnished with a big desk and several well-padded leather chairs. He took off his hat and hung it on a hat tree, then asked if he could take John Henry's as well.

"I think I'll just hang on to it if that's all right," John Henry said. "I'm sort of partial to my hat."

"That's fine, Mr. Sixkiller." As he waved John Henry into one of the chairs in front of the desk, the banker went on, "It's early, I know, but I have a bottle of excellent whiskey. . . ."

John Henry shook his head and waved off the suggestion.

"I appreciate the offer, sir, but like you say, it's early." He sat down and balanced his hat on his knee. "What was it you wanted to talk to me about?"

"A man who gets right down to business," Cravens said. "I like that. How would you like to work for me, Mr. Sixkiller?"

"I already told Bouchard—"

"Not for the town," Cravens said as he sat down, "and not for a group of businessmen. For *me.*"

"I'm pretty good at ciphering, but I'm afraid I wouldn't make much of a teller," John Henry said.

Cravens shook his head and said, "That's not what I'm talking about."

"I already said I'm not a hired killer." John Henry let a little edge creep into his voice as he spoke.

"I don't care if you kill anybody or not. I just want this bank protected, whatever it takes. If you can do that without killing, fine."

"I don't understand," John Henry said, even though he had an idea what Cravens was driving at. "You want the bank protected from what?"

Cravens leaned forward slightly and clasped his hands together on the desk in front of him. He said, "I like to think I'm a good judge of character. You have to be in my business. I believe that you're an honest man, Mr. Sixkiller, and not just because you came to my assistance yesterday. *Are* you an honest man?"

"I try to be," John Henry answered honestly.

"I'm going to trust you with some knowledge. Some people would say that I'm foolish for doing so, but I place a lot of faith in my instincts. In a few days there's going to be a great deal of gold in this bank, Mr. Sixkiller. You may have heard rumors about that since you've been here." Cravens smiled. "It's hard to keep a secret in a small town."

"Go on," John Henry said, not acknowledging whether he'd heard any rumors or not.

"The largest mines in this area are the San Francisco, the El Halcón, and the Bonita, owned by Jason True, Arnold Goodman, and Dan Lacey, respectively. They're all quite profitable operations, profitable enough that they have their own stamp mills to process the ore from their shafts into bullion. But once that's done, they still have to get the bullion out. Recently that's proven to be quite a challenge . . . and a dangerous one, at that."

"Because of Billy Ray Gilmore and his gang," John Henry said.

Cravens sighed and nodded.

"If we had some decent law in these parts, it might be different. But Marshal Hinkle is almost useless, and Sheriff Stone up at the county seat isn't much better. We've been left to shift for ourselves down here, and Gilmore has had a free hand. The mines have sent out a few small shipments, but most of them have been held up and stolen. Because the owners are afraid to risk much at a time, the bullion has built up to the point that it's too risky to keep it at their mines. They have to get it out somehow."

"Hire shotgun guards," John Henry suggested, still playing along with Cravens, even though he already knew all of this.

"People are afraid of Gilmore and his butchers. Too many men who rode shotgun with those gold shipments have been killed. But True, Goodman, and Lacey have hit on a plan. They've pooled their resources and are paying top wages. They've hired enough men to protect the bullion when it's brought down from the mountains, from each of the mines in turn. They're putting it here, in my bank, making up a massive shipment that's worth it for Wells Fargo to send a small army of men to transport it to the railroad at Lordsburg."

"Sounds like a good idea," John Henry said. "But you're worried about the gold being safe while it's here?"

"That's right. The value of the bullion will be so high that it'll be a very tempting target for the lawless."

"You say Gilmore's been holding up the shipments on their way down out of the mountains," John Henry said. "Why won't he just hit these shipments as well?"

"Because there'll be too many guards. That's the advantage the mine owners have from working together, instead of as rivals. They can get the gold here, and Wells Fargo can get it to Lordsburg, but there's that window of time . . . less than twenty-four hours . . . when I'll be responsible for it. And to tell you the truth, Mr. Sixkiller, I don't like the responsibility."

"A banker should be used to taking care of other people's money," John Henry pointed out.

"And I am. But these are special circumstances."

"So you want to hire me to guard the gold?"

"That's right."

"What about all the guards bringing it down from the mines? Can't they protect it while it's here, too?"

"They'll be posted all around the bank," Cravens said. "To tell you the truth, I don't see how anybody could get to it. But that doesn't stop me from worrying. I want a man here inside the bank, a good man to serve as a last line of defense. That man should be you, Mr. Sixkiller."

Now that he'd learned more details of the plan put together by the mine owners, John Henry didn't see how Gilmore—or Sophie and Mitchum, for that matter—could hope to steal the gold. True, Goodman, and Lacey appeared to have every angle covered.

And yet they were still worried, or at least Jason True was, or he wouldn't have written to Judge Parker asking for help. Cravens was scared, too. Seventy-five thousand dollars' worth of bullion was enough to make anybody nervous, John Henry supposed.

If a whole gang of outlaws managed to get into the bank, one man wouldn't be enough to stop them, no matter how good he was. John Henry knew that. He had to keep playing the game, had to try to keep manipulating the situation so things never got that far.

Cravens had just dealt him another card, and John Henry already had a glimmering of how he was going to use it.

"How about it?" Cravens prodded. "What do you think, Mr. Sixkiller?"

John Henry smiled and said, "I think you've just hired yourself a last line of defense."

Chapter Twenty-one

Considering that he'd been in Purgatory less than twenty-four hours, John Henry thought he wasn't doing too badly. He had uncovered two people plotting to steal the gold—Sophie Clearwater and Doc Mitchum—and been taken into the confidence of the banker in whose safe the bullion would reside for a short time, all without having to reveal his true identity as a deputy United States marshal.

Now there was Billy Ray Gilmore to deal with.

All in good time, though. John Henry spent the morning checking on Iron Heart at the stable, then walking around Purgatory in an apparently aimless fashion.

In truth, though, there was nothing aimless about his wanderings. He was familiarizing himself with the town as much as he possibly could, committing to memory everything about the buildings, the streets, the alleys, and anything else that might come in handy to know. He paid particular attention to the area around the bank, where the guards would be posted.

The bank had two stories, with offices on the second floor where a couple of lawyers and a bookkeeper conducted their business. The only other two-story buildings in town were the Silver Spur, which was up the street, and the Barrymore House, which sat directly across from the bank.

John Henry looked from the bank to the hotel, his eyes narrowing as he considered the possibilities. Then he moved on to check out the other businesses around the bank. Riflemen on the roofs of those buildings might be able to pick off some of the guards, and then a concerted rush by the rest of Gilmore's gang could overwhelm the others.

While John Henry was at the bank, Joseph Cravens had spoken with justifiable pride about the strength of the safe. According to him, only two people knew the combination, him and his chief teller, Harley Smoot. John Henry immediately decided that that made both Cravens and Smoot very important in his preparations. He had to find out if pressure could be brought on either man to force him to open the safe.

Of course, a gun to the head would probably work, but threatening the families of the two men would be an even more surefire method of insuring their cooperation.

Cravens had gone on to say that a dynamite blast

strong enough to blow the door off the safe would destroy the room around it. He seemed to think that would discourage any would-be robbers from employing that tactic.

John Henry had his doubts about that. He figured Gilmore would be willing to level the whole bank if it got him what he wanted. Bars of gold bullion, unlike paper money, wouldn't be destroyed in such a blast. The heat might melt them a little, but the damage probably wouldn't be too much.

The one thing John Henry could be sure of was that if Gilmore made it to the safe, he would find a way to get into it and loot the gold, no matter what it took.

The trick would be to keep him from ever getting to it.

That meant a trap of some sort. . . .

John Henry ate lunch at the Red Top Café, and the food lived up to expectations. The steak and potatoes were filling enough that he felt a little drowsy after he ate, so he returned to the hotel, intending to take a short nap before he set out on the rest of the activities he had planned for the day.

This time he didn't find anyone waiting in his room, which was a relief. He was able to stretch out on the bed and doze for a couple of hours without being disturbed.

When he woke up, he splashed some water on his face from the basin on the washstand. Refreshed and alert, he buckled on his gun belt, settled his hat on his head, and set out for the Silver Spur. Billy Ray Gilmore might not be there right now, but John Henry was confident the boss outlaw would show up at the saloon sooner or later. He might as well pass the time pleasantly while he waited, he thought.

The honey blonde, Della, was at the bar when John Henry came in. She picked up a tray with a bottle of whiskey and several glasses on it and said to him, "Wait until I deliver this to one of the tables, and I'll be right back."

"All right," John Henry said. He gave the bartender, Meade, a pleasant nod and added, "I'll have a beer."

Meade filled a mug for him, slid it across the hardwood, and said, "That'll be four bits."

"The days of free drinks are over, eh?" John Henry asked with a grin.

"You'll have to take that up with Mr. Bouchard."

"No, it's fine," John Henry said as he dropped a coin on the bar. "I was just joshing you."

That was liable to be a waste of time, he thought. Meade didn't appear to have much of a sense of humor. That probably went with being a bartender and having to listen to people's troubles all the time, as well as witnessing some pretty sorry behavior now and then.

Della came back carrying the empty tray. She handed it across the bar to Meade, then turned to John Henry with a smile on her face.

"I wasn't sure you were still in town," she said.

"Why would I leave so soon?" he asked. "I just got here."

"Riding into a town and having people trying to kill you isn't that unusual for you?"

"Well, I wouldn't say that," John Henry replied. "But I'm not in the habit of running away from a little trouble, either." He paused. "Speaking of which . . . have you seen Billy Ray Gilmore around today?"

Della frowned and asked, "Why in the world would you want to have anything to do with Gilmore?"

"I thought maybe I'd talk to him again. Maybe try to clear the air between us. I'd just as soon not have to be looking over my shoulder the whole time I'm here in town."

Della shook her head.

"It's too late for that. You killed two of his men. You can't make any sort of deal with him now."

"Don't be so sure of that," John Henry said. "I've got a hunch Gilmore would make any kind of deal as long as he thought it benefited him."

"What have you got that Gilmore might want?" Della asked with a curious frown.

"Well, if we called a truce, I could stop killing his men."

Della looked at him oddly for a moment, then suddenly laughed.

"You're serious, aren't you?" she said.

"Shooting people is serious business."

"I suppose so." She shook her head. "To answer

your original question, no, I haven't seen him today. It's a little early yet for him and the rest of that bunch. They'll be more likely to show up after dark."

"I guess I could come back then."

Della's pink tongue came out and darted over her lips for a second.

"If you want to wait here, I can think of some ways you could pass the time."

"I don't know if that would be a good idea," John Henry said. He was thinking about Sasha Quiet Stream, back home in Indian Territory . . . but keeping her in mind was getting to be more difficult.

"You know, if you keep saying no, eventually the offers will stop coming," Della said with a trace of exasperation creeping into her voice.

"Believe me, I know," John Henry said. "I've just got a lot on my mind these days."

Della's shoulders, which the low-cut dress she wore left bare, rose and fell slightly in a shrug that made her breasts do interesting things.

"Just so you have a good idea what you might be missing out on."

Before John Henry could say anything else, she turned and moved away, heading for one of the tables where several men were drinking. They welcomed her exuberantly and one of them patted her on the rump, which Della didn't seem to mind at all. John Henry sipped his beer and wondered if he'd done the right thing or just made a blasted fool of himself.

Royal Bouchard came down from upstairs a short time later. By then John Henry had drifted over to one of the poker tables and sat down to join the game when one of the players cashed in and left.

John Henry wouldn't describe himself as a serious poker player, but he enjoyed a good game from time to time. He played carefully and didn't plunge, even when he had strong hands, and as a result he was a few dollars ahead after an hour or so. That was enough for him. He gathered his winnings and joined Bouchard at the bar.

The saloon keeper had an unlit cigar in the corner of his mouth. He smiled around it and said, "I'm glad that you've joined us again, Sixkiller. Anybody try to kill you today?"

"Not so far," John Henry said. "But it's early yet."

"That was my hunch, since I hadn't heard any shooting." Bouchard signaled for Meade to bring him a drink. "I spoke to Della a little while ago, upstairs."

John Henry had noticed that Della wasn't downstairs anymore, but he didn't know where she had gone. Now he did.

"She says you want to talk to Gilmore and try to make peace with him," Bouchard went on. "It can't be done. You can talk to him, but he's still going to try to kill you."

"Even if I appeal to reason and show him that we'll both be better off if the killing stops?"

"You think you could appeal to reason with a lobo wolf? Gilmore's even worse than that."

"I just thought it might be worth giving it a try."

Bouchard shook his head and said, "I'd advise against it."

John Henry wasn't going to stand around arguing the matter with Bouchard. He was saved from the necessity of doing so by a voice he didn't recognize that declared, "I want to talk to John Henry Sixkiller."

Chapter Twenty-two

What now? John Henry asked himself as he turned around. The man who had spoken his name didn't sound particularly threatening, so he didn't reach for his gun, but he kept his hand near the Colt's butt anyway.

John Henry immediately recognized one of the three gents he had noticed in the hotel dining room the previous evening. The man was tall, with a stiff stance, iron-gray hair, and a neatly clipped mustache. When he'd seen them in the dining room, John Henry had pegged this one as possibly being Jason True, Judge Parker's old friend.

"I'm Sixkiller," he said. "What can I do for you?"

"I'd like to have a word with you," the man said. "In private." He looked over at Bouchard. "Do you have a room we can use?"

"Of course, Mr. True," Bouchard answered, confirming John Henry's hunch. "There's a private room we sometimes use for high-stakes games."

That was appropriate, John Henry thought. With $75,000 worth of gold bullion involved, those were sure enough high stakes.

"That'll do fine," True said, his voice about as stiff as his backbone appeared to be. As a rich mine owner, he probably didn't like having to ask a favor of a mere saloon keeper. He added to John Henry, "If that's agreeable to you."

"Sure," John Henry said easily. He was curious to hear what Jason True wanted to say to him.

The three men drew quite a few interested looks as they crossed the room to a door Bouchard opened. The chamber on the other side of the door was dark, but Bouchard stepped in ahead of John Henry and True and struck a match to light a pair of oil lamps in wall sconces, one on each side of the room.

The room was windowless and well furnished, John Henry saw in the glow of the lamps. In its center was a poker table covered with green felt and surrounded by comfortable chairs. A well-upholstered sofa sat on the other side of the room, beyond the table. A pair of armchairs were to the right, with a small round table between them, and to the left was a sideboard where drinks could be prepared. Brass cuspidors tucked into the corners gleamed in the lamplight.

"I don't suppose you'd like to play a few hands while you're having your talk," Bouchard said. "I could fetch a new deck, and I'd be glad to deal."

"I don't gamble with cards," True snapped, leaving the impression that he confined his gambling to other things.

"Fine." Bouchard shifted the cigar from one side of his mouth to the other. "In that case, I'll leave you gentlemen alone. Let me know if you need anything."

When Bouchard was gone, True motioned to the armchairs. John Henry sat down in one of them and balanced his hat on his knee.

"We haven't been introduced," True said. "My name is Jason True. I own the San Francisco Mine."

"John Henry Sixkiller," John Henry said. "But you already know that."

"I suspect that just about everyone in Purgatory knows who you are, Mr. Sixkiller," True said, which wasn't the first time John Henry had heard that sentiment expressed. "You've cut quite a wide swath through the town since your arrival yesterday."

"That wasn't exactly my intention."

"Our intentions in life usually have very little to do with what actually happens."

"That's true," John Henry said. "I doubt if you wanted to discuss philosophy with me, though, Mr. True."

"No, I'm here to talk about gold," True said. "Specifically, the shipment that will be held in the bank here for Wells Fargo in a few days' time. I spoke to Joe Cravens a short time ago, and he told me that he's hired you to help guard that gold."

John Henry nodded and said, "That's right. We came to that agreement."

"Cravens should have consulted with me and the other mine owners before he offered you that job," True said with anger in his voice.

"I guess he figured that it's his bank."

"Yes, but it's our gold. And we don't know you, Sixkiller. We don't know you from Adam. All we know for sure is that you're fast with a gun."

"And reasonably accurate with it, too," John Henry said with a faint smile, "since I'm still alive and two other fellas aren't."

"I don't hold with bragging about killing," True snapped.

"I'm not bragging, just stating a fact." John Henry paused, then said, "Look, I understand your reservations, Mr. True. Like you said, you don't know me. You don't have any reason to trust me. But look at it this way: I'm going to be inside the bank, and all those guards you and your friends have hired will be outside. I've seen the safe where the gold's going to be stored. I can't carry it off. I couldn't budge it. And if I got it open, I couldn't carry but a small fraction of the bullion inside it."

"I suppose that's true. But I still don't like it."

"You and the other mine owners are going in together to hire guards to bring the gold down from the mountains, right?"

True grimaced and said, "Did Cravens tell you everything about our plans?" He waved off the question before John Henry could answer it. "Yes, we're hiring guards, as many of them as we can. Good, tough men."

"Do you know each and every one of them?"

True hesitated for a second before replying, "Well . . . no. Some of them were recommended by guards that we've used in the past."

"So you have to trust them."

"I suppose you could look at it like that."

"Mr. Cravens trusts me," John Henry said.

"Only because you saved him from two of Billy Ray Gilmore's ruffians!"

"It's as good a reason as any, I guess."

True frowned at John Henry for a long moment before he said, "Very well. You make a good point. But you should be fully aware of this, Mr. Sixkiller . . . if you double-cross us and cause us to lose that gold, I'll have you hunted down and brought to justice if it takes every penny I have."

"Fair enough," John Henry said. "When's the gold coming down?"

True didn't answer right away. John Henry began to think that he wasn't going to. But finally, Jason True said, "The day after tomorrow."

John Henry couldn't keep the surprise out of his voice as he said, "That soon."

"Yes. We'll be ready to put our plan into operation by then. We'll start early in the morning, and it'll take all day to get the bullion from all three mines into the bank. Wells Fargo will have armored wagons here the next morning to pick it up and transport it to Lordsburg under heavy guard."

"So the bank will have to keep it safe overnight."

"That's right."

John Henry scratched at his jaw and frowned in thought.

"What's to stop Gilmore from hitting the bank during the day, after the first shipment gets here? That would still be a big haul for him and his gang."

"Not as big as if he waited until all three shipments are there. But of course, there's no way to be sure how the mind of a bandit is going to work."

"And your guards are going to be busy taking care of the other two shipments," John Henry mused. "That would be a good time to hit the bank."

"We'll have some men on hand during the day," True said. "And there's you."

John Henry chuckled.

"Yeah. There's me."

True leaned back in the armchair and regarded him with an intent gaze for several seconds.

"You seem sincere," the mine owner finally admitted. "Perhaps you really are an honest man."

"I'd like to think so."

John Henry knew he could set True's mind at ease and erase all the man's suspicions instantly if he just revealed that he'd been sent here by Judge Parker in answer to True's request for help. But so far no one in Purgatory knew who he really was, and John Henry wanted to keep it that way. His ability to play the different factions against each other, if that's what he wound up needing to do, depended on his real purpose here remaining a secret.

Jason True stood up and said, "Just remember what I said about having you hunted down if you betray us. I meant every word of it."

"I imagine you mean just about everything you say," John Henry replied as he got to his feet as well.

For the first time, a hint of a smile appeared on True's face. He extended his hand and said, "I certainly do."

John Henry grasped the mine owner's hand. True gave him a firm shake and a nod, and then left the room.

John Henry waited a moment and then followed him out. Quite a few furtive looks were sent in his direction. People knew he had been in that room talking to one of the richest, most powerful men in these parts, and naturally they were curious about what had gone on between them.

Bouchard waved John Henry over to the saloon keeper's private table. He asked, "You and Mr. True get everything hashed out?"

"Maybe," John Henry said. "I got the feeling he thought I might be an outlaw who's after his gold."

"Well, you could be," Bouchard said with a grin. "None of us around here really know any better, do we?"

"I reckon that's right. But don't I have a trustworthy face?"

"Shakespeare said that a man can smile and smile, and still be a villain," Bouchard pointed out. "In fact, there's a good example of that coming in right now."

John Henry glanced at the entrance and saw Billy Ray Gilmore pushing his way through the bat wings.

Chapter Twenty-three

According to what Della had said earlier about when the outlaws usually showed up, Gilmore was early today. The slightly-built boss outlaw crossed to the bar, seemingly oblivious to the frightened looks that some of the saloon's other customers gave him as they moved quickly out of his way. John Henry was willing to bet that Gilmore noticed the reactions, though, whether he appeared to or not.

He had a hunch that Billy Ray Gilmore didn't miss much.

John Henry started to stand up. Bouchard said, "There's not going to be any gunplay in here, is there?"

"I sure hope not," John Henry said. "But I reckon nothing in life is guaranteed, is it?"

Bouchard made a face, and his teeth clamped harder on the cigar clenched between them.

John Henry walked toward the bar. People didn't react quite as skittishly to him as they had toward

Gilmore, but they still got out of his way without wasting any time.

As John Henry moved up to the bar next to Gilmore, Meade sidled slowly toward them on the other side of the hardwood. The bartender like looked like he would have rather been just about anywhere else right now.

"What can I get you, Mr. Gilmore?" Meade asked after he swallowed hard.

"It's a little early in the day for whiskey," Gilmore replied. "Reckon I'll just have a beer."

"Same here," John Henry said.

Gilmore turned his head to look over at him.

"I don't recall askin' you to have a drink with me, Sixkiller."

"I don't want to intrude," John Henry said, "but I thought it might be a good idea if you and I had a talk."

"I can't think of anything I've got to say to you."

"Are you sure about that? I have an idea that you and I could do each other some good."

Gilmore cocked one eyebrow in a surprised, quizzical expression.

"Is that so?" he murmured. "I don't see how. You killed two of my friends last night."

"Did you send them after me?" John Henry asked. "Or just not get in their way?"

Meade set the two mugs of beer he had filled on the bar in front of John Henry and Gilmore. He opened his mouth to say, "That'll be—" then thought better of it, muttering instead, "Oh, the hell with it."

Gilmore didn't answer the question John Henry had asked. He picked up his beer and took a sip of it. Then he said, "You're either a mighty brave man or a damned fool, Sixkiller."

"You're not the first person to make that observation. To tell you the truth, the same thought has crossed my mind from time to time."

"And what did you decide?"

John Henry grinned and said, "I haven't made up my mind yet."

That brought a grudging chuckle from Gilmore. He said, "Right now let's say you're a brave man and reserve judgment on the other. What is it you want from me?"

"Like I said, we can do each other some good."

"How so?"

"You don't want to keep losing friends, and I don't want to have to keep on killing them."

"Things might work out different next time."

"They might," John Henry admitted. "But do you want to take a chance on that right now?" He lowered his voice. "Especially when you've got such a big job coming up?"

Something flickered in Gilmore's eyes. Not surprise, really, just a tiny reaction to show that he was off balance for a second. He recovered quickly, though, and said, "I don't know what you're talking about."

John Henry took a sip of his beer and said, "I

think you do. No point in us not being straight with each other, Billy Ray. You're after the same thing that brought me to Purgatory."

And that wasn't a lie, now was it, John Henry thought.

He went on, "I don't see any point in the two of us working against each other when we could be working together."

"I don't know you," Gilmore said. "I never even heard of you until you showed up here and started causin' trouble for me."

"Maybe not, but you've got eyes. You've seen for yourself what I can do. You'd be smart to take advantage of that, wouldn't you?"

Gilmore didn't say anything. John Henry couldn't tell if the outlaw was thinking about what he had said, or if Gilmore was just so surprised by the offer of a partnership that he didn't know what to say.

After several moments, Gilmore took another long swallow of beer and lowered the mug.

"We'll talk again tonight," he said. "But not here. We need more privacy. I've got a reputation to uphold, you know."

"Name the place," John Henry said, well aware that he might be cooperating in an attempt to set up a trap for him. He had to run that risk. He couldn't play the cards in this game as close to the vest as he had when he was playing poker earlier.

"The livery stable. Eight o'clock."

"I'll be there."

"Fine." Gilmore drained the rest of the beer and

set the empty mug on the bar with an emphatic thump. He turned and walked out of the saloon without looking back. No one who watched him go could have guessed from his demeanor that he and John Henry had discussed working together.

John Henry returned to the table where Bouchard sat. The saloon owner said, "Looked like that didn't work out too well. I didn't figure it would. But I guess you're no worse off than you were to start with."

"I reckon we'll find out," John Henry said.

After remaining a short time longer at the Silver Spur, he returned to the hotel and had dinner in the dining room. For once the redheaded waitress wasn't there. A pleasant, middle-aged woman took his order and brought him his food instead: fried chicken, potatoes, greens, apple pie for dessert. After he'd eaten, he lingered over a second cup of coffee, knowing that he was in no hurry. It was a good meal.

John Henry hoped it wouldn't be his last.

After eating, he went back upstairs. He cleaned and oiled his Colt, then took a sheathed knife from his gear and slipped it down inside the top of his boot. His Winchester was leaning in the corner, but he left it there. If there was gun work to be done inside the stable, it would be at close range, too close for the rifle to be very effective.

When he checked his pocket watch and saw that

it was time to go, he put his hat on and set it at just the right angle on his head. He went downstairs and nodded to the clerk as he crossed the lobby. When he stepped out onto the boardwalk, he saw that Purgatory was fairly quiet tonight. A few people strolled here and there, a wagon drawn by a team of tired, droopy-eared mules creaked along the street, and a couple of men on horseback rode up to the Silver Spur and dismounted, leaving their horses at the crowded hitch rack.

John Henry turned the other way and walked toward the stable. As far as he could tell, no one was paying any attention to him, but there could be watchers hidden in the darkness, keeping track of his activities.

There could be gunmen as well, drawing a bead on him at that very moment. He tried to look like he didn't have a care in the world but, inside, his nerves were taut and all his senses were on alert. At the first sign of an ambush, he would have to react instantly.

Nothing happened, though, as he walked the couple of blocks to Patterson's Livery Stable and Wagonyard. The double doors on the front of the big barn stood open. A lantern burned inside, casting a flickering yellow glow.

John Henry knew he would be an excellent target when he stepped through the door. He was still several businesses away from the stable when he suddenly slid into a dark, narrow passage between two buildings.

The shadows here were so thick that he couldn't see more than a foot in front of his face . . . but that meant nobody could see him, either. He kept his right hand on the butt of his gun and the fingertips of his left hand against the wall of the building on that side as he moved silently through the darkness.

When he reached the rear corner, he stopped and listened intently. It was very quiet back here with the businesses closed down for the night. The only sounds were the ones that drifted down the narrow passage from the street.

When he was confident that no one was waiting back here to bushwhack him, John Henry rounded the corner and catfooted along the alley behind the buildings. A minute later, he came to the back of the livery stable. Double doors back here led into a corral, but they were closed at the moment.

Half a dozen horses stood in the corral, dozing. They stirred a little as John Henry bent and slipped through a gap between the poles. He spoke to them in whispers, calming them as he made his way to the stable.

The doors had a narrow gap between them, even when they were closed. John Henry put his eye to it and peered into the barn. He couldn't see much, just a slice of the center aisle between the stalls that was lit by the lantern's glow.

He sniffed, smelling the familiar mixture of straw, manure, and horseflesh that could be found in any stable. Blended with it was the scent of tobacco smoke. That didn't mean anything; the hostler could have been smoking in there, although men who worked in stables tended not to because of all the dry straw scattered around. A carelessly dropped quirly could cause a catastrophe.

John Henry smelled something else, though, that warned him.

Unwashed human flesh. The source had to be close, too, for the smell to be that strong.

Someone coughed, right on the other side of the door.

A faint smile tugged at the corners of John Henry's mouth. He drew his gun and took off his hat. A couple of waves with the hat stirred up the horses again. They began moving around, their hooves thudding against the hard-packed ground.

The man on the other side of the doors called softly, "Hey, Billy Ray, something's got those horses in the corral spooked!"

"It's probably nothin'," Gilmore replied from somewhere else in the barn, his voice faint through the doors. "Better go check it out, though, Rankin."

John Henry heard the man called Rankin mutter a curse, then there was a scraping sound as he moved the bar on the inside of the doors. John Henry moved to the side as one of the doors swung out a little.

The dark shape of the outlaw moved into sight. John Henry waited, silent as the grave, while Rankin stood there just outside the doors, looking around the corral. There was nothing to see except the skittish horses. Rankin took another step forward. In the light that spilled through the opening, John Henry saw that the man held a rifle slanted across his chest.

When John Henry made his move, it was fast. His left arm went around Rankin's throat from behind and closed on it like a bar of iron, so tightly that the outlaw couldn't let out even a squeak. At the same time John Henry reversed the Colt in his right hand and struck with it, crashing the butt against the back of Rankin's head, low enough so that the man's hat wouldn't cushion the blow. Rankin went limp and dropped the rifle. John Henry held his breath as the weapon fell, hoping that the jarring of its fall wouldn't cause it to discharge.

The rifle thudded harmlessly to the ground.

John Henry dragged Rankin's unconscious form to the side, out of the light. The whole thing had been so quick, he doubted that anyone inside had noticed. If they had seen any movement, they wouldn't have been able to tell what was going on. John Henry lowered Rankin to the ground, not bothering to be careful about the piles of horse manure scattered around. The outlaw already smelled like he hadn't had a bath in a month of Sundays, and he could wake up stinking even worse for all John Henry cared. He reached down, pulled Rankin's handgun from its holster, and tossed it off into the darkness.

Then he stepped back to the doors in time to hear Gilmore call, "Rankin, you see anything back there? Rankin?"

Impatient footsteps approached the doors. John Henry stepped inside quickly, leveled his Colt at the startled face of Billy Ray Gilmore, and said, "Rankin can't answer you right now, Billy Ray, but I'm here, and I'm shocked—shocked, I tell you— that it appears you were waiting to ambush me."

Chapter Twenty-four

A couple of seconds ticked past tensely before Gilmore said, "I'd be obliged if you'd put that gun down, Sixkiller. I don't take kindly to havin' weapons pointed at me."

"And I don't take kindly to people who lie to me," John Henry said without lowering the Colt. "I thought I was meeting you tonight so we could talk about a truce, not so you could have your men bushwhack me."

So far John Henry hadn't seen anybody else inside the barn, but he had no doubt that more of Gilmore's men were hidden in the shadows. There was probably somebody up in the loft, too. John Henry made sure his voice was loud enough now to carry to all of them, just in case Gilmore hadn't told his men the truth about what was going on here.

To John Henry's surprise, Gilmore grinned.

"You think I've got men waitin' to ambush you, do you?" he asked.

"That's what I just said," John Henry snapped.

"Yeah, but you're wrong."

"There's a fella out there in the corral with a goose egg on his head that says I'm right."

"You mean Rankin?" A look of concern appeared on Gilmore's narrow face. "You didn't kill him, did you?"

"He's just sleeping in a pile of horse manure. Other than that, he's fine."

"Well, I'm glad to hear it. When I asked him to come with me tonight, I didn't tell him what was goin' on. I'd hate to think that I was the cause of him dyin'."

"You're saying you brought just one man with you?" John Henry asked.

"It pays to be cautious. How was I supposed to know that you were gonna come alone?"

"I rode into town by myself, didn't I?"

"That don't mean a thing," Gilmore insisted. "You could have a whole gang here in Purgatory, driftin' in one or two at a time so nobody would notice 'em."

Gilmore was right about that, John Henry supposed. Just because he didn't have any obvious allies didn't mean he was alone, even though in truth he was.

"I didn't bring anybody with me," he said. "Why would I do that?"

"Maybe *you* figured on ambushin' *me*. If we're really after the same thing, it'd be a smart move for you to get rid of the competition, wouldn't it?"

"I'd rather get rid of the competition by making partners out of them."

Gilmore shrugged and said, "That's a smart move if you can pull it off. But I've got no way of bein' sure that you're tellin' me the truth."

John Henry took a step backwards, making certain that he was out of Gilmore's reach. He hadn't seen or heard any signs that more of the gang were here in the barn. Maybe it was time to take a chance. If he was wrong, Gilmore would be the first to die. John Henry would make sure of that.

He holstered his Colt and said, "All right. We'll talk. I haven't forgotten that you brought Rankin with you, though, when you were supposed to come alone."

"Strictly a precautionary measure," Gilmore said. "And seein' as how you're the one who snuck in here and buffaloed him, I'd say it wasn't an unreasonable thing for me to do."

John Henry shrugged and said, "Let's get down to brass tacks. We've both talked about the thing we're after. We might as well put a name on it: gold."

"Gold," Gilmore agreed with a nod.

"Seventy-five thousand dollars' worth of the stuff."

"With just a fraction of that, a man could live out the rest of his life in ease," Gilmore said. A certain dreamy quality came into his voice as he went on, "Get a little hacienda somewhere south of the border, with some sweet Mexican gals to take care of me and keep me happy."

"I can help you get that," John Henry said.

"I don't recall sayin' that I needed your help, Six-killer. I've got plenty of good men with me already. What do you bring to the table?"

"I'm working for Cravens, the banker."

Gilmore was the sort of man who kept himself firmly under control all the time, but again John Henry saw a flicker of reaction in the outlaw's eyes. After a second, Gilmore said, "Now that's somethin' I did not know."

"True, Goodman, and Lacey have thrown in together to hire plenty of guards," John Henry said, "but Cravens decided he wanted somebody working for him, too, looking out for the bank's best interests. He got it in his head that since I'd tangled with your bunch twice and come out of it alive, I was that man." He smiled. "So I guess I really ought to be grateful to your men, Gilmore. They helped get me a job."

"How much is Cravens payin' you?"

"A whole lot south of what a share of $75,000 would be."

"So you're lookin' to pick up somethin' on the side."

"That's the idea," John Henry said. "I can't do that by myself, and I can't do it if I'm having to look over my shoulder all the time for you and your boys. That's why I suggested we team up. I get some peace of mind, and you get an inside man."

Gilmore tried to look casually dismissive of the

idea, but John Henry could tell that he was thinking about it.

"My men wouldn't go along with it," Gilmore said. "You killed Junior Clemons and Jack Bayne, and Duke Rudd and Sam Logan won't ever be the same after what you done to 'em. No, the gang wouldn't stand for it."

"Who gives the orders?" John Henry prodded. "You or the bunch you run with?"

"You're tryin' to get under my skin, Sixkiller, and I'm not gonna let you do it."

"It's an honest question," John Henry insisted. "If you tell them you're working with me, and you're really the boss, they won't have any choice but to go along with it."

He could tell that he was getting to Gilmore. The outlaw was intrigued by the idea of having a spy who could tip him off about everything the mine owners and their guards planned to do. Of course, John Henry intended for the information to wind up working against the gang, but Gilmore didn't know that.

Gilmore was stubborn, though. He said, "I've got to show some loyalty to my men. You may not understand that, but I do. They'll never trust you."

At that moment, John Henry heard a dragging footstep and a groan behind him. He took a fast step back and to the side, turning as he palmed out his Colt. He could see that Rankin had just stumbled back into the barn, hatless, and with manure smeared on his coat.

John Henry had expected Gilmore to use that distraction to make a try for his gun, but the boss outlaw hadn't budged. That was more evidence Gilmore actually was considering the proposal John Henry had made. John Henry was between the two men and didn't particularly care for that position, but Rankin's holster was still empty and he hadn't picked up the rifle, which meant he was unarmed. They couldn't catch John Henry in a crossfire.

Rankin's bleary eyes suddenly focused on John Henry.

"You!" he exclaimed. "You son of a—"

"Take it easy, old hoss," Gilmore said. "Sixkiller and I are just talkin'."

"But the varmint hit me over the head! Knocked me out and dumped me in a big pile of horse apples!"

"Actually, I thought it might improve the way you smelled," John Henry drawled. "It doesn't seem to have worked, but it was worth a try, anyway."

Rankin started toward him, but Gilmore lifted a hand to stop him.

"Settle down," he said sharply.

Rankin didn't look like he was going to settle down any time soon. He was a big man, broad across the shoulders, with a prominent jaw on which a dark, close-cropped beard sprouted. His arms were long and powerful. John Henry could tell that he wouldn't have had such an easy time with Rankin if he hadn't taken the man by surprise and moved fast enough to take advantage of that.

"What're we doin' here, anyway?" Rankin asked. "I thought we were gonna bushwhack this hombre!"

"Only if he tried anything funny," Gilmore said. "Turns out, he really did just want to talk."

"About what?"

"Now, see, that's the really interestin' part. He wants to work with us and help us steal that gold, Rankin."

A fresh surge of anger made Rankin's face flush even darker with rage as he glowered at John Henry.

"Work with us?" he repeated as if he couldn't believe it. "He killed Junior and Jack! He crippled Duke and Sam!"

"That's what I just told him. I said that you and the rest of the boys wouldn't be willin' to work with him after what he done."

Rankin flexed his fingers, opening and closing his big, apelike hands.

"That's for damned sure," he growled. "All I'd be willin' to do is kill him."

"You may get your chance," Gilmore said, "because I've got an idea."

John Henry didn't like the sound of that. Any idea Gilmore had probably wouldn't be good for him. But there was nothing he could do except ask, "What's your idea, Billy Ray?"

"I was thinkin' that nobody gets into this gang without a little . . . trial by fire, let's call it. You gotta earn your way in."

"What do you want me to do?" John Henry asked derisively. "Go steal an apple from the general store to prove that I'm worthy to be one of you?"

"No, I was thinkin' more along the lines that you'd fight Rankin here."

John Henry shook his head and said, "He doesn't have a gun."

"I'm not talkin' about guns. I'm sayin' that you should take him on barehanded."

A grin suddenly spread across Rankin's ugly face. Clearly, he liked that idea.

"If I do that, he's liable to break my neck," John Henry objected.

"Break your back, that's what I'll do," Rankin said with his teeth bared in a snarl. "I'll tear you plumb in half!"

"You survive, you'll have proved your courage," Gilmore went on to John Henry. "Anybody who can stand up to Rankin, well, I reckon I can talk the rest of the boys into acceptin' him, no matter what else he's done. Sound like a challenge you're willin' to accept, Sixkiller?"

"It sounds pretty loco to me," John Henry said, although he was starting to see that there might not be any way out of this if he wanted to proceed with his plan.

"You already said yourself that you can't hope to steal that gold on your own," Gilmore pointed out. "You need some partners . . . and we're the best ones you're gonna get."

John Henry wasn't sure about that. He still had

Sophie Clearwater and Doc Mitchum to consider.
But this was the main part of his plan, right here.

"How do I know you won't try to gun me down as
soon as I pouch this iron?" he asked.

"Well . . . if we're gonna work together, I reckon
you're gonna have to start trustin' me sometime,
aren't you?"

Gilmore was right about that, at least as far as
appearances went. In reality, John Henry didn't
intend to trust the wiry little outlaw for even a
second.

If he could pull this off . . . if he could survive a
tussle with Rankin . . . he would have the in with
the outlaws that he needed. So there wasn't really
any choice, he told himself.

He lowered his Colt, slid it into leather, and
started to unbuckle the gun belt.

"You've got yourself a deal," he told Gilmore, figuring there would be a few more preliminaries
than that.

But as soon as the gun belt came loose around
John Henry's hips, Rankin bellowed, lowered his
head, and charged like a maddened bull.

Chapter Twenty-five

John Henry dropped the gun belt and tried to brace himself to meet Rankin's attack. He wasn't quite fast enough. Rankin slammed into him and drove him backwards, off his feet. John Henry's hat went flying in the air.

If he'd landed on the hard-packed dirt with Rankin's weight smashing down on top of him, the impact probably would have cracked some of his ribs and maybe ended the fight then and there. As luck would have it, they toppled onto a pile of straw instead, and that cushioned the landing.

Even so, that was enough to knock all the air out of John Henry's lungs and leave him gasping for breath.

Dust from the straw filled his nose, along with the stench from Rankin, made worse by the manure smeared on his clothes. John Henry gagged and coughed. The stable seemed to spin crazily around him for a second. When he looked up, he saw Rankin's face, leering with hate as it loomed over him.

Rankin lifted his right fist high above his head, ready to bring it down in a pile driver punch that would crush John Henry's face. John Henry didn't give him a chance to launch that blow.

Instead, he shot a straight left up into Rankin's jaw. That rocked Rankin's head back and drew his throat tight. John Henry whipped the edge of his right hand across Rankin's throat in a slashing thrust.

Rankin clutched at his neck and fell back. John Henry heaved and bucked and sent the bigger man flying off of him. As Rankin tumbled to the right, John Henry rolled to the left to put a little space between them.

John Henry made it to his feet first with room to swing a fist. His right looped around and caught Rankin on the cheekbone just as Rankin surged upright. The punch staggered Rankin but didn't knock him down. He got his boots under him and charged again, trying to curse but unable to get anything through his damaged throat except some incoherent croaks.

John Henry was ready for this assault. He went low, tackling Rankin around the knees. Rankin's weight and momentum sent him toppling over John Henry's back. John Henry scrambled out from under Rankin's legs before he could be trapped there and pushed himself up again.

From the corner of his eye, he saw Billy Ray

Gilmore standing off to the side, watching the battle. Evidently, Gilmore intended to stay out of this fight, making it a fair match between John Henry and Rankin. As fair as it could be, anyway, considering that Rankin had a couple of inches and probably forty pounds on his smaller opponent.

But size wasn't everything, John Henry knew. He had been in a lot of fights, all the way back to when he was a boy, and he had won most of them through a combination of speed, strength, and the ability to think clearly even when he was in the middle of a desperate struggle.

Rankin was still trying to get up. John Henry clubbed his hands together and brought them down on the back of Rankin's neck. That drove Rankin's face into the ground. When he lifted his head again, blood was pouring from his nose. His throat had started working again; the roar of mingled pain and rage he let out was proof of that.

His hand shot out and fastened on John Henry's left ankle. A hard jerk upended the lawman. John Henry fell on his back and kicked out, driving the heel of his other boot into Rankin's shoulder. That held off the bigger man and prevented him from getting on top of John Henry and pinning him down.

As John Henry scrambled backwards, he ran into one of the beams that supported the hayloft. He grabbed hold of it to brace himself as he climbed to his feet.

His heart was pounding and blood hammered in

his head. He was out of breath. The fight hadn't lasted long so far, but it had been fierce and had taken a toll on him.

The good news was that Rankin appeared to be in just as bad shape, if not worse. Blood from his broken nose was splattered across the lower half of his face. His jaw was already bruised and swollen.

He wasn't ready to give up, though. He got to his feet and bulled in, swinging wild roundhouse punches.

John Henry ducked. Rankin's left fist hit the beam on which John Henry leaned. A knuckle broke with an audible *pop!* Rankin howled in pain.

Boring in, John Henry hooked punch after punch into Rankin's midsection. The bigger man was forced to give ground. With his left hand now broken, he could only punch with his right, and his defense was awkward. In desperation, he lurched forward, got both forearms against John Henry's chest, and shoved as hard as he could. John Henry went backwards and would have fallen if he hadn't caught himself against the beam.

With his back braced, he lifted his right foot and sunk the toe of his boot deep in Rankin's belly as the man attacked again. Rankin doubled over. John Henry laced his fingers together and clubbed Rankin on the back of the head again.

Rankin went down. He was able to catch himself on hands and knees for a second, but then his strength deserted him. He sprawled on his belly and groaned. His fingers dug into the dirt as he tried to push himself up and failed. After a second, he slumped again and then lay still except for his back rising and falling as he heaved in breath. The air made ugly bubbling sounds in his nose.

John Henry leaned against the post and dragged the back of his hand across his mouth. His hair had fallen across his eyes. He tossed his head to throw it back and clear his vision.

He saw Gilmore standing several yards away. The outlaw had picked up John Henry's gun belt and stood there holding it with a smile on his face.

John Henry wondered if he could get the knife out of his boot and use it in time to stop Gilmore from killing him, if that was what the outlaw had in mind.

That didn't seem to be Gilmore's intention, though. As he came toward John Henry, he said, "That was just about the most entertainin' fracas I've seen in a long time." He held out the gun belt, which he had coiled around the holstered Colt. "Here you go, Sixkiller."

John Henry took the belt and buckled it on. He asked, "So, are we partners now?"

"I don't think Rankin'll be too happy about it, but yeah, I reckon we can work together. I'll be keepin' an eye on you, though. If I get the idea that you're tryin' to double-cross us, you won't live very long after that."

"I could say the same thing about you."

"I'd be disappointed in you if you didn't feel that way," Gilmore replied with a chuckle. "Reckon I'd better get a bucket of water and dump it over Rankin, see if I can bring him around. That was some thrashin' you handed him."

"He got in some punishment of his own," John Henry said. "How do we proceed from here?"

"I'll be in touch and let you know what our plans are."

John Henry nodded. He thought about telling Gilmore that the mine owners were going to bring the gold down from the mountains the day after tomorrow, but he decided to hold on to that knowledge for now. That was one of his hole cards, he told himself, continuing to think of this affair as a deadly game.

He smoothed his rumpled hair, picked up his hat, and put it on. With a curt nod to Gilmore, he left the livery barn.

A familiar stocky figure stood on the boardwalk a couple of doors down. John Henry recognized the hostler who had been taking care of Iron Heart. The man said nervously, "Hope you don't hold any grudges against me for lettin' those hombres use my stable, Mr. Sixkiller. When Gilmore came in and told me it'd be a good idea for me to make myself scarce, I didn't know what else to do."

"That's the only thing you could do," John Henry assured the man. "No hard feelings on my part."

"I'm mighty glad to see that you're still alive." The hostler darted a glance toward the livery barn, then lowered his voice to add, "That fella Gilmore, he reminds me of a diamondback rattlesnake."

"That's a pretty apt description," John Henry agreed. "But he and his friend should be gone before long, and you can have your stable back." He handed the man a silver dollar. "That's extra, just for taking such good care of my horse."

"I'm obliged, Mr. Sixkiller."

John Henry went on toward the Silver Spur. He felt the need of a drink.

When he came in, he saw both Royal Bouchard and Della right away. They seemed to be watching the door for him. Bouchard motioned for John Henry to join him at his table, and Della was there, too, by the time John Henry reached the table.

"Did you have your talk with Gilmore?" Bouchard asked bluntly.

"You must not have, since you're still alive," Della added.

John Henry smiled and said, "That's where you're wrong. We worked everything out. There's not going to be any more trouble."

"I'll believe *that* when I see it," Bouchard said skeptically.

The saloon keeper didn't know it, but John Henry was in complete agreement with that sentiment.

Chapter Twenty-six

Marshal Henry Hinkle rattled the doorknob of the hardware store, making sure it was locked. That was part of his nightly rounds, checking to see that all of Purgatory's businesses were secure. Strolling around town in the evening when things were quiet and peaceful for the most part was one of the few things about his job that he actually enjoyed. Maybe the only thing.

The other advantage to this particular chore was that a doorknob had never taken a shot at him. There was certainly something to be said for that. A lot to be said for it, in fact.

He was passing an alley when a voice called softly to him, "Marshal."

Hinkle crouched and froze, not sure whether to run, duck, or make a grab for the gun on his hip, which was just about the last thing in the world he wanted to do. He settled for croaking out, "Who . . . ?"

The man in the shadows laughed.

"Take it easy, Henry," he said. "It's just me."

"Oh." Hinkle straightened from his crouch. "You took me by surprise. Spooked me a little."

Actually, he'd been a lot spooked, and they both knew it. But there was no point in talking about such things as long as they were working together.

"Things have quieted down some today, haven't they?" the man in the alley said.

"Yeah, thank goodness. With everything else that's going on these days, we didn't need any more trouble, especially from that Sixkiller fella."

"But he's still around and I don't trust him, not for a second. He's up to something."

"You really think so?" Hinkle asked.

His partner made a disgusted noise.

"A man who can handle a gun like that? He didn't ride into town a few days ahead of a massive gold shipment by accident, Henry."

"He's got his eye on the gold?"

"That would be my guess. Of course, he's not the only one, is he?"

That brought a rueful chuckle from the lawman.

"Of course not. But we'll need to keep an eye on him anyway."

"The simplest thing to do would be to get rid of him," the man in the shadows mused. "Do you think you could handle that, Henry?"

Fear coursed through Hinkle at the mere thought of facing John Henry Sixkiller in a gunfight. He would be nervous even if the plan was to ambush Sixkiller. If the first shot wasn't instantly fatal, that would give Sixkiller time to fight back. . . .

A shotgun would be best in those circumstances, Hinkle told himself. A double load of buckshot in the back would knock down anybody, and they wouldn't be getting back up again.

The man in the shadows understood Hinkle's hesitation in answering. He said, "Don't worry about it, Henry, I'm not going to ask you to throw down on Sixkiller. There are other ways to make sure he doesn't interfere with us. I just want you to be ready in case we wind up having to do something about him."

"All right," Hinkle said. "I will be."

He was willing to make that promise to keep his partner happy, whether he would ever be able to keep it or not.

"I'll let you finish your rounds. I just wanted to check in with you and see how you're doing."

"I'm fine," Hinkle declared with a lot more confidence than he really felt. "Everything's going to go just like we planned."

"That's right. And then we'll be rich men."

The thought made Hinkle feel stronger. It was a toss-up which emotion was more powerful within him, greed or fear.

For now he was going with greed.

* * *

A short time later, Billy Ray Gilmore was headed for Red Mike's. He had sent Rankin back to the old deserted trapper's cabin in the mountains that they were using as a sort of hideout, although the people in Purgatory and the surrounding vicinity were so afraid of the gang there was no real need for them to hide out.

It wouldn't do any good to tell Rankin to bathe, but at least he could get rid of the clothes he'd been wearing when he went rolling around in horse apples. The way Rankin smelled now, he wasn't really fit to be around anybody.

Gilmore hadn't quite reached the saloon when someone spoke to him from the shadows next to a building.

"Billy Ray."

The outlaw tensed. His hand moved instinctively toward his gun. Then he relaxed and chuckled when he realized who the man was.

"That's a good way to get yourself shot, spookin' me like that," he said.

"That would have been unfortunate for both of us," the man said. "What happened with Sixkiller? I assume he's still alive?"

"He's alive," Gilmore confirmed. "We reached an arrangement, just the way you suggested. We'll be able to keep an eye on him now. That's better than havin' him floatin' around like some sort of wild card."

"That's what I thought."

"But here's somethin' you might not know," Gilmore went on. "Sixkiller's workin' for Joe Cravens."

"The banker?" The other man sounded genuinely surprised by that news.

"That's right. Cravens wants somebody who answers to him to guard the gold while it's in his bank."

"Hmm. But Sixkiller is double-crossing Cravens and joining forces with you?"

"Yeah. *If* we can trust him to follow through on that."

"And that's a big if," the man in the shadows agreed. "I'm not convinced that he's not trying to play all of us for fools."

"Maybe he is," Gilmore said, "but it'll catch up to him sooner or later. And when it does, he'll wind up dead. But maybe we can get some use out of him first."

"That's why I suggested that we not kill him outright. I had a hunch he might prove to be useful. Just be careful in your dealings with him."

"I intend to be," Gilmore said. "There's too much at stake to get careless now."

The other man faded away into the shadows, and Gilmore went on to Red Mike's. With everything he was trying to keep straight in his head right now, he needed a drink to help him clear his thoughts.

John Henry sat in the Silver Spur with Bouchard and Della for a while, sipping a beer and letting his nerves calm down after the battle with Rankin and the deal he had made with Billy Ray Gilmore. When he excused himself to go back to the hotel, Della sadly said, "I know there's no point in asking you if you'd rather come upstairs with me."

"No," John Henry replied, "and you don't know how sorry I am to say that."

She just gave him a rueful smile and shook her head.

As usual, John Henry kept his eyes and ears open as he walked back to the Barrymore House. He thought that he was safe from ambush for the moment, but if he got careless and was wrong about that, he could easily wind up dead.

Along the way he ran into Marshal Henry Hinkle, who appeared to be making his evening rounds. John Henry nodded and greeted him with a polite, "Marshal."

"Mr. Sixkiller," Hinkle replied in a surly tone. "I was hoping you'd decided to move on by now."

"No, I'm going to be around Purgatory for a while longer," John Henry told the lawman. "Sorry to disappoint you."

"I'm not disappointed. You're welcome here as long as you don't break the law, just like anybody else."

"I'll bear that in mind," John Henry promised dryly.

When he went into the hotel, the clerk wasn't behind the desk. That didn't have to mean anything—

the man had probably stepped out to the privy or something—but John Henry was wary anyway as he went up the stairs and along the hall to his room. He didn't trust Billy Ray Gilmore not to go back on the deal they had made.

When he'd left earlier, he had slipped an almost unnoticeable piece of thread taken from his shirt tail into the gap between the door and the jamb so that it hung over the tongue of the doorknob. If the knob was turned and the tongue pulled back, the thread would slip loose and fall to the floor. When John Henry saw that the thread was still in place, he knew no one had been in his room.

He unlocked the door, went in, and lit the lamp. Other than the battle with Rankin, not much had happened today, but that fracas was enough by itself to make him sore and tired. And the complex, ever-deepening labyrinth of false alliances in which he found himself was brain wearying, too. He would be glad to get some sleep.

He had taken off his hat, coat, and gun belt when a knock sounded on the door.

John Henry had hung the gun belt on the bedpost so the Colt would be handy while he slept. He drew the revolver from its holster now as he went toward the door. Knowing the panel wasn't thick enough to stop a load of buckshot or a bullet fired from close range, he didn't bother asking who was there. That would just give away his position.

Instead, he grasped the knob in his left hand,

turned it, and jerked the door open as he thrust the Colt out in front of him, leveling it at the person who stood in the corridor.

"Well," Sophie Clearwater said coolly as she looked down the barrel of the gun, "is that supposed to frighten me?"

John Henry lowered the Colt.

"Most people would be at least a little nervous," he said.

"I'm not most people," Sophie said. "And this isn't the first time I've had a gun pointed at me."

"Somehow I don't doubt that," John Henry said. "What can I do for you?"

"You can let me in, to start with. I don't feel like standing in the hall to do my talking."

John Henry stepped back. Sophie came into the room, and he closed the door behind her.

"Where's your partner?" he asked.

"Doc's asleep, I imagine. He's not as young as he used to be."

"What do you want?"

"That's a little blunt, isn't it? We're supposed to be working together. Can't I come by to see how you're doing?" Sophie frowned slightly as she studied his face. She asked, "Have you been in a fight?"

"You could say that. I had to tangle with one of Gilmore's men who was almost as big as a bear and smelled even worse than one."

"Why? Was it another ambush?"

John Henry shook his head.

"No, that was Gilmore's idea of making me earn my way into his gang."

Sophie's eyes widened. She said, "You're a member of Gilmore's gang now?"

"Well . . . we're allies, I guess you could say."

"You're supposed to be working with Doc and me." Sophie's jaw was taut as she spoke.

"I am," John Henry said. "I have to find out what Gilmore's plans are some way. This seemed like as good a way as any."

"So you're not really throwing in with him."

"That's right."

"And how are Doc and I supposed to know that you're not planning to double-cross us, too?"

John Henry didn't have to come up with an answer for that, because just then someone else knocked on his door.

"Are you expecting anyone?" Sophie asked in a whisper as she tensed even more.

John Henry shook his head and whispered back, "I wasn't even expecting you."

He still had the gun in his hand at his side. He lifted it as he motioned with his other hand for Sophie to move over so that she would be behind the door when he opened it.

Just as he had when he answered Sophie's knock, he jerked the door open and leveled the Colt. Della gasped as she took an involuntary step back.

"Good Lord, John Henry," she said. "You scared me. What are you doing with that gun?"

John Henry hadn't expected to see the saloon

girl again tonight. He lowered the revolver and instead of answering her question he asked one of his own; the same one he had asked Sophie, in fact.

"Della, what are you doing here?"

She stepped into the room, lifted her arms and wrapped them around his neck, and said, "I'm here to give you one more chance to come to your senses, John Henry Sixkiller, and take me to bed."

Chapter Twenty-seven

Before John Henry could say anything, Della lifted herself slightly on her toes, which brought her mouth within reach of his. She pressed her lips to his and let her body mold itself warmly against him.

Della's eyes were closed in passion, but John Henry's were still wide open. He looked past the saloon girl's honey-blond head and saw Sophie standing against the wall behind the door, looking equally surprised.

But then Sophie's eyes started to narrow, and she began looking more angry than surprised. John Henry tried to shake his head in a signal for her to be quiet, but that was hard to do with Della kissing him so passionately.

It became even more difficult when she cupped one of her hands against the back of his head to hold him still as the kiss grew even more urgent.

Sophie said in a loud, clear voice, "John Henry, who in the hell is *this*?"

At the sound of the other woman's voice, Della jumped back a few inches and gasped. She let go of John Henry so she could whirl around and confront Sophie. They glared at each other with open hostility, blonde versus brunette.

"Now I understand why you kept turning me down, John Henry," Della said when she had recovered enough from her surprise to speak. "You already had a floozy of your very own stashed here in your hotel room."

"Floozy?" Sophie repeated, her voice rising with anger. "You're a fine one to talk, dear, dressed—or should I say undressed—the way you are. Don't you ever get cold with all that hanging out like it is?"

"You can't talk to me that way—" Della began.

"I'll talk to you any way I please. You're the one who's intruding."

Della tossed her hair defiantly.

"I'll bet I have just as much right to be here as you do," she said.

Sophie smiled coldly and said, "I doubt that. You see, John Henry is my husband."

There she went with that lie again, John Henry thought. He wasn't in any mood to let Sophie get away with it.

"I'm not her husband," he said to Della. "I swear we're not married."

"We might as well be," Sophie insisted, "considering all the things that have gone on between us. Or have you forgotten about all that, John Henry?"

He knew she was talking about the gold and their supposed partnership to steal it, although Della would probably take the statement to mean something else. He said, "I haven't forgotten about anything."

"So there *is* something between the two of you?" Della demanded.

"Nothing romantic—"

"Call it whatever you want," Sophie broke in. "If that's how little I mean to you, maybe we'd better just forget it."

"Now, hold on," John Henry said. He wasn't sure what to do about this. He was more accustomed to dealing with situations that required guns or knives or at least fists. He didn't want Sophie to get mad over nothing, though, and jeopardize his plans.

"I won't bother you anymore," Della said as she took a step toward the doorway. She paused, looked at him, and added, "Unless you'd rather get rid of this woman and spend some time with me instead. I can promise you wouldn't regret it, John Henry."

"You just get out of here right now," Sophie said furiously.

"I think John Henry should be the one to decide that," Della responded. "It's his room, after all."

"Ladies—" John Henry began.

Sophie stepped forward and grabbed Della's arm. She shoved Della toward the door as she said, "I told you to get out!"

"Oh!" Della cried. "Let go of me, you . . . you . . ."

Evidently, she couldn't find a word bad enough to describe the way she felt about Sophie. So instead she balled up a fist and swung it at Sophie's head.

Sophie saw the blow coming and jerked aside with a startled yell. She launched a blow of her own and slapped Della across the face.

That was a mistake. The hard life Della had led had made her quick to defend herself. She shoved Sophie back, then went after her, slapping and clawing.

John Henry moved toward them, intending to break up the fight. That might be more difficult than it sounded. As a lawman back in Indian Territory, he had gotten in the middle of plenty of ruckuses, but they were always between men so he didn't have to worry about being too careful with them. He could wallop a few heads with his gun barrel if he couldn't make the combatants listen to reason any other way.

He couldn't do that with Sophie and Della. He had to try to stop them from hurting each other without inflicting any damage on them himself.

Before he could manage to get between them, Sophie lowered her head and tackled Della around the waist, forcing her to stagger backwards. The back of Della's knees hit the edge of the bed. She fell across the mattress, and Sophie sprawled on top of her, striking at her with both hands.

John Henry got hold of Sophie's waist and dragged her off the other young woman. He turned so that his body was between them, and when Della came up off the bed with fire in her eyes and tried to get to Sophie again, John Henry fended her off with one arm while he kept the other arm looped tightly around Sophie. She was struggling to get loose from his grip so that she could resume the battle.

"You two just stop it right now!" John Henry commanded. His voice was loud with exasperation. "Neither one of you has any reason to be acting like this."

"I don't like her!" Della said. "She's a nasty, stuck-up bitch!"

"At least I'm not a two-bit tramp like you!" Sophie shot back at the blonde.

"You're probably not *worth* two bits! No man in his right mind would pay that for you. She's a cold fish, John Henry. You can tell that by looking at her."

John Henry didn't think any such thing was true, but he didn't figure saying that would help the situation. So instead he said, "Just be quiet, both of you. You're going to disturb the other folks in the hotel. This ruckus has gone on long enough."

"It was just getting started," Sophie said through clenched teeth.

"Well, it's over now," John Henry insisted. "Della, I think you should go."

She stared at him coldly.

"So you're picking her over me?"

"I'm not picking either of you," John Henry said. "I just don't want both of you leaving at the same time and starting this fight all over again out in the hall."

"You're going to make me leave, too?" Sophie demanded.

"I think we've said everything to each other that we have to say right now."

"Maybe for good, if that's the way you feel," Sophie threatened.

John Henry still didn't want that, but he couldn't have the two women trying to kill each other in his hotel room, either.

Della said, "Fine. I'm not going to stay where I'm not wanted."

"You're not wanted here, I can promise you that," Sophie said. "John Henry, let go of me, damn it!"

"In a minute," he told her. "Della, you go on now. I'll see you sometime at the Silver Spur."

Della stalked out of the room, throwing one last murderous glance over her shoulder. John Henry used a foot to nudge the door closed behind her. Only when the door was firmly shut between Sophie and Della did he let go of Sophie.

She straightened her dress, pushed back some of the rich brown hair that had fallen in front of her eyes, and glowered at him.

"I thought you had better taste than that, John Henry, I really did."

"You've got it all wrong, Sophie. There's nothing going on between Della and me."

"Not for lack of her trying, I'll bet," Sophie snapped.

John Henry shrugged. It was true that Della had made it abundantly clear from their first meeting that she was interested in him. That didn't mean he returned the interest in anything other than a friendly way.

"This doesn't have to have any effect on matters between us," he said.

"I'm not so sure about that," she replied coolly. "If we're going to work together, we have to trust each other, and I'm not sure I trust you anymore."

"Just because some saloon girl set her cap for me?" he asked in amazement as he spread his hands. "How is that my fault? I don't have any control over that."

"You could have told me about her."

"I didn't see any point in it. It just didn't seem important. It doesn't have anything to do with us."

Sophie regarded him with narrow eyes.

"I'm not sure there is any 'us' anymore," she said. "I'm going to have to think about it."

"Don't think too long," John Henry said bluntly. "They're bringing the gold down from the mountains the day after tomorrow."

Her breath seemed to catch in her throat.

"How do you know that?" she asked.

"I've got sources," he said, not wanting to admit just yet that Jason True had told him.

"You're sure of the information?"

"Pretty sure."

"Then we really don't have much time, do we?"

"That gold will be here before you know it," John Henry said.

"And the gold is the important thing." Sophie nodded slowly, as much to herself as to him. "All right. I guess I just lost my head there for a minute. It's none of my business what you do with women like that."

"I haven't done anything," John Henry said.

"You don't have to lie. I really don't care anymore."

"I'm not—" John Henry stopped. Let her think whatever she wanted, he told himself. Like she said, it didn't really matter. "Was there anything else we need to talk about?"

"I suppose not. Not right now, anyway. The three of us will have to get together tomorrow to discuss our plans."

"You mean you, me, and Doc?"

Sophie sniffed and said, "I certainly didn't mean you, me, and . . . what was that creature's name? Della? The three of us are *not* going to be doing anything together, John Henry. You might as well get that thought out of your head right now."

"It was never in there," John Henry promised

her. His only thoughts were of how to protect that gold bullion until it was in those armored, well-guarded Wells Fargo wagons and on its way to Lordsburg.

That was plenty as far as he was concerned.

Chapter Twenty-eight

Della was still seething as she walked back toward the Silver Spur. She had slipped out of the saloon the back way so that Royal Bouchard wouldn't see her leaving and want to know where she was going. Bouchard was a good man, not without his flaws, certainly, but nowhere near as abusive as some of the men she had worked for in the past.

One of his flaws, though, was curiosity. If he had known that she was on her way to throw herself at John Henry Sixkiller one last time, he probably would have tried to talk her out of it. For her own good, he would have said.

The way things had turned out, maybe that would have been better, Della thought. Then she wouldn't have felt like such a fool when she saw that stuck-up brown-haired witch in John Henry's hotel room.

She hadn't heard the woman's name and didn't know who she was or why she'd been there. She'd been slightly relieved when John Henry insisted that the brunette wasn't his wife, but clearly there was some sort of relationship between them, something deeper than the friendship that evidently was the only thing he felt for her.

Della sighed. With the sort of life she had led, she should have known better than to let herself feel anything genuine for a man. That always caused trouble in the long run, and sometimes in the short run as well.

She hadn't reached the Silver Spur yet. In fact, she was just passing the saloon called Red Mike's, when two men slapped the bat wings aside and stepped out onto the boardwalk, blocking her path. From their reactions when they saw her, Della could tell that they hadn't gotten in her way intentionally, but that didn't make them move. They stayed right where they were, so that she would have had to step down into the street to go around them.

"Well, howdy," one of the men said with a grin that was half leer. He squinted at her in the light that came through the grimy front windows of Red Mike's. "You're one of them fancy gals from up at the Silver Spur, ain't you?"

"Excuse me," Della said. "Could you let me by?"

"No, I don't rightly think I could," the man said. Della recognized him now as Ben Morton, one of Billy Ray Gilmore's men. The other one was part of Gilmore's gang, too. After a moment she came up with his name: Wes McCallum. Morton went on, "I want to talk to you for a minute."

Della wished she had put on a jacket or a shawl of some sort before leaving the Silver Spur. The way both men were looking at her bare shoulders and the exposed upper portion of her bosom made her uncomfortable.

After all the men she'd been to bed with, that didn't seem like it should be possible, but this was different somehow. For one thing, she was out on the street tonight, not in the familiar confines of the saloon where help was just a quick shout away in case anything went wrong.

"What do you want to talk about?" she asked, hoping she could get rid of them quickly.

McCallum said, "We wouldn't mind availin' ourselves of the pleasure o' your company for a spell, missy."

"Come on up to the Silver Spur, then," Della said. "I'm sure we can work something out."

"What's wrong with right here?" Morton demanded.

"On the boardwalk? That's sort of public, isn't it?"

"I was thinking more of over there," Morton said as he gestured toward the nearby mouth of an alley.

"You've got me pegged wrong, mister," Della snapped, somewhat offended by the suggestion. "I'm not some sort of two-bit—"

She stopped. She'd been about to say that she wasn't a two-bit tramp, but that was exactly what the brunette in John Henry's room had accused her of being, she thought. Maybe that's all she really was. She had no right to put on airs of any kind.

Alleys were smelly, dirty, and uncomfortable, though, and a girl had to have *some* standards, even a saloon girl. She shook her head.

"You'll have to come up to the Silver Spur," she insisted.

Morton moved closer to her, close enough for her to smell the whiskey on his breath as he said, "You don't understand. I said here."

"And I said no," Della shot back with anger flashing in her eyes.

McCallum growled, "Hell, don't argue with the slut, Ben. Just take her if you want her."

"That's just what I'm gonna do," Morton said.

He lunged at Della, who tried to twist away but couldn't escape him. He grabbed one of her arms, spun her around so that he was behind her, and clapped his other hand over her mouth so she couldn't cry out.

"Gimme a hand with her, and you'll get a turn, too," Morton told his companion.

McCallum chuckled and said, "Sounds good to me."

He took hold of Della's other arm, and together they dragged her toward the alley. She squirmed and tried to get away, but her strength was no match for theirs. As the darkness of the alley swallowed up the three figures, she wished she was back in John Henry's hotel room, even if that infuriating brunette was still there.

At this moment, though, John Henry Sixkiller

might as well have been a hundred miles away for all the good he could do her.

Della didn't put up a fight for very long. For one thing, she knew that if she gave the two outlaws too much trouble, they would be more likely to hurt her. It would be easy enough for them to kill her if they wanted to, and nobody in Purgatory would do anything about it or even care, except maybe Royal Bouchard. To everybody else she would be just a dead whore, a nuisance to be consigned to an unmarked and forgotten grave on Boot Hill.

So she calmed her raging temper and resigned herself to cooperate with them. The sooner this ordeal was over with, the better.

Not surprisingly, that didn't take long. Both of them were drunk and eager, and Della knew all the tricks of the trade. When they were both finished, she started straightening her clothes while the men stumbled off toward the back end of the alley.

They stopped to roll and light quirlies, and McCallum said, "Once we've got our share of that gold, we can buy ourselves better whores than that one."

Della felt a surge of resentment at those overheard words, then told herself she was crazy to care what a couple of dumb brutes like those two thought of her.

Besides, the word "gold" had caught her ear.

With their lust satisfied, Morton and McCallum

had already forgotten her. She slipped closer to them as they smoked and talked.

"Once we've got our share of the gold, we can buy damn near anything we want," Morton said. "Even divvied up, $75,000 goes a long way."

Della's breath froze in her throat. Seventy-five thousand dollars was a lot more money than she would ever make in her life. It was a lot more than she would even lay eyes on. She could barely imagine that much money.

Like everybody else in Purgatory, she had heard whispered rumors that the three big mine owners, Jason True, Arnold Goodman, and Dan Lacey, were talking about combining their bullion into one big shipment. That would amount to a fortune like the one Morton and McCallum were talking about, so she had a feeling the rumors were true.

From the sound of what they said, the thing was going to happen soon. And it was no wonder that Billy Ray Gilmore's gang planned to go after it. That much gold would be too tempting a target for any outlaw to ignore.

Hell, Della thought, other than whoring she'd always been pretty law-abiding, and it was more than enough to tempt her.

Maybe lucky for her, she wouldn't have any idea how to go about stealing a big pile of bullion like that. So her thoughts turned to some other way she might be able to make some money off of this situation. Maybe the mine owners would give her a reward if she tipped them off to what the outlaws were planning.

On the other hand, True, Goodman, and Lacey weren't fools. They would have to be aware already that Gilmore might make a try for the gold. So it probably wouldn't work for her to approach them, she thought . . . unless she had some really specific information to sell to them, information that would allow them to thwart whatever Gilmore had in mind.

Shoot, she would take just one bar of that bullion as a reward. That would be just fine with her, she told herself as she slipped closer to the two men who stood at the end of the alley, smoking. She didn't want to miss anything they might have to say.

"You really think we'll be able to get our hands on it?" McCallum asked.

"I don't see why not. You know Billy Ray always gets what he goes after. And this time he's got that fella Sixkiller workin' as an inside man at the bank."

Della's breath froze in her throat. John Henry was one of the outlaws? She couldn't believe that. It didn't make any sense. He had killed Junior Clemens and Jack Bayne, after all, and shot that varmint Duke Rudd and his dim-witted friend Sam Logan. He couldn't be part of the gang.

"Yeah, well, I don't much like that," McCallum said. "It's a mistake lettin' Sixkiller in on the deal. I don't trust him."

"Neither does Billy Ray, but if he can help us get our hands on that bullion, I reckon I can put up with him for a while." An evil-sounding chuckle came from Morton. "At least until we've got the gold. Then it'll be easy enough to put a bullet in Sixkiller's back. Pay him off in lead instead of bullion."

"Yeah, I like the sound of that," McCallum agreed.

Della's heart slugged in her chest. She didn't want to believe that John Henry was working with these outlaws, but they seemed convinced of it. And even though she prided herself on being a good judge of men's character—she saw so much of it, and so much bad—she had known John Henry for only two days. She supposed she could be wrong about him.

"Yep, two days from now we'll all be rich men," Morton mused as he flicked away the butt of his smoke. The orange coal at the end of it made an arc through the air. "Hit the bank as soon as the last part of the shipment gets here, before the guards have a chance to get set. That's mighty smart of Billy Ray, setting it up like that."

There was the information she needed, Della thought. She could tip off Mayor Cravens, as well as the three mine owners, about the precise time the Gilmore gang intended to strike. They ought to be grateful enough to her for that to make it worth her while. She was still shocked and disappointed that John Henry was part of the plot, but she forced that out of her mind as she began to slide along the wall toward the street.

Maybe she ought to go to John Henry first. He

wasn't actually a member of the gang; he was just working with them. If she told him that they planned to double-cross him and kill him as soon as the robbery was successful, maybe he would drop out of the plan. Yes, she decided, she would go back to the hotel first and hope that brunette harpy was gone by the time she got there.

"Hey," Morton said suddenly, "where'd that whore go?"

Della froze in the shadows.

"Why?" McCallum asked with a chuckle. "You ain't ready for another little fandango with her this soon, are you?"

"It ain't that. I just don't want her eavesdroppin' on what we were just talkin' about."

"Oh, yeah," McCallum said, sounding a little worried now. "Billy Ray told us to keep our traps shut, didn't he? I guess between the whiskey and the lovin', my mind got a mite muddled." He paused. "Reckon it's all right, though. She probably skedaddled back up to the Silver Spur as soon as we were finished with her."

"Maybe," Morton said. "But come to think of it, we didn't pay her. You ever know a whore to take off when you hadn't crossed her palm with gold or silver?"

"Well . . . no," McCallum said. Their boots thudded on the hard-packed dirt of the alley as they came toward her. "Strike a match, Ben, so we can take a look around."

Della knew she couldn't afford to wait any

longer. If she could reach the street, she could probably give them the slip. And if she got back to the Silver Spur, she would be safe.

She turned and dashed through the darkness toward the faint glow from the street that marked the end of the alley.

Behind her, a match rasped to life and its harsh glare split the shadows. One of the outlaws yelled, "Hey! There she goes!" and the other one called out, "Stop her!"

Guns crashed, and the roar of shots just made Della run faster, lifting her skirts so that her legs flashed back and forth in the gloom.

She was about halfway to the street when something smashed into her with stunning impact.

Chapter Twenty-nine

John Henry was just about to doze off when he heard the shots somewhere not far off. He lifted his head from the pillow and frowned.

Of course, it wasn't unusual to hear shooting in a frontier settlement, especially one where there were plenty of saloons. Men got liquored up, fell into some sort of argument, and settled it with six-guns. The results were sometimes tragic, but they weren't uncommon.

On the other hand, something about the brief flurry of shots he heard made John Henry's instincts stir uneasily. He had no reason to believe that the outbreak of violence had anything to do with him, but the hair on the back of his neck stood up for a second anyway.

The shooting stopped and wasn't repeated. Whatever it was, it seemed to be over. John Henry settled back down and told himself to go on to sleep while he had the chance.

Once again he had almost dozed off when a sound roused him. This time it wasn't shots from somewhere else in Purgatory.

It was a faint scratching on his own door.

John Henry sat up quickly in bed, his hand reaching unerringly for the butt of the Colt, even in the dark. He pulled the revolver from the holster hanging on the bedpost as he swung his legs out of bed and stood up wearing only the bottom half of a pair of long underwear.

Silently, his bare feet padded across the room to the door. The insistent scratching sound had stopped. John Henry leaned closer, putting his ear to the narrow gap between the door and the jamb.

He knew he was taking a chance. Somebody might start shooting through the door, thinking that the little noise would be enough to intrigue him and make him come over here—and they would be right about that, of course—but he didn't think that was going to happen.

Instead, he heard what sounded like harsh, ragged breathing, and then a little moan.

Somebody was hurt out there.

The next instant he knew who it was, as a familiar voice whispered with obvious effort, "John . . . John Henry . . . please . . ."

Even knowing it might still be a trap, knowing that the woman in the hall might be a Judas goat, he twisted the key in the lock and jerked the door open.

Della fell into his arms.

John Henry caught her, and as he wrapped an arm around her, he felt a warm, wet stickiness on her side. She was alone in the hall, and she was hurt.

Picking her up was awkward with a gun in one hand, but he managed. She didn't weigh much, or at least she didn't seem to at this moment. He kicked the door closed and carried her to the bed. The likelihood of getting blood on the sheets never even crossed his mind as he gently placed her on the mattress.

He set the gun on the little table next to the bed, found the tin of matches next to the lamp, and got it lit. As he lowered the glass chimney and the yellow glow of the flame filled the room, he saw how pale and drawn Della's face was. She wore the same dress she'd had on earlier, but now there was a large, dark bloodstain on the left side of it.

John Henry didn't waste any time. He needed to know how badly she was hurt before he went to fetch a doctor. There might not be time for that much delay. He took hold of the dress with both hands and ripped it down the side, peeling it back to reveal the wound.

So much blood had welled from the bullet hole that it was difficult to see how bad the injury really was. John Henry grabbed the sheet and swabbed away some of the gore.

He felt a slight sense of relief when he realized that the slug hadn't penetrated deeply into Della's body. Instead, it had plowed a raw, ugly furrow that ran for several inches along her side. The wound was messy and she was weak and disoriented from losing so much blood, but he didn't think she was in any danger of dying right away. The injury certainly needed medical attention, though.

Della looked like she had passed out from the shock of the wound. John Henry started to turn away so he could get dressed and go find a sawbones for her.

She surprised him by lifting a hand and clutching feebly at his arm. Her eyelids fluttered open as she husked, "J-John Henry . . ."

He leaned over the bed and told her, "I'm right here, Della. You're going to be all right. I'll fetch a doctor—"

"No!" The exclamation sounded urgent. "No . . . doctor . . . please."

"But you're hurt," he protested. "You've got a bullet wound in your side. That happened a few minutes ago, when I heard those shots, didn't it?"

"Can't you . . . patch me up? I don't want them to know . . . that I'm still alive."

John Henry started to ask whom she was talking about, who it was that had shot her. But right now that didn't matter, he realized. Blood was still oozing from the gash in her side. It needed to be cleaned and bandaged as soon as possible.

He tore a piece of fabric off the sheet and soaked it in the basin. Then as carefully as he could he wiped the blood away from the wound. He got another piece of the sheet and folded it into a pad. As he pressed it against the gash, he said, "Can you hold this in place? Press tight on it."

"I'll . . . try," Della said.

"I'll be right back."

"John Henry . . . don't . . . leave me."

"I'm just going down to the lobby. I won't be gone more than a couple of minutes."

Clearly, she didn't like the idea, but she said, "All right. H-hurry."

John Henry pulled on a pair of trousers and a shirt and stuck the Colt in his waistband. He locked the door behind him when he left. Della was worried that whoever had shot her might come after her, and John Henry didn't want the bastard, or bastards, to find her.

He hurried downstairs. The lobby was empty. The clerk, as usual, it seemed, was not behind the desk. John Henry went back there to look around on the shelves below the counter where the registration book lay.

"Hey! What are you doing?"

The startled question came from the clerk, who emerged from a hallway leading toward the rear of the hotel. He stopped short at the sight of John Henry behind the desk.

"I'm looking for a bottle of whiskey," John Henry said. He had glanced up when the clerk spoke, but now he went back to his search.

"What makes you think I'd have any liquor back there?" the clerk asked. He tried to sound indignant and offended, but it didn't go over too well since being around John Henry obviously made him nervous.

John Henry reined in his impatience and said, "I imagine the nights get pretty long while you're working. A little nip now and then might help you get through them."

"Well . . ."

"I'm not trying to get you in trouble with the owners. I just want that whiskey."

John Henry took a ten-dollar gold piece from his pocket and let it drop in the counter to reinforce the request.

If that didn't work, he might have to see if a closer look at the Colt would make the clerk more cooperative.

He didn't have to go that far. The clerk hurried behind the desk, shoved aside some boxes, and brought out a half-full bottle of amber-colored liquid.

"It comes from Red Mike's, so it's not the best quality," he said. "You can get better at the Silver Spur."

"No time for that." John Henry took the bottle out of the clerk's hand and turned toward the stairs.

"Is . . . is there trouble of some sort, Mr. Sixkiller?"

"No trouble," John Henry said curtly over his shoulder. He took the stairs two at a time.

When he got back to his room, Della's eyes were closed and the makeshift dressing had fallen away from the wound when her grip on it relaxed. For a second, he was afraid she had died, despite not seeming to be that seriously injured, but then he saw her chest rising and falling and the flutter of a pulse beat in her soft throat. She had passed out or possibly even gone to sleep.

She might be better off if she'd passed out. If she was just asleep, the fiery bite of the whiskey on her raw flesh would wake her up.

He wiped away the blood that had seeped out while he was gone, then soaked another rag in the whiskey and used it to clean deep in the wound. Della gasped and arched her back, but her eyes remained closed.

John Henry cleaned the wound thoroughly, then fashioned another dressing and bound it tightly in place with strips of cloth cut from the sheet. When this assignment was over, he would have to see to it that Judge Parker reimbursed the hotel for the damage he was doing. It was more important to save Della's life than to save a few pennies, though.

When he was finished, she let out a little moan and stirred. Her eyes opened again. After a moment, she focused on him and said, "Wha . . . what happened?"

"I'm hoping you can tell me," John Henry said as he pulled one of the chairs over to the bed and sat down on it so he could lean close to her. "Somebody shot you. Do you know who it was?"

She lifted her head enough to look down at herself.

"I'm . . . practically . . . naked."

"Modesty had to take a backseat to patching you

up," John Henry told her. He pulled what was left of the sheet over her.

"You didn't . . . bring a doctor up here . . . did you?"

"Nobody knows that you're here except me," he assured her. "Unless somebody saw you coming in."

She shook her head.

"No, I was . . . careful. I came up . . . the back stairs. I was afraid . . . I might pass out . . . before I got here . . . but I was determined . . . to hang on."

"You made it, all right. Now tell me what happened?"

She licked her lips and asked, "Can I get . . . something to drink first?"

"Water or whiskey?"

"Better make it . . . whiskey."

The bottle was still about a fourth full. John Henry slipped a hand behind Della's head and lifted it enough for him to tip the bottle to her lips. She took a small swallow from it and shuddered.

"That's not from . . . the Silver Spur . . . is it?"

John Henry had to smile.

"No, I got it from the clerk downstairs, and he said it came from a place called Red Mike's."

"I'm not . . . surprised. Royal wouldn't . . . serve swill like that."

John Henry took a swig from the bottle and made a face.

"You're right," he said. "It's not very good."

"But it's . . . booze. Gimme another."

John Henry let her drink, then set the bottle aside. Her color looked a little better now, he thought.

He eased her head back down on the pillow. She looked at him and said, "You know . . . this is one hell of a way . . . to finally get you to put me in your bed."

That brought an outright laugh from John Henry. He pushed her honey-blond hair back from her sweaty forehead and said, "You need to tell me what happened now. I want to know the name of the varmint I have to hunt down, so I can settle the score for what he did to you."

Della's expression grew serious again.

"There were two of them," she said, "and it shouldn't be . . . too hard for you to find them, John Henry. They're your . . . partners."

He frowned and asked, "What are you talking about?"

"Their names are . . . Morton and McCallum. They're part of Billy Ray Gilmore's gang." She lifted a hand and clutched at his arm again. "But you have to be careful, John Henry. Once you've . . . stolen the gold . . . they plan to double-cross you and put a bullet in your back!"

Chapter Thirty

John Henry couldn't help but stare at her for a moment in surprise. Somehow she had found out a lot in a hurry. He was convinced that when she left here earlier, she hadn't known a thing about his connection to Gilmore's gang.

He asked himself if he should tell her that it was all a sham, maybe even reveal his true identity as a deputy U.S. marshal. No, not yet, he decided. At least not until he had more of the story from her.

"Go on," he urged. "Tell me what happened after you left here."

"You mean after you kicked me out . . . in favor of that brown-haired witch?"

"She left right after you did," John Henry told her. "I don't care what she said, there's nothing going on between us."

"But you know her." Della's eyes widened. "Is she part of the plan . . . to steal the gold, too?"

"I'll get to all that," John Henry promised.

"Men," Della said with a sigh. "You always want what you want . . . when you want it."

He smiled and said, "I'll tell you all about it, but I want to hear your story first."

"All right . . . I ran into Morton and McCallum outside Red Mike's . . . on my way back to the Silver Spur. They wanted to have some fun, and I'm . . . a sporting girl . . . so I told them to come to the Silver Spur with me. But they didn't want to. They wanted to . . . take me in the alley right there."

John Henry's jaw tightened with anger.

"I don't even know these hombres, and I don't like 'em," he said.

"You don't know . . . all the members of the gang?"

"My arrangement is with Gilmore himself," John Henry admitted. He would give her that much if it kept her talking.

"Well, you haven't missed much . . . by not knowing those two. They're sorry bastards. Morton grabbed me . . . and dragged me into the alley. They . . . took what they wanted."

"They'll pay for that," John Henry promised.

That made Della laugh.

"They sure as hell . . . didn't pay me," she said. "When they were finished . . . they wandered off to have a smoke . . . and that's when they started talking about the gold . . . and about you working with the gang. They said . . . you're going to be the inside man at the bank. Is that . . . true, John Henry?"

"It's true," he told her, his face and voice grim. He didn't like the idea of her believing that he was an outlaw, but for now she didn't really need to know the truth. She might even be better off if she didn't.

"Well, I don't guess I can . . . blame you," she said. "Seventy-five thousand dollars is an awful lot of money. If I was a man . . . I might be trying for a share of it, too."

"Why did those two varmints start shooting at you?"

"Because they realized . . . I had overheard what they were saying. Gilmore warned them . . . not to talk about it. I guess they thought . . . if they killed me . . . he'd never have to know." Della's mouth twisted bitterly. "After all . . . who'd give a damn about a dead whore?"

John Henry stroked her forehead again.

"I'm glad they didn't kill you, that's for sure," he said. "How did you get away from them?"

"I was hit . . . but I managed to stay on my feet and keep running. I made it to the street ahead of them . . . but I knew they'd catch up if I tried to outrun them . . . all the way to the Silver Spur. So I ducked down . . . the next alley . . . and hid. Got behind . . . a rain barrel . . . and prayed they wouldn't find me." Della laughed softly. "Guess that's pretty funny . . . somebody like me . . . praying."

"Not funny at all," John Henry said quietly. "And since you're here, I'd say it's likely Somebody heard those prayers."

"I . . . hope so. Anyway, I heard them . . . looking around. One of them even came into the alley where I was hiding . . . but he didn't see me in the dark. I held my breath . . . until he was gone. It was hard not to cry . . . because my side hurt so bad . . . but I didn't."

"I'm proud of you," John Henry told her.

"When they were gone . . . I decided to come here. I had to warn you . . . about what they were planning. I stayed in the shadows . . . came up the back stairs like I told you . . . but when I got here . . . I was too weak to knock. So I just . . . scratched at the door . . . and hoped you would hear. . . ."

She had started to look pale and weak again. Talking so much had worn her out, John Henry knew. He gave her another sip of the whiskey and told her, "You should rest now. That wound's not too bad. You just need to take it easy and let it heal."

"John Henry." She made an obvious effort to talk. "John Henry, if they think I got away, they'll know I might tell you about the double cross. They might . . . go ahead and kill you. We've got to . . . make them believe I'm dead."

John Henry thought about what she said and realized she was right. He said, "Can we trust Bouchard?"

"I do. For a saloon keeper . . . he's a good man. And I think he . . . likes me."

"All right. I'll talk to him. We'll figure something out."

"That sounds good." She moved a hand, and he took hold of it in both of his hands. "Thank you . . . for saving my life."

"Thank you for saving mine," he told her, even though he never would have trusted Billy Ray Gilmore, even without her warning, and would have been ready for a double cross. It was good to have those suspicions confirmed, though.

"This is . . . the worst damn timing in the world."

"What do you mean?"

"Here I am in your bed . . . and we can't even . . . do anything."

"I wouldn't say that," John Henry told her. "We can do this."

He leaned closer to her and pressed his lips to her forehead. She closed her eyes and sighed, and he sat there and held her hand until she fell into a deep, natural sleep this time.

Marshal Henry Hinkle was at the desk in his office the next morning, sitting there sipping a cup of coffee from the pot on the stove, when the door opened and a middle-aged man with a brown brush of a mustache strode in like the place belonged to him.

Dislike made Hinkle frown as he set his cup down and stood up.

"Sheriff Stone," he said. "What are you doing here?"

"This whole county's my bailiwick, ain't it?" Sheriff Elmer Stone asked. "Part of my job to come check on the outlyin' settlements from time to time."

Hinkle didn't think it was a coincidence that his fellow lawman had shown up in Purgatory just now, when rumors were flying fast and furiously about the big gold shipment being put together by the three mine owners. Stone was a politician; if something important was going on, he wanted to be on hand for it. That might mean a few extra votes for him when it came time to run for re-election.

There had been a time when Hinkle planned to oppose Stone in that campaign. Lately, though, he'd been leaning toward the opinion that it wasn't worth it. He had his sights set on something bigger than being sheriff of some backwater county in New Mexico Territory.

"Well, if there's anything I can do to help you, just let me know," Hinkle said, but the surly tone of his voice made it clear the offer wasn't exactly sincere. As far as he was concerned, the sooner Sheriff Stone went back to the county seat, the better.

"I could do with a cup of that coffee I smell," Stone said.

Hinkle nodded toward the stove.

"Help yourself. It was made fresh this morning."

"Much obliged." Stone went to the stove, took a cup from the shelf next to it, and used the thick leather pot holder to grip the handle as he poured. He took a sip of the steaming black brew and nodded. "Just the way I like it. Strong enough to get up and walk around on its own hind legs."

Hinkle wanted to tell the man not to use that folksy humor on him. It wouldn't work the same way it would on the stupid voters. But he didn't say anything as he sat down again.

"I hear tell you've been havin' some trouble down here," Stone went on.

Hinkle shook his head and said, "Not so's you'd notice."

"Really? From what I hear, you've got outlaws runnin' roughshod over the populace and gunfights in the streets."

"It's not that unusual to have a ruckus break out from time to time," Hinkle said defensively. "I'll bet you have them in the county seat, too."

"Well, now and then. Any time a gunfighter rides in, though, me and my deputies make sure he rides on pretty quick-like."

"You think we've got a gunfighter here in Purgatory?"

"Man called Sixkiller. You know him?"

"We've met," Hinkle admitted.

"And he's killed a couple men since he's been here, hasn't he?"

Obviously, the sheriff had someone in the settlement who fed him information about what was happening here. Hinkle wasn't really surprised. A good politician had to have a whole network of spies if he was going to hang on to power.

"I investigated that shooting," Hinkle snapped. "It was a clear case of self-defense. Sixkiller was ambushed, and he defended himself. That's all there was to it."

"Yeah, but can you really consider it self-defense when one of the fellas involved is a gunslinger? Seems to me he should've been jailed, or at least told to move on."

"I won't roust somebody and throw them out of town when they haven't broken the law," Hinkle said.

"Especially when it's somebody who might not take kindly to the effort and fight back, eh?"

Hinkle felt his face warming with anger. He knew Stone was referring to his reputation for cowardice.

Maybe it was true that he went out of his way to avoid trouble sometimes, but there was a good reason for that. He couldn't do anybody any good if he was dead, now could he? So staying alive meant he was a better lawman. That was the way he'd always seen it, anyway.

Still, he couldn't completely contain his anger. He said, "I don't appreciate what you're insinuating, Sheriff."

Stone grunted.

"I'm not insinuatin' anything, Marshal. I'm outright sayin'—"

What Stone was saying went unspoken, because at that moment the office door opened again. Royal Bouchard hurried in, an upset expression on his handsome face. He stopped short at the sight of Sheriff Stone, then gave an abrupt nod and said, "Good. Both lawmen here at the same time."

Hinkle put his hands on the desk and shoved himself to his feet.

"What's this all about, Bouchard?" he demanded. "It better be important for you to interrupt a meeting between me and the sheriff."

"How about murder?" Bouchard said. "Is that important enough for you, Marshal?"

Chapter Thirty-one

"Murder?" Hinkle repeated. That wasn't something he wanted to hear. "What are you talking about?"

Bouchard lifted a hand and rubbed it over his face. He heaved a sigh.

"One of my girls," he said. "Della Turner. She disappeared last night. I went looking for her this morning and found her in the alley between Pratt's Hardware and the apothecary shop. She . . . she'd been shot in the back."

"Good Lord," Hinkle said. "She was dead?"

"Dead as could be," Bouchard replied with a nod. He had a haggard look about him now, as if the strain of the grim discovery was catching up to him.

Stone said, "You're Bouchard, aren't you? Own the Silver Spur?"

"That's right, Sheriff," the saloon keeper replied with a curt nod.

"And this dead girl worked for you?"

"That's what I said, isn't it?" Bouchard asked with barely controlled impatience.

"So she was a—"

"She was a human being, Sheriff," Bouchard said. His voice had a hard edge to it.

"Well, sure," Stone said. "But you know how it is with these gals. They go into an alley with some lowlife cowboy or miner, pert' near anything can happen to 'em. Maybe she tried to rob whoever it was that shot her." The sheriff shrugged. "No way in hell to find out who done it or what really happened."

"That's my decision to make, Sheriff, since it happened here in town," Hinkle said. "I give you my word, Mr. Bouchard, that I'll make a thorough investigation of the matter."

Bouchard grimaced.

"The same way you make a thorough investigation of every other crime that takes place in this town, Marshal? You'll excuse me if I don't hold my breath waiting for you to catch the murderer."

Hinkle flushed angrily again.

"If that's the way you feel," he said, "then why did you come to me in the first place?"

Bouchard shrugged and said, "I thought I ought to report what happened, even though I didn't really expect it to do any good."

"Well, you've reported it," Hinkle snapped. "I'll handle things from here. Where's the body now?"

"Down at the undertaker's. Don't worry, Marshal,

I'll be paying for the burial. The town won't be out any money on a dead whore."

"That's not what I was worried about. I'm . . . sorry, Bouchard. Sorry for your loss."

Bouchard sighed and nodded slowly.

"Thanks for that, anyway," he said. "If there's any way I can help you find out who killed her . . ."

"I'll let you know," Hinkle said.

Bouchard nodded again and went out of the office.

When the saloon keeper was gone, Stone asked, "You're not really gonna try to find out who killed that saloon girl, are you, Hinkle?"

"Like you said, it'd be next thing to impossible," the marshal admitted. "Bouchard was upset, though. It didn't hurt anything to tell him that I'd try."

"No, I reckon not."

For a politician, Stone had been pretty callous about the girl's death just then, Hinkle thought. He supposed that Stone didn't consider the feelings of a saloon owner important enough to worry about. Besides, whores couldn't vote to start with, since they were female, and drunkards usually didn't bother. Stone probably liked to confine his glad-handing and politicking to the more respectable elements of the citizenry.

Hinkle was convinced that he could beat the sheriff if he were to run against Stone in the next election. Right now, he would keep that plan in reserve, in case the other things he had in the works didn't pan out. But if they did . . .

Well, why would a man as rich as he was going to be even want to be sheriff, anyway?

When the quiet tap sounded on the door, John Henry stood up from the chair beside the bed and drew his gun. He waited. Two more discreet taps against the panel came, then a pause, then a final one.

John Henry didn't holster his gun, but he relaxed slightly. It was unlikely that anyone would duplicate by accident the signal he had worked out with Royal Bouchard a short time earlier, when he had filled in Bouchard on what had happened and explained the plan to him. When he opened the door and saw Bouchard standing there, the saloon keeper nodded.

"It's done," he said. "Not only did I report Della's death to Marshal Hinkle, but Sheriff Stone happened to be there to hear about it, too."

"Della's death," said the woman sitting up in the bed with pillows propped behind her back. "I'm not sure I like the sound of that."

John Henry closed the door and grinned at her.

"Neither do I," he said, "but this way is better than if it was the real thing."

Della returned the smile and said, "You won't get any argument from me about that."

Bouchard took out a cigar and offered it to John

Henry, who shook his head. Putting the cheroot in his mouth instead, Bouchard said around it, "I've made arrangements with Cy Shuster, the undertaker. He's going to weight down an empty coffin and bury it later this morning. There won't be much fuss about it. Meade and some of the girls and I will be the only ones there, I'll wager. But folks will see us headed for Boot Hill, and they'll know what's going on. It won't take long for the news to reach Gilmore, if it hasn't already."

"This fella Shuster, can we trust him?" John Henry asked.

Bouchard grunted.

"Cy would say that up was down and the moon was green if you paid him enough. Not only that, but I happen to be aware of a few . . . indiscretions, shall we say? . . . on his part that he wouldn't want getting back to his wife, so I think he'll go the extra mile to make sure he doesn't do anything to annoy me."

"So in other words, you're paying him off *and* blackmailing him at the same time," John Henry said.

Bouchard rolled the cigar from one corner of his mouth to the other.

"I've always liked to cover all my bets," he said. He smiled at Della. "You look like you're feeling better this morning."

"Thanks to John Henry, I am," she agreed. There was quite a bit of color in her cheeks again, and she was wearing a silk robe that Bouchard had brought her. "I think he did as good a job of tending to this wound as any doctor could have. Probably a lot better than what some of those old quacks I've seen would have done."

"I've patched up a few bullet wounds in my time," John Henry said.

"He went down to the dining room and got me something to eat earlier, too," Della went on. "They must have thought you were starving when you got that much food on a tray and brought it back upstairs with you."

"I'm just a growing boy," John Henry said dryly. "Got a big healthy appetite."

"For some things, anyway," Della said.

"That's enough talk like that," Bouchard said. "We need to figure out what we're going to do now."

"You and your people are going to that so-called burial," John Henry said, "and then your part in all this is done."

Bouchard frowned.

"I want to help out all I can," he insisted. "I have a score to settle with those buzzards who hurt Della." He cleared his throat. "No one mistreats one of my girls and gets away with it."

"You've done enough already, or at least you will have once the burying is done," John Henry said. "We've already run a risk by having you come up here a couple of times. That might be enough to make Gilmore suspicious. We want him and all of his men to believe that Della isn't a threat to their plans anymore."

"All right," Bouchard said with obvious reluctance. "But if there's anything else you need, don't hesitate to call on me, any time of the day or night."

"I won't," John Henry promised.

Bouchard went over to the bed and reached down to pat Della's shoulder.

"You get some rest now," he told her gruffly. "That's the best way for you to start getting well."

"Don't worry, Royal," she said. "I'll be back earning money for you in no time."

"Hmmph," he said. "I wasn't worried about that." He reached inside his coat. "Here, there's one more thing I can do." He brought out a two-shot, over-and-under derringer and pressed it into her hand. "Take this, just in case there's any trouble and you need to defend yourself. It's saved my bacon a few times."

Della looked at John Henry and asked, "Do you think I should?"

"It wouldn't hurt," he told her. "You're safe as long as nobody but us knows you're here, but it never hurts to be ready for trouble."

Della nodded. She slipped the derringer underneath one of the pillows at her side.

"You know how to use that, don't you?" John Henry asked.

"Of course I do."

"Ever shot anybody before?"

She fixed him with a level gaze and said, "Don't ask questions you don't really want the answers to."

John Henry returned the look for a second and then nodded.

"Fine, we'll leave it at that. Thanks again, Royal."

"Any time," Bouchard said. He smiled at Della again and left the room.

"That fella likes you," John Henry told her when Bouchard was gone.

"I know. We've always gotten along well."

"No, I mean he *really* likes you."

She made a face and shook her head.

"He may think he does, but he doesn't, not really. No man really feels like that about a girl like me."

"You'd be surprised."

"He knows about the life I've led," she insisted. "How could he ever forget that?"

"Maybe that's the only kind of man who could."

That made her frown in thought. After a moment, she mused, "He *does* know all about me. . . ." Then her expression hardened. "I don't want to think about this now. I just want to stay alive and settle the score with Morton and McCallum. With what they did, on top of the way Rudd and Logan treated me before, I've got a real grudge against that whole gang."

"I don't blame you," John Henry said.

Late that morning, he watched from the window of the hotel room as Cy Shuster's hearse, pulled by a team of six black horses, rolled past on Main Street, heading for the cemetery at the edge of town. Royal Bouchard, the bartender called Meade, several of the women from the Silver Spur who were dressed less provocatively than usual for the occasion, and a handful of men John Henry didn't know followed along on foot.

"Well, how about it?" Della asked from the bed. "Am I getting quite a send-off?"

"There's a decent group of mourners," John Henry told her. "Looks like some of your customers have turned out, too."

"Oh, I'd like to see that! I'd like to know which of them decided to risk their reputation by going to a whore's funeral. But I guess I'd better not come to the window and look out, had I?"

"That would sort of defeat the purpose of all this trouble we're going to," John Henry drawled. He let the curtain fall closed and turned away from the window.

"What now?" Della asked.

"Now we wait," he said.

That's what they did for the rest of the day. John Henry went downstairs and up the street to the Red Top for lunch. He didn't like leaving Della alone in the room, but he had to act like everything was normal and she insisted that she wasn't hungry after the big breakfast he had brought her. She had the derringer, but her greatest safety lay in the fact that no one knew she was there except him and Bouchard.

He was on his way back to the hotel when Mayor Cravens came up to him.

"Mr. Sixkiller," the banker said, "do we still have an agreement? You'll be helping to protect the gold while it's in my bank?"

"That's the deal," John Henry said.

Cravens leaned closer to him and said in a conspiratorial tone, "Then be ready tomorrow. The first load of bullion will be here by mid-morning. I'll expect you at the bank then."

"So soon, eh?" John Henry said, as if he hadn't already been told the schedule by Jason True. He nodded and went on, "All right, Mayor. I'll be there."

"Excellent! Thank you, Mr. Sixkiller."

As John Henry walked the rest of the way to the hotel, he thought about what Della had learned by eavesdropping on Morton and McCallum the night before. Gilmore and his gang planned to strike just as the final load arrived. That was pretty smart. The guards wouldn't have had time to settle into their positions around the bank, and a third of the bullion would already be loaded and ready to go. If a surprise attack wiped out the guards, Gilmore and his men could go into the bank while the rest of the citizens were lying low, trying to stay out of the line of fire, and force either Cravens or Harley Smoot to open the safe. Then they could load the gold onto some more wagons and drive away with the entire shipment.

John Henry hadn't figured out exactly how he was going to stop them yet, but he had some ideas. For one thing he could tip off the guards to be expecting the attack. Without the element of surprise on the outlaws' side, the assault could backfire on Gilmore.

John Henry also didn't know what Sophie Clearwater and Doc Mitchum were planning to do, but he wasn't worried that much about them. They were wild cards, true, but he didn't see how they could possibly steal the gold by themselves.

Della dozed most of the afternoon. At suppertime, John Henry got another big meal on a tray from the dining room downstairs, supposedly just for himself. They shared the food and the pot of coffee he brought up.

After supper, he changed the dressing on Della's wound. The gash in her side still looked ugly and painful, but the blood had scabbed over and the wound was starting to close. Most importantly, John Henry didn't see any signs that it was starting to fester.

"You take good care of me," she told him with a smile. "You should have been a doctor instead of a . . . a whatever it is you are. You just don't seem like an outlaw."

"That's not my chosen profession," he said.

"Sometimes life nudges you into odd corners, though."

"I suppose so—"

She stopped as a knock sounded on the door. John Henry turned to look at it, then glanced back at Della as she mouthed the name *Royal?*

He shook his head and shrugged, put his hand on the butt of his gun as he stood up. He crossed to the door and called softly, "Who is it?"

"Your old pard Billy Ray Gilmore," came the reply. "We need to talk, Sixkiller."

Chapter Thirty-two

John Henry looked over his shoulder at Della. She had heard Gilmore's voice, and her eyes had gone wide with fear. There was no closet or wardrobe in the hotel room, no good place for her to hide.

The only thing she could do was slide off the far side of the bed and stay as low to the floor as possible. That ought to keep Gilmore from seeing her as long as the outlaw didn't actually come into the room.

With a quick motion of his hand, John Henry indicated what he wanted Della to do. She nodded in understanding and climbed silently and carefully out of bed, grimacing as she did so. The unexpected activity probably made the wound in her side hurt. The covers on the bed were messed up, but that just looked like they hadn't been straightened since John Henry got up that morning. Gilmore wouldn't be able to tell from the doorway that he'd slept in the chair the night before.

"Sixkiller?" the boss outlaw's voice came again.

"Hang on," John Henry said. He twisted the key in the lock and opened the door about six inches. As he looked out into the corridor, he asked, "What do you want?"

Gilmore grinned at him.

"Is that any way to say howdy to your partner? We *are* still workin' together, aren't we?"

"Sure we are," John Henry said. "I'm not about to back out of our deal now. How about you?"

"No, sir. That's why I'm here." Gilmore's eyes narrowed slightly as he looked at the way John Henry was standing, blocking most of the view of the room. "Am I interruptin' something? You got company in there, Sixkiller? Mind you, it's all right with me if you do, as long as it ain't anybody you're plannin' on double-crossin' me with."

John Henry grunted, moved back a step, and swung the door open so that Gilmore could see the bed.

"Does it look like I have company?" he asked.

"No, I reckon not. How about lettin' me in so we can talk about what's gonna happen tomorrow?"

"How about we go somewhere and have a drink while we're talking instead?"

Gilmore shook his head.

"You don't want to be seen drinkin' with me. That'd be too likely to get folks suspicious of us. But if it's booze you want, I can go get a bottle and come back. I used the back stairs, so it ain't likely anybody's gonna see me."

"No, that's all right," John Henry said, realizing that he wasn't going to get rid of Gilmore easily. It might be best to keep this conversation as short as possible. Hoping that Della would understand what she needed to do, he continued, "Come on in, I guess."

He moved back, stepping all the way over beside the bed. As he glanced down, he saw the covers swaying slightly where they were draped over the side of the mattress. Della had crawled underneath the bed in time. It must have been painful for her and might have even broken the wound open and started it bleeding again, but that was better than letting Gilmore see her and realize she was still alive.

John Henry nodded toward the door and said, "Shut that, would you?"

He glanced around the room, searching for any signs that Della was here. The dishes and coffee cups from supper were already gone, so Gilmore wouldn't be able to tell that John Henry had eaten with someone in here. He had snuck some clean sheets from the hotel's linen closet earlier in the day, so the torn, bloody ones were no longer in evidence. Bouchard had taken Della's dress away with him earlier to dispose of it, along with the sheets. As far as John Henry could see, everything was clear.

Gilmore closed the door and turned to face John Henry.

"Maybe I should have gone to get that bottle

after all," he said. "Then we could drink to our mutual success tomorrow."

"We'll drink to it afterward," John Henry suggested. "We'll be rich enough we can afford the finest champagne there is."

"That's true. We'd better go over the plan." Gilmore's voice hardened slightly. "Start by tellin' me what you know about what's gonna happen tomorrow."

John Henry's voice also held an edge as he said, "I could ask you to do the same thing."

"Oh, I'll share what I know, don't worry."

John Henry shrugged and said, "Fine. The gold's coming down from the mines in three loads, one from each mine. I don't know the order, but the first load of bullion is supposed to arrive at the bank at mid-morning, accompanied by armed guards. They'll unload it from the wagons into the bank's safe, then go back up to the next mine and load up again. Cravens wants me inside the bank when the first load gets there, and I'll stay inside from then until the Wells Fargo agents load it up the next morning to take it to Lordsburg."

"That agrees with what I've been told," Gilmore said with a nod.

"Told by who?"

Gilmore just smiled and shook his head without saying anything.

John Henry narrowed his eyes and said, "I'm not the only inside man you've got working with you, am I? You've paid off one of the guards, too."

"I didn't say that. But I do have my sources of information," Gilmore acknowledged. "And they tell me that if everything goes as planned, the third and final load of bullion will arrive in Purgatory late tomorrow afternoon. As soon as the wagons pull up in front of the bank with the third load, that's when we're gonna make our move. Some of the guards will be inside. It'll be your job to take care of them while we're dealing with the men outside. They won't be expectin' trouble from you, so you shouldn't have much trouble with 'em."

"That almost amounts to cold-blooded murder."

Gilmore put on a show of pretending to think about it and then nodded.

"I suppose you could call it that. I like to think of it as a necessary chore that'll pay off in $75,000 worth of bullion."

"That's a better way to think of it, all right," John Henry said. "How are you going to haul all of it away?"

"The last load will already be on the wagons. I've got four more wagons lined up, good teams of horses, and good men to handle them."

"Are you taking the gold back up into the mountains to hide out?"

Gilmore shook his head.

"We'd have to move too slow on those steep roads. A posse might be able to catch us, that is, if Marshal Hinkle could stop tremblin' in his boots long enough to get a posse together. No, we'll be lightin' a shuck for a flag stop west of Lordsburg. It's all set up with a fella who works for the railroad. There'll be a westbound train that stops early the next morning. We load the gold onto it, get on board ourselves, and ride in style all the way to California. Some fellas there are gonna take the gold off our hands for a good price, and from there it'll be simple to get across the border into Mexico. We'll have enough money to live like kings there for the rest of our lives."

"You've thought it all out," John Henry said with what appeared to be an admiring nod. "I'll be coming with you to California?"

"Unless you'd rather go somewhere else and have me send your share to you later."

John Henry chuckled and shook his head.

"No offense, Billy Ray, but I like the idea of not letting you out of my sight until I've got my share."

"I'd feel the same way, if I was you," Gilmore said. "You got any questions?"

John Henry shook his head.

"I think you covered it all pretty well. The plan sounds like it should work . . . unless those guards put up too much of a fight for your gang."

"My boys can handle them," Gilmore said confidently.

"You're down a few men, remember?"

"And whose fault is that?"

"In my defense, when I shot those hombres I

didn't know you and I were going to wind up working together," John Henry said.

"I know that. That's the only reason you're still alive." Gilmore paused. "That and the fact that it's gonna come in mighty handy havin' you inside that bank tomorrow afternoon."

John Henry hoped Della was doing all right under the bed. So far she hadn't made a sound. He had kept Gilmore talking and spouted quite a few words himself to cover up any tiny noises she might make. Now that he knew the details of the plan, it was time to get Gilmore out of here.

"Sounds like everything's squared away and ready to go," he said. "Anything else we need to talk about?"

"No, I think we're done." Gilmore extended his hand. "Partner."

John Henry gripped the outlaw's hand without hesitation and said, "Partner." He didn't like giving his word when he had no intention of keeping it, but he figured that was a necessary evil in this case.

"We'll have that drink in California," Gilmore went on. "A couple of rich swells, sippin' fancy booze."

"Sounds good to me," John Henry agreed. He wondered if Gilmore was lingering because he was suspicious, or if the man was just talkative.

"Ah, well," Gilmore said. "We'd better both get some rest. We're gonna need to be fresh tomorrow."

It was an effort, but John Henry managed to stay

nonchalant and unhurried as he showed Gilmore out of the room. Gilmore checked the hall first, so that no one would see him leaving John Henry's room, then slipped out. John Henry eased the door closed behind the boss outlaw.

He didn't say anything. He went over to the bed, hunkered on his heels, and lifted the dangling covers. He leaned over to look and saw Della peering out at him, her eyes wide.

He put a finger to his lips indicating that she should be quiet, then reached under the bed so she could take his hand and let him help her out of her hiding place. When he had her clear, he put his arms around her and lifted her. She gasped softly against his ear, so he knew the movement hurt her.

"Sorry," he whispered. He lowered her to the mattress as gently as he could.

Her robe was covered with dust from under the bed. She looked down at it in dismay.

John Henry was more worried about the wound in her side. He motioned for her to stay where she was and went to the door. His concern was that Gilmore might be lurking out there in the corridor with his ear to the door, listening to see if anyone else really was in here, as he had suspected at first.

With his hand on his gun, John Henry opened the door a couple of inches and looked out. Not seeing anything, he opened it wider and stuck his head out. The corridor was empty. He closed the door and locked it.

"Are you all right?" he asked quietly as he returned to Della's side. "I need to check that wound."

"It hurt some, but I don't think it started bleeding again," she said.

"I want to take a look for myself."

"The worst part was the dust. I thought I was going to sneeze several times, and I really had to fight to keep it in."

"I'm glad you did," John Henry told her with a smile. "That would have been sort of awkward. I don't think Gilmore would have said God bless you."

"More than likely he would have said go to hell and tried to send us both there."

"More than likely," John Henry agreed.

It took a few minutes to check the dressing on Della's wound. A little fresh blood had seeped from it, but not enough to worry about, John Henry decided. In order for him to do that, she had to take off her robe, so he shook it out to remove the dust while she had it off.

Dressed only in a thin shift, she watched him and said, "I heard everything that Gilmore was saying, John Henry. You really are an outlaw, aren't you? You're working with him to steal all that gold."

"Things aren't always what they seem to be."

"Maybe not, but this is pretty damned obvious. You even called each other partner. I'll bet you were even shaking hands at the time."

John Henry shrugged.

Della looked up at him and shook her head. She said, "I just never really had you pegged as that sort. Lord knows, that much gold is tempting. Like I said, I'd be tempted to go after it myself if I was a man."

"Maybe I could take you to California with me," John Henry suggested. "Or you could meet me there later."

She looked at him for a moment, then shook her head.

"No?" he asked.

"No," she answered. Her voice was firm and decisive. "I said I'd be tempted, not that I'd do it. I'm a whore, not a thief. I know some soiled doves rob their customers, but I'm not one of them. I never have been. A man like you might not be able to understand this, John Henry, but—and Lord knows I never thought I'd be saying *this*—I'm an honest woman. You do what you have to, but I don't want any part of that blasted gold robbery."

John Henry reached a decision and said, "I'm glad to hear you say that, Della . . . because I'm really a deputy United States marshal."

Chapter Thirty-three

She gaped up at him for a couple of seconds, then said, "You're really a crooked lawman?"

"I don't know about the crooked part," John Henry said with a smile, "but I'm definitely a lawman. I can show you my badge and bona fides if you want."

She shook her head to indicate that wasn't necessary.

"But you're going to help Gilmore and his gang steal that gold!"

John Henry shook his head.

"No, Gilmore just thinks I'm going to."

The light of understanding dawned in Della's eyes. She said, "You're working undercover." She giggled suddenly, unable to hold in the reaction. "That's something you and I have in common, I guess."

"You need to stop thinking all the time about

what you've been doing for a living. There's a lot more to you than that."

She shrugged and said, "I don't know about that, but right now I don't care. You were sent here to get Gilmore?"

"I was sent here to protect the gold. Gilmore's just the main threat to it."

But not the only one, he thought, remembering Sophie Clearwater and Doc Mitchum. He wondered what they were up to tonight.

"Making Gilmore think that I wanted to work with him seemed like the best way to find out what his plan was," John Henry went on. "You heard for yourself how well that worked."

"He told you everything, all right. But what if he was lying? He might not trust you enough to tell you the truth."

"Some things you just have to take on faith," John Henry said. "Besides, I'm convinced he believes what I've told him. Things will go easier for him if he's got a man inside the bank, and I'm that man."

"But he's planning to double-cross you and kill you as soon as he's got the gold."

"I'd expect as much from a skunk like him, even if I really was as crooked as you thought I was."

"You convinced me, all right," Della said. "Does anybody else know about this? Have you told the marshal?"

"You're the only one. Once I saw what sort of hombre Marshal Hinkle is, I figured I couldn't count on any help from him."

"That's the truth," she said emphatically. "He's useless. He's worse than useless."

"What about Sheriff Stone? He's here in town right now, too, according to Bouchard."

Della shook her head and said, "I don't really know much about him, but from everything I've heard he's more of a politician than a real lawman. He might risk his hide to help you because those mine owners are so wealthy and influential, but again, you can't count on that."

"So I'm going to have to handle Gilmore and his gang by myself," John Henry mused. "Well, with some help from the guards hired by True, Goodman, and Lacey, of course."

"You should tell Royal about this," Della suggested. "He'll back your play. He's a good man . . . for a saloon-keeping, whoremongering gambler," she added with a smile.

"I'll keep that in mind, but for right now I'm going to keep on playing a lone hand."

"That's a good way to lose. And you've got a pretty big wager on the table."

John Henry nodded and said, "I know. Seventy-five thousand dollars in gold bullion."

"I was talking about your life," Della said.

She tried to convince him to share the bed with her—just for sleeping, she insisted, nothing else—but John Henry spent the night in the chair again. He was up early the next morning. By sundown, if everything went as planned, the main threat to the gold would be eliminated, so he told Della, "I'm going to stop by the saloon and let Royal know that he can come here this evening and get you. It'll be safe by then for you to go back to the Silver Spur."

"What if your plan doesn't work and Gilmore gets away with the gold?"

"Well, in that case, you won't really be a threat to him anymore," John Henry said. "Either way, you ought to be safe again."

"But you'll probably be dead if that's the way it turns out."

"I suppose you can't have everything," John Henry said.

She rolled her eyes at him.

John Henry went downstairs to the dining room to get a breakfast tray. The redheaded waitress was there, and she said, "If I didn't know better, Mr. Six-killer, I'd say you have someone else up in your room."

"You're welcome to come take a look for yourself," he told her with a meaningful smile.

As he expected, she got a little skittish when he pretended to take her flirting seriously and returned it. She said, "I, uh, can't do that. I have to work."

"That's a real shame."

"Goodness, I can't stand around talking all day!" She bustled off, and John Henry tried not to grin at how well his ploy had worked.

After breakfast he told Della, "Sorry, but I'm

going to have to leave you now. I have a lot to do this morning, between now and the time I need to be at the bank."

"What *are* you going to do?"

"Get ready to give Gilmore and his men a warm welcome this afternoon," John Henry said. He didn't go into detail, and Della didn't press him.

She looked nice, wrapped in her robe and sitting up in the bed. John Henry went over to her, bent down, and pressed his lips to her forehead.

"That's the best I'm ever going to get, isn't it?" Della asked with a sigh. Without waiting for him to answer, she went on, "Whoever that girl is, back where you come from, she's mighty lucky."

"I hope she feels the same way," John Henry said. "Don't forget what I told you about Royal. You ought to give him a chance."

Della still didn't look convinced that the saloon keeper could really care about her, but she promised, "I'll think about it."

Figuring that a man who ran a saloon might still be asleep at this time of day, John Henry's first stop was the general store. In a town like Purgatory that depended heavily on the mines in the area, the store naturally carried quite a bit of mining equipment, and it had what John Henry needed. He was sure the clerk was curious about what he intended to do with his purchases, but John Henry didn't offer any explanations.

And since he was known as the man who had survived a bushwhacking by two of Billy Ray Gilmore's outlaws, none of the citizens were about to give him any trouble over anything he did.

With the things he had bought in a canvas sack, he stopped at the livery stable to check on Iron Heart. The horse nuzzled his hand happily, glad to see him again.

"You've been stuck in here the whole time we've been here, haven't you?" John Henry said. "If I'd known I wasn't going to be riding the range any, I might not have brought you. You're probably ready to get out and stretch your legs again. Soon, old friend, soon. This is almost all over."

He hoped that turned out to be true.

From the stable he went down the street to the undertaking parlor, where he introduced himself to Cy Shuster. Most people thought of undertakers as cadaverous themselves, but Shuster was short, plump, and jolly. Bouchard had kept John Henry's name out of the ruse concerning Della, so Shuster didn't know about his connection to that. He knew who John Henry was, though, just like nearly everybody else in Purgatory.

Since part of the undertaker's job was making coffins, he was good at carpentry and working with wood. As John Henry explained what he wanted, Shuster frowned, obviously puzzled, but he nodded and said, "Sure, I reckon I can do that, Mr. Six-killer. How soon do you need those things?"

"Just as soon as you can have them ready," John Henry said. "Later this morning, if possible."

"Well, if I hurry that much, it won't be a fancy job."

"It doesn't have to be fancy," John Henry said. "It just has to work."

Shuster nodded and said, "All right. Give me an hour."

John Henry carefully lifted the canvas sack and asked, "Can I leave this here until I come back for the other things?"

"Sure."

"Don't look in it or jostle it around," John Henry warned.

Shuster held up his pudgy hands and shook his head. He said, "Whatever's in there is your business, not mine." He hesitated. "It won't bite, will it?"

John Henry chuckled.

"No, but you still wouldn't want to stick your hand in there."

He left the undertaking parlor and spent the next hour strolling around town, apparently idly. Actually, he was studying everything about Purgatory as he had before, making sure he had things clear in his mind. Once the trouble started, he might not have time to wonder where he was or which way he needed to head next.

He also went by the Silver Spur and talked to Royal Bouchard, telling him that it would be safe that evening for Bouchard to bring Della back to the Silver Spur.

"You're sure about that?" Bouchard asked.

"Positive," John Henry said. "One way or another, she'll be out of danger by then."

Bouchard shook his head and said, "I don't know how I can ever thank you for what you've done for that girl, John Henry."

"Give me one of your cigars, and we'll call it square."

"A cigar?" Bouchard asked as his eyebrows rose in puzzlement. "That's not much."

"It's enough," John Henry insisted.

"Well . . . all right."

Bouchard handed John Henry a cigar. John Henry smelled it appreciatively, then slid it into his shirt pocket.

"I'll smoke it later," he said. "There's one other thing, Royal."

"Anything," Bouchard said.

"If I was you, I'd get around to telling Della how you really feel about her sooner rather than later."

He left Bouchard staring after him in surprise.

When John Henry returned to the undertaker's, Shuster greeted him with "Was this what you wanted?"

John Henry looked over the hastily fashioned items for a moment before nodding in satisfaction.

"These ought to work for what I need," he said. "How much do I owe you?"

Shuster waved away the offer of payment and said, "I used scraps for most of it, so it didn't really cost me anything but time. I'm just curious to find out what you're planning. Or do you intend to keep it a secret?"

"Not for too much longer," John Henry said. "Do you have something I can use to wrap all this up?"

"A burial shroud. Would that do?"

"Strangely appropriate," John Henry said with a nod.

This time when he left Shuster's place, he went out the back. Carrying the bag from the general store and the shroud-wrapped bundle of the things the undertaker had made for him and sticking to the alleys, he made his way to the rear of the bank and gently set everything on the ground. He had noticed a ladder leaning against the wall a few businesses away, so he fetched it now and leaned it against the bricks.

Being careful, he took the things he had rounded up this morning up the ladder to the building's flat roof. Staying low and keeping to the middle of the roof so no one on the ground would be likely to notice him, he catfooted to the front of the building and made a few more preparations, then left them there where they would be ready for him later.

Since he couldn't materialize a troop of cavalry or a posse of deputy U.S. marshals out of thin air, he had done what he could to get ready for what was going to happen today, he told himself as he climbed down the ladder.

He just had to hope it would be enough.

* * *

John Henry checked his pocket watch: eleven o'clock. The wagons bringing down the first load of bullion from the mountains ought to be here soon. He'd really expected them to show up earlier than this.

"I know," Mayor Cravens said as John Henry put his watch away. "I thought they'd be here by now, too." The banker took out a handkerchief and mopped sweat from his forehead, even though the day was cool. "Maybe Gilmore decided one load was enough and hit them in the mountains."

"I don't think so," John Henry said. "He wouldn't be satisfied with a third of what he could get if he waited until all the gold is here."

The bank was closed for business today, and the front door was locked. The head teller, Harley Smoot, had come in to work, though, and stood at the windows looking out at the street. He turned suddenly and said in an excited voice, "They're here, Mr. Cravens!"

"Thank God!" Cravens muttered. "It's about time."

He hurried toward the door to unlock it.

John Henry was right behind the banker. He stepped out onto the boardwalk to watch the impressive procession coming down the street.

Two wagons drawn by teams of six strong mules rolled toward the bank, each driven by a hard-faced man who wore two revolvers. Beside each driver rode an equally grim guard also armed with a pair of six-guns and a double-barreled Greener.

Two Winchesters lay on the floorboard. That was a lot of firepower.

It was just the start, though. Four men, each of them heavily armed as well, rode in front of the lead wagon. Four more guards were positioned between the wagons, and a final four brought up the rear. Twelve guards on horseback, four more on the wagons themselves, counting the drivers. If they were attacked, they could put up a fight, that was for sure.

In front of both wagons and all the guards came a buggy with two more men in it. One was another shotgun-wielding guard. The man holding the reins was Jason True, and he handled the team of two black horses pulling the buggy briskly and efficiently. So the first load of bullion came from True's San Francisco mine, John Henry thought.

He looked along the street and saw that the boardwalks were unusually empty. Once he thought about it for a second, he understood why. Rumors must have been flying about the gold being brought to town today; with that many guards working for the mine owners, it would have been impossible to keep the schedule a total secret. And the townspeople had to figure that Billy Ray Gilmore probably had his eye on the bullion. The citizens of Purgatory were going to keep their heads down, well out of the line of fire, until that gleaming fortune was gone from their town.

That was good for his purposes, John Henry told

himself. When hell broke loose, there would be less chance of an innocent bystander getting hurt.

And hell *was* going to break loose. He had no doubt of that.

Jason True brought his buggy to a halt in front of the bank. The gold-laden wagons pulled up behind him. John Henry could see now that canvas was stretched over the bed of each wagon, but there were enough gaps around it that stacks of wooden crates were visible. Each crate would have several ingots of bullion inside it, he knew.

"Thank God you're here safely," Cravens greeted True. "Did you have any trouble?"

"Not a bit," True said as he looped the reins around the buggy's brake lever. With the agility of a younger man, he jumped down from the vehicle. "We just got a bit later start than we'd intended." True looked at John Henry and nodded to him. "Sixkiller. How does everything look?"

"Good," John Henry said. "I don't think you're going to have any problems."

He knew good and well that wasn't true, but he didn't see any harm in saying it.

Jason True grunted and said, "I'll believe that when I see it." He turned and gestured to his men. "Let's get it unloaded and inside the bank."

The guards dismounted. Half of them arranged themselves around the wagons, holding rifles slanted across their chests and facing outwards so their eyes could constantly scan the buildings along the street, alert for any signs of trouble. The other guards began hauling the crates into the bank.

"How many men are you leaving with me?" Cravens asked True.

"There will be four guards around the bank."

"Four?" Cravens repeated. "Is that all? Gilmore has at least a dozen men!"

"That's all we can spare," True said. "Not as many men showed up as we were expecting. I suppose they decided double wages weren't enough for risking their lives." He nodded toward John Henry and added dryly, "But you have your own special guard as well."

"It's not enough," Cravens insisted.

"We do the best we can. There are a lot more places up in the mountains where Gilmore and his gang could ambush the wagons. We need the guards there. I'll be staying here, too, Joe. We'll be all right."

Cravens sighed and said, "I don't know why Wells Fargo couldn't just meet you here today and take charge of the gold right away."

"They have limited manpower as well, and besides, they couldn't leave with it until tomorrow morning anyway."

"I suppose. I won't rest, though, until it's out of my safe and on its way to Lordsburg."

Neither would he, John Henry thought.

Chapter Thirty-four

The air of tension inside the bank and elsewhere in town grew even stronger as the day went on. By the time the second load of bullion arrived shortly after one o'clock in the afternoon, this one from Arnold Goodman's El Halcón mine, the boardwalks were completely empty.

Except for the activity around the bank, Purgatory looked like a ghost town.

"Did you encounter any trouble?" Jason True asked Goodman as they watched the guards unloading the gold.

The stocky, bulldog-like mine owner shook his head.

"No sign of Gilmore or any other desperado," he said. He looked at John Henry and went on, "This is the gunslinger Cravens hired?"

"That's right. John Henry Sixkiller, this is Arnold Goodman."

Goodman didn't offer to shake hands. He looked

at John Henry with narrow, suspicious eyes and said, "I don't like the idea of trusting a man who makes his living with a gun."

"Some people feel the same way about men who make their living sitting in boardrooms," John Henry said.

Goodman's heavy features flushed with anger.

"I didn't always sit in a boardroom," he snapped. "If you want I'll prove it."

"Settle down, Arnold," True said. "Let's worry about Gilmore, not about fighting with someone who's here to help us."

"How do we know he's here to help us?" Goodman demanded.

True looked at John Henry and said, "If he's not, then God help him, because he'll regret it."

John Henry kept his face impassive and didn't say anything. They would all know the truth about him soon enough, he thought.

Once Goodman's gold was unloaded and stowed away in the safe, the wagons and their accompanying guards would head up into the mountains once more, bound for Dan Lacey's Bonita mine where they would pick up the final load of bullion.

Four guards posted around the bank wouldn't be enough to fight off Gilmore's gang, John Henry thought. Cravens had been right about that. He checked the street again, then went over to True and Goodman.

"I think you ought to leave more men here this

time," John Henry told them. "Since there's more gold here now than the wagons will be bringing down, the odds have tipped the other way. This is where the greatest danger is."

Of course, he knew from talking to Gilmore when the outlaws planned to strike, but he wasn't quite ready to reveal that. For one thing, he was convinced that Gilmore had another inside man, and John Henry didn't know that man's identity. He didn't want anybody tipping off Gilmore that the plan was compromised.

Also, there was always the chance that Gilmore had lied to him and planned to rob the bank before the third load got here. In that case, having some extra guards on hand might save the day.

Goodman said, "I'm not sure we should be taking advice from a—"

"Hold on," True broke in. "Sixkiller may be on to something there. If Gilmore was to hit the bank after the wagons start back up to Lacey's mine, he could get twice as much bullion here than he could if he made a try for the wagons."

"He wants it all," Goodman insisted.

"You're probably right. But it won't hurt to leave a few more guards here. In fact, let's split them and keep eight men here while eight go with the wagons."

Goodman didn't look happy about it, but he reluctantly went along with the idea.

"This had better not backfire, though," he said. "If it does, I'm blaming you and Sixkiller."

John Henry didn't give a damn about blame. He just wanted to get this over with.

Something else was nagging at him. He hadn't seen Sophie Clearwater or Doc Mitchum since the night before last. He didn't know if they were even still in Purgatory, or if they had given up the idea of stealing the gold and left town. With all the plans he had made, those two were still wild cards, and they could ruin everything if they interfered at the wrong time.

It was too late to do anything about them. In a few hours, the third load of bullion would be here and Billy Ray Gilmore would make his move. That is, if he didn't strike before then. . . .

With approximately half as many guards as they'd had before, the empty wagons left Purgatory and started back up the winding trail into the mountains where the mines were located. The bank's front door was locked and two of the extra guards were stationed at the door of the room containing the safe. The rear door was not only locked but had a heavy bar across it. No one would be getting in that way without a considerable amount of trouble or a fistful of dynamite.

Couldn't rule anything out, John Henry thought with an ironic smile as he looked at that rear door. If Gilmore had been telling the truth, though, he intended to come in the front, after slaughtering the guards.

He had paid attention to the time it was when the

wagons left after delivering the load from the San Francisco and when they got back with the bullion from El Halcón. He asked True and Goodman, "Is Lacey's mine closer to the settlement or farther from it than yours?"

"It's the farthest of the three, a couple of miles farther from town than mine," Goodman answered. "Why?"

"Just trying to figure out how long it's going to take for the wagons to get back."

True took out his pocket watch, flipped it open, and said, "They ought to be back here by five o'clock."

"The shank of the afternoon," John Henry mused.

"Why is that important?" Goodman wanted to know. Clearly, he was still suspicious of John Henry.

"Just curious," John Henry said. He was going to wait as long as he could before springing the truth on them, even though he had decided that the guard who was in Gilmore's pay probably wasn't here in the bank. Gilmore's plan called for him to eliminate all the guards inside the building, which would have put the spy at risk. More than likely the man was outside, where he could abandon his post and scurry for cover as soon as the shooting started.

Time dragged by. Cravens mopped his sweating face and asked, "What if they don't show up? What if Gilmore decided it's too risky and he isn't even going to make a try for the gold?"

"Then we'll count our blessings," True said. "I can't bring myself to believe that's the case, though."

"Neither can I," Goodman said. "They'll be here. It's just a matter of when."

John Henry knew the when, or at least thought he did. He kept checking his watch, and so did the other men.

At a quarter to five, he approached True, Goodman, and Cravens, who were standing together near the front windows, watching the street for the arrival of the wagons.

"There's something I need to tell you," John Henry said.

Goodman instantly looked suspicious again. He said, "I knew it. You're double-crossing us."

"Not exactly." John Henry slipped a hand inside his coat. The three men tensed, no doubt thinking he was about to draw some sort of weapon.

Instead he brought out a leather folder and flipped it open. On one side was pinned his badge, and the other held the card identifying him as a deputy United States marshal.

"A lawman!" Cravens exclaimed. "Good Lord! All this time you've been a lawman?"

"That doesn't mean anything," Goodman said stubbornly. "Anybody can have a badge and a piece of paper."

"But only somebody who really is who he says he is would know about that letter you wrote to Judge Parker in Fort Smith, Mr. True," John Henry said.

"Letter?" Goodman said. "What letter?"

A look of mingled surprise and relief was on True's stern face. He asked John Henry, "You work for Isaac?"

"Yes, sir, I do."

True looked at the other mine owner and the banker and said, "I was worried that our preparations wouldn't be enough, so I wrote an old friend of mine who's a federal judge and asked if he could send someone to help us." He frowned at John Henry. "Of course, I expected more than one man, and I didn't expect the man who showed up to masquerade as a gunslinger!"

"I reckon I'm the only one the judge could spare right now," John Henry drawled, "and as far as acting like a gunslinger, that allowed me to partner up with Gilmore."

"You . . . you . . ." Goodman sputtered. His eyes were practically bulging from their sockets.

John Henry held up a hand and said, "Hold on. You'll bust a vein, Mr. Goodman. I should have said, that allowed me to *pretend* to partner up with Gilmore. He thinks I'm going to double-cross you fellas and kill the guards in here when he and his gang attack the rest of the guards outside, as soon as the wagons get here with the last of the bullion."

"He told you this?" True asked shrewdly. "He let you in on his plans?"

"That's right. And having him reveal that was *my* plan."

"They're attacking as soon as the wagons get here with the third load?" Cravens said. "We've got to do something. That could be any minute now!"

"I know," John Henry said. "That's why I want you to let me out the back door, then lock it and bar it behind me."

"You're running out on us?" Goodman asked.

"No, I just need to get outside where I can move around easier. Plus I've put together a little welcome for Gilmore."

Cravens said, "I don't know about any of this—"

"Do what Sixkiller says, Joe," True snapped. "If he works for Isaac Parker, I have complete faith in him."

"He's been fooling us all along," Goodman protested. "How do we know we can trust him now?"

"What other choice do we have?"

The other two men didn't have an answer for that. Cravens said, "All right, Mr. Sixkiller, I'll let you out the back. I guess you weren't ever really working for me, were you?"

"I'm afraid not, Mayor, but we're after the same thing: protecting that gold and putting a stop to the threat of Billy Ray Gilmore and his gang."

Cravens led John Henry to the back door. John Henry removed the bar, and Cravens unlocked the door. John Henry slipped out into the alley behind the bank. The ladder was right where he had left it that morning. He climbed to the roof while Cravens relocked the door and replaced the bar across it.

A short wall surrounded the flat roof. The things John Henry had placed beside that wall at the front of the building were still there, too. Staying low again because he didn't want to be spotted, he hurried over to them and knelt there to unwrap them from the burial shroud.

The bow he pulled out of the cloth was a crude one, nothing like the bows his father's people made back in Indian Territory. Cy Shuster had fashioned it in his carpentry shop, turning a length of supple wood on a lathe to round it, then stringing it with cord instead of animal gut. The half-dozen "arrows" John Henry unwrapped were actually just short lengths of wooden poles notched to fit the cord. They didn't have any fletching, so accuracy might be a problem, but luckily they wouldn't have to go very far.

John Henry reached into the canvas sack that held his purchases from the general store. He used twine he had bought to lash a single stick of dynamite to each of the makeshift arrows. To each stick of dynamite he attached a blasting cap and a short fuse. He set them down, lining them up in a row within easy reach.

Now it was just a matter of waiting for the right time to use them.

He didn't have to wait for very long. The sound of wagon wheels came to his ears. He took off his hat and lifted his head enough to look along the street.

The wagons were on their way. He could see

them entering the edge of town, along with the guards riding around them.

John Henry watched as the wagons came closer and closer. One of the men riding in front of the lead wagon wore an expensive suit and hat, and a watch chain glittered where it looped across his vest. John Henry recognized the man he had seen having dinner with True and Goodman a few nights earlier and knew he had to be Dan Lacey, owner of the Bonita mine. The third load of bullion was here.

Below John Henry, the front door of the bank opened. The wagons came to a halt, and the riders reined in. Jason True stepped out onto the board-walk and called urgently, "Lacey! Get inside the building! Hurry!"

Lacey hesitated, looking confused. He said, "Jason, what's wrong?"

The answer to that question came in the form of hoofbeats as a large group of horsemen surged around a corner two blocks away. John Henry saw Billy Ray Gilmore in the lead. He was shocked to realize that the gang was even larger than he'd expected. At least two dozen men were with Gilmore, maybe more than that.

That ought to make things more interesting, John Henry thought as he took the cigar he had gotten from Bouchard out of his pocket, put it in his mouth, and lit it.

Down below, men yelled in alarm and scattered for cover as the outlaws opened fire and charged toward the wagons.

John Henry picked up the closest dynamite arrow and puffed on the cigar, making the tip glow red. He held the fuse to the coal and saw sparks as it sputtered to life.

Then he stood up, drew back the bow, and yelled, "Bank's closed!" around the cigar.

He let the arrow fly.

Chapter Thirty-five

The arrow didn't travel quite as far as John Henry hoped it would, landing well in front of the onrushing outlaws. He had cut the fuse the correct length, though, because the explosive detonated at almost the exact same instant it hit the ground, throwing dirt high in the air and causing a cloud of dust to billow up.

By that time, John Henry had adjusted his aim and had two more of the arrows arcing through the air. Gilmore's men were trying to slow their charge, but momentum carried them forward so that those two sticks of dynamite exploded among them. The blasts shredded man and horseflesh alike and blew several of the would-be gold robbers right out of their saddles.

John Henry didn't slow down his barrage. As the gang scattered, he raised the angle of his shots even more and rained down death and destruction through the swirling clouds of dust. Firing all six arrows had taken less than a minute, and during that time the street had been plunged into chaos.

He spat out the cigar, turned, and ran to the back of the bank building. As quick as he could, he climbed down the ladder, leaping off of it when he was still a few feet from the ground. He landed running and darted around the corner to head for the street.

The outlaws were demoralized and disoriented by John Henry's explosive counterattack, but the ones who were still alive weren't giving up, not with the lure of $75,000 in gold bullion to keep them fighting. Shots roared as the men who were still mounted veered around the bloody craters in the street and continued their charge toward the bank.

John Henry saw that when he reached the front of the building. He had drawn his Colt as he ran along the alley. It bucked against his palm as he fired and knocked one of the outlaws out of the saddle. The man hit the dirt and rolled over several times before he came to a stop on his back with his arms outflung and blood welling from the hole John Henry's bullet had left in his chest.

John Henry crouched as a slug whined over his head. He shifted his aim and pulled the trigger again. This shot wasn't quite as accurate. Instead of boring through its target's heart, the bullet shattered the outlaw's left shoulder. That was enough to make him slew around sideways in the saddle and drop his gun. A second later, before the outlaw could recover, one of the guards at the bank blew his brains out with a Winchester.

A furious bellow from the side made John Henry twist around. He saw the giant outlaw Rankin, the brute he had battled in the livery stable to earn entrance to the gang, leave his horse in a diving tackle. John Henry didn't have time to get out of the way before Rankin crashed into him and drove him off his feet.

The impact was so stunning that John Henry blacked out for a second. He came to with Rankin on top of him. The big man's weight kept him from drawing breath, and the force with which he had landed had driven all the air from John Henry's lungs.

Some instinct, though, had enabled John Henry to hang on to his gun. He still clutched the Colt in his right hand. He brought it up and smashed it against Rankin's head just above the big man's ear. That drove Rankin to the side and allowed John Henry to roll in the other direction. His chest heaved as he gulped down a deep breath.

While John Henry was doing that, Rankin scrambled back to his feet first. John Henry tried to swing up the revolver, but Rankin's foot lashed out in a kick that connected with John Henry's wrist. John Henry yelled in pain as the Colt flew from his grip.

Rankin pulled a massive bowie knife from a sheath at his hip and roared, "I'm gonna cut you into little pieces, you son of a bitch!" He raised the knife high and lunged at John Henry.

Rankin's head jerked before the slashing blow could fall. His face blew apart as a heavy slug crashed through his head from behind. Blood and brain matter sprayed over John Henry, who still had to throw himself aside quickly to avoid being crushed by Rankin's toppling body. That knife still represented a threat, too.

John Henry neatly avoided that danger and leaped to his feet. His first thought was that one of the guards at the bank had shot Rankin, but suddenly he realized that the angle was wrong for that. The shot had come from somewhere else, most likely across the street. He looked toward the Barrymore House and saw a curtain flutter in one of the hotel's second-floor windows.

Whoever was up there had quite possibly saved his life. John Henry lifted his left hand in a wave of thanks as he reached down with his right to scoop up his Colt. He didn't linger.

There were still outlaws to battle . . . and he didn't know if Billy Ray Gilmore was dead or alive.

He felt the wind-rip of a bullet past his ear and whirled to see one of the gang charging him. John Henry's return shot punched into the man's chest and made him rock back in the saddle. The man didn't fall, but he was only half conscious and bleeding badly as he galloped past.

"Sixkiller, you son of a bitch! You double-crossed me!"

John Henry heard that strident shout over the roar of shots and the thundering hoofbeats. He recognized Billy Ray Gilmore's voice and searched for the boss outlaw in the roiling clouds of dust and powdersmoke. A spurt of muzzle flame guided him. Gilmore's bullet sang over his head.

John Henry triggered a couple of shots, and then his hammer fell on an empty chamber. Twisting aside as another slug sizzled past his ear, he darted into the scanty cover of the building's corner and reached for the cartridge loops on his gun belt.

As he reloaded with the ease of long practice, he risked a glance around the corner, not needing to see what he was doing as he thumbed fresh rounds into the Colt's cylinder. He spotted Gilmore right away.

The outlaw had been unhorsed in the chaos and confusion. He had lost his hat, too, and his thick dark hair was wildly askew. He ran toward a riderless horse, obviously intending to swing up into the saddle and make a getaway.

John Henry burst from cover and went after Gilmore. He snapped a shot at the fleeing man, who was moving so fast that John Henry knew his earlier shots had missed. Gilmore twisted as he ran and flung a couple of rounds at John Henry, who had to dive to the ground as the bullets cut through the air just above him.

That gave Gilmore enough time to reach the horse, which was dancing around skittishly, and seize the reins. He brought the animal under control and grabbed the saddlehorn. A vault put him into the saddle, where he leaned far forward over the horse's neck as he kicked the animal into a gallop.

Gilmore headed for the edge of town, leaving his surviving men behind him. Obviously, his hide was worth more to him than the rapidly fading chances of him getting his hands on any of that bullion.

Gilmore was already too far away for John Henry to waste a shot with his Colt. He ought to just let the outlaw go, he told himself. After all, Judge Parker had sent him here to protect the gold, and clearly Gilmore's plans to steal it were wrecked.

John Henry knew that . . . but he grabbed the reins of another riderless horse anyway and leaped into the saddle. Leaving things unfinished went against the grain for him. He sent the horse lunging after Gilmore.

Purgatory fell behind the two men as the shooting began to dwindle. John Henry wouldn't have left if he hadn't seen that Gilmore's gang was practically wiped out and no longer a real threat.

Gilmore headed west out of town, toward the mountains. He was following the same road the wagons had used to bring the gold down from the mines. The road quickly began to slant upward, and John Henry felt the horse laboring underneath him.

Gilmore's mount was struggling, too, though. As his horse slowed, he twisted in the saddle to look behind him. John Henry saw a couple of jets of flame and smoke as Gilmore fired down at him. The shots didn't come anywhere close. They struck rock and whined off harmlessly into the distance.

John Henry holstered his Colt. The hurricane deck of a galloping horse was no place for accurate shooting. Let Gilmore waste bullets if he wanted to.

John Henry didn't know if his mount was fresher or just stronger to start with or both, but he began to cut into Gilmore's lead. Gilmore slammed his heels against his horse's sides and slashed at the animal's head with the reins, but the animal could only go so fast, especially uphill like this. John Henry continued to close in.

They had actually climbed quite a bit, he saw when he glanced to his left. The ground fell away from the road at a steep slant, dropping seventy or eighty feet to a point where it leveled off. That drop continued to increase slowly.

Gilmore kept shooting. He emptied his revolver, but none of the bullets came close enough to worry John Henry. He saw Gilmore jam the iron back into its holster, then lean forward to concentrate on his riding.

The road took a bend up ahead. Gilmore had to slow down for that. John Henry closed in even more. He could see the sweat on Gilmore's face now when the outlaw looked back over his shoulder. John Henry urged the last bit of speed out of his horse.

He drew even with Gilmore, to the outlaw's right. Gilmore had drawn a knife from somewhere and slashed at John Henry with it. John Henry ducked the blade, kicked his feet free of the stirrups, and left the saddle in a diving tackle that sent him crashing into Gilmore.

Both men fell, and for a split-second John Henry wondered if they were both going to go off the side of the drop-off. Then they slammed into the ground at the side of the road, with a hundred feet of mostly empty air only a couple of yards away from them.

Gilmore had managed to hang on to the knife. John Henry saw steel glitter as the blade came flashing toward his face. He got his left hand up and grabbed Gilmore's wrist, stopping the thrust when the knife was scant inches from his throat. He brought up his right fist in a straight punch that landed solidly on Gilmore's jaw and twisted him to the side.

John Henry rolled after him, holding on for dear life to the wrist of Gilmore's knife hand. Gilmore brought a knee up in a crushing blow that would have incapacitated John Henry if he hadn't writhed aside at the last second to take it on his hip and thigh. As it was, the vicious attack left his leg momentarily numb.

With his free hand he hammered punches into Gilmore's head and body. Gilmore was fighting with the strength and rage of the insane, though, and he threw John Henry off. A quick roll put him on top of the lawman. He drove the knife down with all his power. John Henry was barely able to hold it off. The blade's razor-sharp point pricked John Henry's throat and drew a drop of blood.

"You . . . double-crossed me!" Gilmore panted. "Were you . . . workin' for the mine owners . . . all along?"

"I work for . . . Uncle Sam," John Henry responded, equally breathless. "I'm a . . . deputy . . . U.S. marshal!"

That took Gilmore by surprise. John Henry could tell by the way the outlaw's eyes widened. But the revelation didn't shock Gilmore into slipping. If anything, he struggled even harder to plunge the knife into John Henry's throat.

In a desperate move, John Henry brought his right leg up and hooked it in front of Gilmore's throat. He arched up off the ground as he straightened the leg and drove Gilmore backwards.

John Henry scrambled to his feet, and Gilmore did likewise. Gilmore still had the knife. He swung it wildly. John Henry ducked under the sweeping blow, stepped closer, and brought his right fist almost from the ground in an uppercut that caught Gilmore under the chin and lifted him as he flew backwards.

When he came down, there was no ground

under his feet anymore. John Henry had knocked him right off the edge of the road.

Gilmore had time to scream for a couple of heartbeats before he struck the steeply slanting slope about halfway to the bottom. He bounced, flew into the air, and hit a couple of more times, turning as limp as a rag doll by the time he came crashing down on the level ground. John Henry, chest heaving as he dragged air into his lungs, looked down at the sprawled form, saw the grotesquely sharp angle at which Gilmore's head now rested on his neck, and knew that the outlaw hadn't survived the fall.

The horses hadn't gone very far. When he had caught his breath, John Henry mounted one of them and led the other as he started back down toward Purgatory. He could see the town below him..The late afternoon air was quiet now. The battle against Gilmore's gang was over.

He thought suddenly about all that gold bullion, and about Sophie Clearwater and Doc Mitchum as well. Then he heeled the horse to a faster pace, feeling an urgent need to get back to town and make sure everything was all right.

Chapter Thirty-six

By the time John Henry reached Purgatory, Marshal Henry Hinkle and Sheriff Elmer Stone were making themselves visible, striding around Main Street issuing orders about the disposal of all the dead bodies littered about. John Henry didn't recall seeing either of the lawmen during the battle, but they were certainly in evidence now.

He ignored them and proceeded straight to the bank, where Jason True greeting him by exclaiming, "Marshal Sixkiller! No one knew where you were. I was afraid you'd been killed."

"I went after Gilmore," John Henry explained. "Probably shouldn't have. Is the gold all right?"

True nodded and said, "All stowed away in the bank's safe. What about Gilmore? Did he get away? Do we have to worry about him coming back?"

John Henry shook his head.

"No, in fact, Cy Shuster's going to have some work waiting for him out of town, once he's through here. That is, if the scavengers haven't dragged off Gilmore's carcass by then."

"I hate to celebrate the death of any man, but in Billy Ray Gilmore's case, I'll make an exception."

John Henry thought that was allowable, especially when True went on to tell him that three of the guards had been killed in the fighting. That paled next to the number of casualties among the outlaws, though. Eighteen of them were dead, and the five prisoners were all wounded, three of them seriously. Those dynamite arrows of John Henry's had wreaked some serious havoc among the desperadoes.

With more than a dozen guards left to take care of the gold, John Henry figured it was safe to leave the bank. Dusk was beginning to settle over the town as he headed for the hotel. When he reached his room, he found the door open. Della was still sitting up in his bed, and Royal Bouchard was in the chair beside her, holding her hand.

"John Henry!" Della cried. "Thank God you're alive. Royal saw you from the window when you rode back into town and said that you looked like you were all right. You *are* all right, aren't you?"

John Henry grinned and said, "I'm fine. And you don't have to worry about Gilmore. He and most of his gang are dead."

"Good riddance," Bouchard said. "I can take Della back to the Silver Spur now—"

"Actually, I've been thinking," John Henry said. "It would probably be better if she wasn't moved just yet, so why don't the two of you just stay here for a few days? Meade can take care of the saloon, can't he?"

Bouchard grinned and said, "He sure can. And I can take care of Della."

"Is that what you really want, Royal?" she asked.

He didn't hesitate in nodding and saying, "It surely is." His hand tightened on hers.

"But what about you, John Henry?" Della asked. "Where will you stay?"

"I figured I'd spend the night at the bank. There's still a fortune in gold bullion over there, and my job is to protect it until Wells Fargo takes over in the morning."

Bouchard frowned and said, "You don't think anybody else is going to make a try for it, do you? Nobody else in these parts had a big enough gang but Gilmore."

"Sometimes it doesn't take a gang," John Henry said.

Three of the guards were in the bank along with John Henry that night. Fortified with good meals and several pots of coffee, they were ready to stay there until morning, when the Wells Fargo wagons would arrive. John Henry didn't really expect any trouble, but as long as the gold was here, it was a target.

He was surprised when someone knocked on the front door about ten o'clock.

Only a small lamp was burning on one of the desks. John Henry motioned for the guards to stay where they were and drew his Colt as he approached the door. The curtains were drawn over the glass in the door so nobody could look in. He flicked one of the curtains aside and looked out.

Jason True, Arnold Goodman, and Dan Lacey stood on the boardwalk, along with Marshal Hinkle and tall, spare, middle-aged Harley Smoot, the bank's head teller.

John Henry had no idea why the mine owners would be here, unless they wanted to check on the gold. That was feasible, he supposed . . . but why were Hinkle and Smoot with them?

John Henry turned the key and opened the door slightly.

"What's wrong?" he asked.

"We need to check the safe," Dan Lacey said urgently. "There's been some sort of trick. Something's been substituted for the bullion!"

"That's loco," John Henry said. "It's just not possible. The gold's been locked up in the safe all day."

"We just want to look to be sure, Marshal," Jason True said. "We brought along Mr. Smoot to open the safe. Once we've seen for ourselves that everything is all right, we won't bother you again."

"Well . . . all right." The gold belonged to them, after all, John Henry thought. He didn't see any way he could refuse to let them look at their own gold. He stepped back. . . .

Lacey lowered his shoulder and drove forward, slamming the door open so that it struck John Henry and knocked him backwards. John Henry caught his balance, but before he could raise his gun he found himself looking down the twin barrels of the sawed-off shotgun that Lacey clutched in both hands.

Hinkle had charged into the bank right behind Lacey. He leveled another shotgun he held at the guards and yelled, "Don't move!"

Wisely, the guards obeyed. At this range, the sawed-off in Hinkle's hands could sweep all of them off their feet in a deadly lead hailstorm.

True and Goodman stepped into the bank, prodded from behind by Harley Smoot, who also carried one of the shortened shotguns. John Henry knew as soon as he saw that that Gilmore's other inside man had been Smoot, not one of the guards.

"Sorry, Marshal," True said. "They forced Arnold and me to cooperate."

"Drop your gun, Sixkiller," Lacey ordered.

"What if I don't?" John Henry asked coolly.

"Then I'll blow your head off and we'll kill those guards and True and Goodman as well. I'll say that we caught you and the guards trying to steal the gold yourselves, and Jason and Arnold were killed in the crossfire before the marshal and I cut you down. Who's going to doubt me?"

John Henry knew that was true. Lacey's story was plausible enough to be believed, especially with Hinkle and Smoot to back him up.

"On the other hand," Lacey continued, "if you do what you're told, all we do is take the gold and nobody has to die."

"You'd steal your own gold?" John Henry asked.

That brought a derisive laugh from Lacey.

"What gold?" he said. "Those boxes of mine are filled with lead ingots, not gold. My mine played out months ago. I've just been biding my time, waiting to make a big haul from the other two mines. Gilmore was supposed to help me do that, but you ruined that plan. Luckily, I had something else in mind in case Gilmore failed."

"Yeah, me," Hinkle said with a note of bitterness in his voice. "I might not be too happy about you playing both sides, Lacey, if I wasn't going to come out of this a rich man."

"And in the end, that's all that matters, isn't it?" Lacey said. "So what's it going to be, Sixkiller? Are you going to be reasonable?"

Slowly, John Henry reached over and laid his Colt on a nearby desk.

"Good," Lacey said. "Back away from it. Go over there with the guards. All of you drop your guns, and be quick about it."

Facing the terrible threat of the sawed-offs, the men had no choice but to comply. They set their rifles aside and unbuckled their gun belts. At this range, the bank would look like a charnel house if those scatterguns started bellowing.

"Now we're going to put you to work," Lacey said. "There are three wagons parked in the alley out back. You'll load the boxes from the San Francisco and the El Halcón into them. Just leave the ones from the Bonita. They're not worth a damn anyway."

"You paid off your miners to go along with the sham?" John Henry asked.

"As long as they got their wages, they didn't care," Lacey snapped. "Now move. With six of you working, it won't take long to get the wagons loaded."

And when that chore was finished, Lacey, Hinkle, and Smoot would kill all of them, John Henry thought. They wouldn't want to leave witnesses behind to testify about who was really responsible for the robbery, although when the three men dropped out of sight anybody with half a brain could figure it out. In a court of law, though, there wouldn't be any evidence to convict them.

Knowing that to finish the chore would be to sign his death warrant, John Henry didn't get in any hurry to load the bullion on the wagons parked behind the bank once Smoot had opened the safe. The other guards seemed to have figured out the same thing he had, because they were dragging their feet, too. Of course, the crates containing the gold were heavy. The men couldn't move too fast with them.

Lacey grew more and more impatient. He stood beside the wagon with the scattergun leveled and said, "Hurry up, damn it! I want to be a long way from here by morning."

"You won't get away with this," True growled.

"Of course I will," Lacey said with supreme confidence.

"No, you won't. I'll hunt you down."

Lacey didn't seem bothered by that threat. He just said, "We'll see," which reinforced John Henry's conviction that the renegade mine owner didn't intend to leave any of them alive to seek vengeance on him.

He was watching for an opportunity to make a play, but so far Lacey and his confederates had been too careful. Lacey stood beside the wagons, Smoot was just outside the doorway, and Hinkle was inside at the safe.

Most of the bullion was loaded. They were working on the third wagon now. John Henry knew he would have to take a chance soon.

He got help from an unexpected source. He and one of the guards were just about to swing another crate up into the wagon bed when a voice suddenly ordered, "Drop those guns!"

Lacey whirled toward the sound. At the same time Smoot took a step out from the doorway. Smoot was closer, so John Henry swung the crate toward him. The guard caught on instantly and helped. Smoot's shotgun boomed, but the charge struck the crate instead of scattering, and an instant later the heavy crate slammed into the treacherous head teller and knocked him over backwards.

A pistol cracked and Lacey's shotgun roared almost at the same time. John Henry left his feet in a diving tackle that caught Lacey around the knees from behind and upended him. Lacey went down hard, but he kept his hold on the shotgun and twisted around to slam the weapon's butt against John Henry's shoulder. John Henry gasped but got his other hand on the shotgun's cut-down barrels. He thrust them skyward as Lacey triggered the other load.

Lacey let go of the now empty shotgun and slashed a punch across John Henry's face. He heaved his body upward and threw the federal lawman to the side.

Hinkle rushed out into the alley through the bank's rear door and swung his shotgun toward John Henry. With John Henry and Lacey so close together the blast would probably kill the mine owner as well, but Hinkle was obviously panic-stricken and ready to pull the triggers.

Shots cracked from both sides of him, making him stumble. The shotgun's barrels sagged. Two more shots split the night, and Hinkle fell, jerking the triggers as he collapsed. The double load of buckshot blew both of his feet off, but he was beyond caring. He hit the ground with a soggy thud.

Lacey lunged at John Henry and grabbed the empty shotgun again. He forced it down against John Henry's throat in an attempt to crush his windpipe. John Henry had both hands on the shotgun, too, and he held it off as Lacey bore down on it. For long, desperate seconds, the two men struggled. Then Lacey's muscles abruptly weakened, and John Henry grunted with effort as he shoved the gun upward. The stock crashed into Lacey's jaw. John Henry felt bone shatter under the impact. Lacey toppled to the side, moaning.

John Henry figured all the fight had gone out of Lacey with that broken jaw. The trouble might not be over, though. The next moment a match rasped and a lantern sputtered to life. Doc Mitchum held the lantern high, and the glow it spread over the alley revealed not only the revolver in his other hand but also the pistol held firmly in the grasp of Sophie Clearwater as she stepped forward.

"Don't try to get up, Mr. Lacey," Sophie ordered. "I'd hate to have to kill you because I want to see you behind bars, but I will if I have to."

Realization burst on John Henry like an artillery shell. He looked up at Sophie and said, "You're law."

A faint smile curved her red lips.

"Not the same sort as you, Marshal," she said. "Doc and I work for Wells Fargo. We were sent ahead to make sure the gold stays safe until our wagons get here for it. But when we found out a deputy U.S. marshal was on the job, too, we figured we'd let you do most of the work for us."

John Henry grabbed hold of a wagon wheel and hoisted himself to his feet.

"You knew I was a lawman?" he asked.

"Not all the time. We just got word yesterday. You may not be well known in New Mexico Territory,

Marshal, but you sure are back in Indian Territory, and Wells Fargo has contacts all over the country."

John Henry looked over at Mitchum and asked, "Was that you who made the shot from the hotel that killed Rankin?"

"That big bruiser about to wade into you with a bowie?" Doc asked with a chuckle. "No, that was Sophie. She's a crack shot with a rifle, too."

John Henry turned his gaze back to the lovely brunette and said, "You're just full of surprises, aren't you, Miss Clearwater?"

"Life's more interesting that way, wouldn't you say, Marshal Sixkiller?" she asked right back at him.

She had a point there, John Henry thought.

Marshal Henry Hinkle was dead, and so was Harley Smoot. The crate full of gold bullion had landed on Smoot's chest when he fell, and it was heavy enough so that several of his ribs had fractured under the impact. The sharp end of one of them had skewered his heart.

That left Dan Lacey as the only one of the plotters still alive. He would live to stand trial, and since his scheming had cost a number of innocent men their lives, John Henry thought there was a good chance Lacey would spend a long, long time behind bars, where he deserved to be.

The armored, heavily guarded Wells Fargo wagons rolled out of Purgatory the next day, bound for Lordsburg with the $50,000 worth of bullion from the mines belonging to Jason True and Arnold Goodman. John Henry was glad to see them go.

His job here was over, so he stopped by the hotel to say so long to Della and Bouchard before he pulled out. He shook hands with the saloon keeper and kissed Della on the forehead.

"The two of you take care of each other," he told them.

"I think that's just what we'll be doing from here on out," Bouchard said with a broad smile.

"Royal insists I'm going to retire," Della said. "I'm willing to go along with that as long as he'll still let me hang around the saloon and look pretty."

"No one's more qualified for that job than you are, my dear," Bouchard told her.

"I'm pretty good when it comes to dealing cards, too, so I might work at that. I don't want life to get too settled and boring."

"Not much chance of that in a town called Purgatory," John Henry said with a grin.

He said his farewells and went downstairs, and when he reached the hotel lobby he was surprised to see Sophie Clearwater sitting in one of the chairs. She stood up and came toward him.

"I thought you and Doc left with the gold wagons," John Henry told her.

"Doc did. I told him I'd meet him in El Paso. I was hoping you and I could travel that far together."

"That's a nice idea," John Henry said, "but I'm

not taking the stagecoach back to Lordsburg. I've got my horse with me."

"I can get a horse," Sophie said. "I'm a very good rider, you know."

John Henry chuckled and said, "Somehow that doesn't surprise me. I don't think it would do your reputation much good to spend a couple of nights on the trail with a man you're not married to, though."

"I'm a lady detective. I don't have much of a reputation to start with, Marshal . . . or should I call you John Henry?"

He thought about it for a second, then reached a decision. He hoped he wasn't being too disloyal to Sasha back in Indian Territory when he smiled and said, "Well, if we're going to be traveling together, I reckon you'd better call me John Henry."

Turn the page for an exciting preview!

The families Jensen and MacCallister are two of the most legendary clans in frontier fiction. Now, the USA Today *bestselling authors of* A Lone Star Christmas *bring them together once more—in a gripping tale of tragedy, survival, love, betrayal, and maybe even a miracle. . . .*

Three days before Christmas, Matt Jensen is traveling the Denver and Pacific railway when an avalanche slams down onto the train, trapping it in desolate Trout Creek Pass. But it wasn't an act of nature that caused the accident; it was a gang of outlaws attempting to rescue their leader, who is being taken to Red Cliff to be hanged.

As Smoke Jensen and Duff MacCallister frantically try to make their way to the scene, Matt struggles to save the survivors, among them a beautiful young woman with a dark past, a merchant seaman turned rancher, and a senator with his very ill young daughter. Starving under a bitter, driving snow in the brutal, unforgiving Rocky Mountains, and surrounded by armed and desperate outlaws, Matt still dreams of making it home for Christmas. But unless fate lends a hand, nobody will.

A ROCKY MOUNTAIN CHRISTMAS
by William W. Johnstone
with J. A. Johnstone

On sale November 2012 wherever
Kensington Books are sold.

Prologue

Rebecca Daniels Robison awaited her flight in the comfort of the Admiral's lounge. A huge Christmas tree sparkled with blinking lights and shining ornaments, and Christmas music played softly over the lounge speakers. Rebecca was reading the newspaper when she was approached by a very attractive young woman.

"Ambassador Robison? My name is Margaret Chambers, and I'm a reporter for the *St. Louis Globe-Democrat.* I wonder if you would consent to an interview?"

"Why would you want to interview me, dear? I'm no longer an ambassador."

"No, but you are still active on the international scene, and a recent poll put you as the country's most admired woman."

"Nonsense, my dear. Eleanor Roosevelt is the most admired woman."

Margaret laughed. "You came in second, and Mrs. Roosevelt doesn't count. She's been the most admired woman for the last thirteen years."

"And rightly so," Rebecca said. "She has certainly been most gracious to me, over the years."

"Attention passengers, all flights are on temporary hold until the runways can be cleared of snow."

"I was about to say that there wouldn't be time for an interview," Rebecca said. "But it appears that my flight has been delayed, so I would be happy to talk to you. I suppose you want to hear about my time as ambassador to Greece."

"No, ma'am," Margaret said. "I'm doing a story for our special Christmas edition. I understand that you once had a most harrowing Christmas experience when you were a child."

"Harrowing? Yes, I suppose it was, though that's not exactly the word I would use. But it was also the most uplifting experience of my life."

"Could you share that story with our readers?"

"How much do you know about that incident?" Rebecca asked.

"Hardly anything—just that you've been very reluctant to discuss it all these years and that you've turned down every request for it. Your father was a U.S. senator then. . . ."

"A state senator in Colorado," Rebecca corrected her.

"Yes, thank you. According to what little information exists, you and your family were on a train going from Pueblo to Red Cliff, Colorado, during a blizzard."

"That's correct," Rebecca said. "But that is only part of the story. If I told you everything, I'm afraid you would have a very difficult time believing it. Which is why I have never told the story before."

Margaret held her little narrow reporter's pad on her knee, and raised her pencil, poised to take notes. "Why don't you try me? I would love to hear the entire story," she said.

"Margaret, is it?"

"Yes ma'am."

"Well, since my plane is delayed, Margaret, I will tell you the whole story of that Christmas so long ago. I'm eighty years old now, and I don't much care if people think I'm a crazy old lady or not. I guess now is as good a time as any to finally tell it."

"Thank you, Ambassador Robison."

"Let's sit down, Margaret. And please, no questions until I am done."

Chapter One

The *Delta Mist* was moored to the bank, running parallel with Tchoupitoulas Street. Matt Jensen showed his ticket to the purser, then boarded the vessel. Instead of going directly to his stateroom, Matt stood along the rail of the Texas deck, looking back toward the city of New Orleans, at the flower-bedecked ironwork trellises and balconies, and the belles of New Orleans strolling the streets in butterfly bright dresses under colorful parasols.

Of all the cities Matt had ever visited, New Orleans was one of the most remarkable. Although it was an American city, it retained much of its French heritage, and although it was a Southern city, it had its own unique culture, making it stand apart from all the other cities of the South. From the city wafted the aromas of food, flowers, and a "perfume" that was distinctive only to New Orleans. From a river- front bar on Tchoupitoulas Street came the sound of music, interspersed with the loud guffaws of the men, and the high trills of the women laughing.

The captain of the boat was standing on the lower deck, frequently pulling out his pocket watch to check the time. It was obvious that he was waiting for someone, and whoever it was was late, contributing to an increasing agitation.

Then Matt saw a cab approaching the river, the horse in a rapid trot. The cab pulled to a stop at the river's edge and a woman got out, handed a bill to the driver, then hurried across the gangplank and onto the boat.

"Uncle, I'm so sorry. I was shopping and I lost track of the time," the woman said.

"Jenny, I can't hold up the entire boat because my niece can't keep track of the time," the captain said.

From here, Matt was able to examine the woman rather closely. She was an exceptionally pretty woman with red hair, a peaches-and-cream complexion, blue eyes, and prominent cheekbones. If one had asked her about her lips, she might suggest that they were, perhaps, a bit too full.

"Mr. Peabody!" the captain called.

"Aye, sir," one of the other officers answered.

"Away all lines, pull in the gangplank."

Matt maintained his position at the rail on the Texas deck, watching as the boat crew performed the ordered tasks. Captain Lee had, by now, reached the wheelhouse and once the boat was free of its restraints, a signal was sent to the engine room. Smoke belched from the twin, fluted chimneys, and the stern wheel began to turn, pushing the boat away from the bank and out into the middle of the Mississippi River. They turned upstream, and the great red-and-yellow paddle wheel began spinning rapidly, leaving behind the boat a long, frothing wake.

Off Memphis—July 11, 1889

Jenny Lee worked for her uncle as a hostess in the Grand Salon of the *Delta Mist,* a packet boat that made the run between St. Louis and New Orleans. Over the last two days, the boat had been averaging 12 miles per hour and was now just approaching Memphis, which was 704 miles, by river, from New Orleans. Jenny was passing pleasantries with some of the passengers, when a loud, angry voice got the attention of everyone in the salon.

"No man is that lucky! You have to be cheating!" a man shouted angrily.

The speaker was standing at one of the tables, and the object of his anger and the subject of his charge was Matt Jensen. Matt was sitting across the table from him, and unlike the angry man, Matt's composure was calm.

Not so for the other two players who, at the outburst, had stood up and backed away from the table so quickly that they knocked over their chairs.

For a long moment there was absolute silence in the Grand Salon, with nothing to be heard but the sound of the engine, the slap of the stern paddle, and the whisper of water rushing by the keel.

"Mister, nobody cheats me and gets away with it," the man said, addressing his hostility toward Matt.

"You're out of line, Holman," Dr. Gunter, one of the other players, said. "Nobody has been cheating at this table."

"The hell there ain't nobody been cheatin'! I ain't won a hand in the last hour. And he's won the most of 'em." Holman reached for the money that was piled up in the middle of the table. "I'm just goin' to take this pot to make up for it."

"That's not your pot," the other player said. This was Jay Miller, a lawyer from St. Louis.

"Yeah? Well, we'll just see whose pot it is," Holman said contemptuously as he started to put the money in his hat.

"Leave the money on the table, Holman," Matt said. Those were the first words he had spoken since the challenge.

"The hell I will. This money is mine, and I'm takin' it with me."

Jenny hurried over to the table then.

"Mr. Holman, please," she said. "You are creating a disturbance, and your behavior is making the passengers uneasy."

"Yeah? Well, to hell with the passengers. What kind of boat is this, anyway, that you allow cheaters in the games?"

"I wasn't cheating," Matt said.

"Mr. Jensen is tellin' the truth, Miss Lee," Dr.

Gunter said, pointing toward Matt. "He wasn't cheatin'."

"What do you say, Mr. Miller?" Jenny asked the third man.

"I've played a lot of cards in my day, and I think I can tell when someone is cheating. I don't believe he was."

Jenny looked back at the angry gambler. "These gentlemen don't agree with you."

"Of course, they don't. They are probably in on it. I wouldn't be surprised if they didn't all get together later on and divide up the money. *My* money. And like I said, I'll be taking this pot."

"Miss Lee, I've played cards with Mr. Jensen," a passenger who wasn't currently in the game said. He pointed at Matt. "I've never known him to be anything but honest."

"Same here," another put in. "I wasn't in this game, but I've played a few hands with him since we left New Orleans, and I found him to be an honest man. And if these two gentlemen, who were in the game, say he wasn't cheating, then I would be inclined to believe them."

"Mr. Holman, that makes four people who say that Mr. Jensen wasn't cheating. When you play cards for money, you are accepting the possibility of losing. The only thing that protects the game is the honesty, integrity, and the honor of the players."

"You!" Holman said, pointing at Jenny. "You are in it, too, aren't you? You are all in it together."

"Look. We were in the same game as you. You

think we would take up for him if he was cheating? Hell, we lost money, too," Miller said.

"Yeah, well, neither one of you lost as much money as I did."

"That's because neither of them is as bad at cards as you are," Matt said.

"What do you mean, I'm a bad player? Why, I'm as good at cards as any man."

"No, you aren't," Matt insisted. "You can't run a bluff, you raise bets in games of stud when the cards you have showing prove you are beaten. You should find some other game of chance, and give up poker."

Jenny turned to Matt. "Mr. Jensen, I believe the pot is yours." She reached for the money to slide it across the table toward Matt, but Holman pushed her back away from the table so hard that she fell.

He pointed down at her. "Keep your hands off my money. Like I said, I'm takin' this pot, and there's nobody here who can stop me."

Matt and another passenger helped Jenny get up.

"Thank you for interceding, Miss Lee," Matt said. "But I think you had better let me handle this now."

"Ha!" the angry gambler said. "You are going to handle this? What do you plan to do?"

"Oh, I'll do whatever it takes," Matt said.

Matt's calm, almost expressionless reply, surprised the angry man and the shock showed in his face. Then the shock was replaced by an evil smile. He stepped away from the table, and flipped his jacket back, showing an ivory-handled pistol in a tooled-leather holster.

"Mister, maybe it's time that I tell you who I am. My name ain't John Holman like I been sayin'. My actual name is Quince Justin Holmes, only some folks call me Quick Justice Holmes because I tend to make my own justice, if you know what I mean."

"Quick Justice Holmes?" one of the other passengers said in awe. "That's Quick Justice?"

"This is gettin' downright dangerous," another said.

"What do you say now?" Holmes asked.

"I say the same thing I've been saying. You aren't getting that pot," Matt said, resolutely.

"It won't matter none to you whether I get the pot or not, 'cause you ain't goin' to be around to see it," Holmes said, his voice menacing.

"Does this mean you are inviting me to the dance?" Matt asked.

Holmes laughed. "Yeah, you might say that. I'll even let you make the first move."

Despite his offer, Holmes's hand was already dipping for his pistol, even as he was speaking. He smiled as he realized that his draw had caught Matt by surprise. But the smile left his face when he saw Matt's draw.

To the witnesses, it appeared that Matt and Holmes fired at the same time. But in actuality, Matt had fired just a split second sooner than Holmes and the impact of his bullet took Holmes off his aim. Holmes's bullet whizzed by Matt's ear, then punched through the glass of one of the windows of the Grand Salon.

"I'll be damn! I've been kilt!" Holmes said as he staggered back from the blow of the bullet.

"You could have prevented it at any time," Matt said.

Holmes dropped his gun and clamped his hand over the wound in his chest. Blood spilled through his fingers, and he opened his hand to look at it before he collapsed.

Matt returned his pistol to his holster. Looking over toward Jenny, he saw a horrified expression on her face.

"I'm sorry about this, Miss Lee," he said.

"No," Jenny replied in a small voice. "You—had no choice."

Because the shooting happened just off Memphis, the boat put in there, and a coroner's inquest was held. There were enough witnesses who testified that Quince Justin Holmes had instigated the shooting incident that the hearing concluded: *Quince Justin Holmes died as a result of a .44 ball which was energized to terrible effect by a pistol held by Matthew Jensen. This hearing concludes that Mr. Jensen was put in danger of his life when Holmes drew and fired at him. It is the finding of this hearing that this was a case of justifiable homicide, and no charges are to be filed against Mr. Jensen.*

The hearing took less than an hour, and Matt was welcomed back aboard the *Delta Mist* by those who had witnessed the shooting, as well as those who had only heard about it. Matt apologized to the boat captain for having been involved in the incident.

"Nonsense," Captain Lee replied. "Why, you've made the *Delta Mist* famous. People will be wanting to take the boat where the infamous Quick Justice Holmes was killed. To say nothing of the fact that he was killed by Matt Jensen. You are truly one of America's best-known shootists, as well known for your honesty and goodness of heart, as you are for your prowess with a pistol."

"Hear, hear!" someone called, and the others cheered and applauded.

For the next 575 miles, the distance by river from Memphis to St. Louis, passengers vied for the opportunity to visit with Matt, or better, to play poker with him. Matt's luck wasn't always as good as it had been for the first 705 miles from New Orleans to Memphis, so that by the time the boat docked up against the riverbank in the Gateway City, Matt had no more money with him than he had when he left New Orleans.

Jenny Lee was standing by the gangplank, telling the passengers good-bye as they left the boat, and thanking them for choosing the *Delta Mist*.

"Mr. Jensen, I do hope you travel with us again. You managed to make this trip"—Jenny paused in mid-sentence and smiled broadly—"most interesting."

"Perhaps a little too interesting," Matt suggested as he took the hand she had offered him.

Chapter Two

The ship was the *American Eagle*, a four-masted clipper in the Pacific trade. As much canvas as could be spread gleamed a brilliant white in the sunshine, and the ship was lifting, falling, and rolling from side to side, as it plowed over the long, rolling swells of the Pacific. The propelling wind, spilling from the sails, emitted a soft, whispering sigh.

The helmsman stood at the wheel, his legs slightly spread as he held the ship on its course. Working sailors were moving about the deck, tightening a line here, loosening one there, providing the exact tension on the rigging, and angle on the sheets to maintain maximum speed. Some sailors were holystoning the deck, while others were manning the bilge pumps.

The ship was heeling from the wind and Luke Shardeen, the first officer, was standing on the leeward side on the quarterdeck, his hands resting lightly on the railing. He examined the barometer for the third time in the last thirty minutes. There was no doubt that it was falling, and that could only presage bad weather. Leaving the quarterdeck, he tapped on the door of the captain's cabin.

"Yes?" the captain called.

"Captain, permission to enter?" Luke called.

"Come in, Mr. Shardeen."

Luke stepped into the captain's cabin, which was as large as all the other officers' quarters combined. Captain Cutter was bent over the chart table with a compass and protractor.

"Captain, the barometer has fallen rather significantly in the last half hour. I've no doubt but that a storm is coming."

"Do you have any idea how fast we are going, Mr. Shardeen?"

"It would only be a guess."

"We are doing nineteen knots, Mr. Shardeen. Nineteen knots," Captain Cutter said. "It's my belief that if we can maintain this pace, we'll outrun the storm."

"We won't be able to maintain this pace, Captain, if we rig the storm sails."

"I have no intention of rigging the storm sails," Captain Cutter said. "Certainly not until it is an absolute necessity."

"Very good, Captain," Luke said, as he withdrew from the captain's cabin.

"Mr. Shardeen," the bo'sun said when Luke returned to the quarterdeck. "Will we be taking in the sail, sir?"

Luke shook his head. "Not yet."

Luke looked out over the water. The sea was no longer blue, but dirty gray, and swirling with white caps. This kind of sea was referred to by the sailors as "green water," and it was so rough they dropped off in a trough and took green water over the entire deck as they started back up.

Then the storm was on them, with wind and rain so heavy that it was impossible to distinguish the rain from the spindrift.

"Captain, we have to strike sail!" Luke shouted above the noise of the gale.

"Aye, do so," Captain Cutter agreed, and Luke sent men aloft to strike sail, praying that no one would be tossed off by the bucking ship. They managed to strip the masts of all canvas without losing anyone, but the storm continued to build until by mid-morning, it was a full-blown typhoon. Fifteen-foot-high waves crashed against the side of the two-hundred-ten-foot-long ship, and the *American Eagle* was in imminent danger of foundering.

"Captain, we have to head her into the wind!" Luke Shardeen, shouted.

"No, even without sail we're still making headway," Captain Cutter shouted back.

"If we don't do it, we'll likely lose the ship!"

"I'm the captain of this vessel, Mr. Shardeen. And as long as I am captain, we'll sail the course I've set for her."

"Aye, aye, sir."

The huge waves continued to crash against the side of the ship and the rolling steepened, once going over as far as forty-five degrees to starboard where it hung for so long that there was the sure and certain fear that it would continue to roll to starboard until it capsized.

"Everyone to port side!" Luke shouted through the megaphone and, though the sailors found it difficult to climb up the slanted deck, they did so, their combined weight helping to bring the ship back from the brink of disaster.

Belowdecks in the mess, cabinet doors swung open and plates, cups, and bowls fell to the floor. The dishes slid back and forth, crashing against the starboard. Then when the ship rolled back, they tumbled to port, breaking into smaller and smaller shards as they did so until there was nothing left but a jumbled collection of bits and pieces of what had once been the ship's crockery.

Above deck the yardarms were free of sail except for the spanker sail, which had been left rigged, and was now no more than tattered strips of canvas, flapping ineffectively in the ninety-mile-per-hour wind.

Captain Cutter was standing on the quarterdeck when a huge wave burst over the side of the ship. The captain and three sailors were swept off the deck, into the sea.

"Cap'n overboard!" someone shouted, and Luke ordered the helmsman to turn into the wind. That kept them in place and stopped the terrible rolling of the ship, which began to pitch up, then down, by forty-five degrees. Luke put the men to the rails to search for those who had been washed overboard. They found and recovered two of the sailors, but there was no sign of the third sailor, or the captain.

By late afternoon, the storm had abated, and Luke ordered the ship to remain in place to continue the search. For the next two days, in calm winds and a placid sea, they searched for the captain and the missing sailor, but found no sign of either of them. Finally, Luke ordered the ship to continue on its original course. They raised San Francisco twenty-three days later.

They were met in the bay by a tugboat which shot a line up to them to be made fast, and, with all sail gone, they were towed into the bay and up to the docks where they dropped anchor. As soon as the ship was made fast by large hawsers, a ladder was lowered for the officers, and a gangplank to be used by the men to offload their cargo of tea.

Luke sat in the outer office of the headquarters for the Pacific Shipping Company. The walls were decorated with lithographs of the company's ships, including one of the *American Eagle*. Beside each ship was a photograph of the captain, and Emile Cutter's face, stern and dignified looking in his white beard, was alongside the picture of the ship Luke had just left.

"Captain Shardeen, Mr. Buckner will see you now," a clerk said.

Luke wasn't a captain, but he assumed the clerk either didn't know that, or had called him captain because he had assumed command of the ship to bring it home.

Although Richard Buckner had become a millionaire from his shipping empire, he had never been to sea. Nevertheless, his office was a nautical showplace, replete with model ships, polished bells engraved with the names of the ships from which they came, and the complete reconstruction of a helm, with wheel and compass.

Buckner was a man of average height, but in comparison to Luke Shardeen's six-foot, four-inch frame, he seemed short. He greeted Luke with an extended hand.

"Mr. Shardeen, you are to be congratulated, sir, for an excellent job of bringing the ship back safely. Please, tell me what happened."

Luke told about the storm, and how a huge wave hit them broadside, washing over the captain and three other sailors. Luke made no mention of the argument he had with Captain Cutter about bringing the ship into the wind.

"We rescued two of the sailors right away, and we stayed on station for two days, but we never found Captain Cutter or Seaman Bostic."

"Thank you. I'm sure that Mrs. Cutter will be comforted to know exactly what happened, and will be grateful for the effort the entire ship showed in trying to rescue her husband."

"I wish we had been successful."

"Yes, well, such things are in the hands of God. Now, Mr. Shardeen, if you would, there are some reports we will need for you to fill out. And after you are done with the reports, please come back into the office. I have something I want to discuss with you."

"Aye, sir," Luke said. He normally didn't use "aye" except when he was at sea, but he knew that Buckner enjoyed being addressed in such a manner.

As he was filling out the reports, he was given a stack of letters that had been held for him until the ship's return. One of them was from a lawyer's office in Pueblo, Colorado. Luke had never been to Pueblo, Colorado, and as far as he was aware, didn't know anyone there. He wondered then why he would be the recipient of a letter from a Pueblo lawyer. His curiosity was such that he interrupted the paperwork in order to read the letter.

Dear Mr. Shardeen:

It is with sadness that I report to you the death of your Uncle Frank Shardeen Luke, who passed away on the 5th of August instant, from an infirmity of the heart.

As you were his only living relative, you are the sole beneficiary of his will, in which he leaves you the following items:

18,000 acres of land
A four-room house
All the furniture therein
A bunkhouse
A barn
1500 head of cattle
20 horses with saddles and tack
$1017.56 (remaining after all final expenses)

In order to claim your inheritance, you must present yourself at the Pueblo courthouse on, or before, November 1st, 1890.

> *Sincerely,*
> *Tom Murchison*
> *Attorney at Law*

The letter came as a complete surprise. He had not seen his Uncle Frank in over ten years, and had no idea that he lived in Colorado, or that he even had anything valuable enough to leave in a will.

And, Uncle Frank left everything to him! He felt conflicting emotions of elation and guilt—elation over what appeared to be a rather substantial inheritance, and guilt because he had not only not seen his Uncle Frank in the last ten years, he had only corresponded with him three or four times in all that time.

When he was finished with the paperwork, he returned to Mr. Buckner's office as requested.

"Mr. Shardeen," Buckner said. "With the unfortunate death of Captain Cutter, we are going to have to find a new captain for the *American Eagle*. You know the ship and the men, and you brought her successfully through a terrible storm. I would like for you to be her new captain."

Had this offer been made to Luke one month earlier—or even one hour earlier—he would have accepted it immediately. But the letter from Tom Murchison changed all that.

"I thank you for the offer, Mr. Buckner. I am extremely flattered by it," Luke said. He took a deep breath before plunging on. "But I believe I will leave the sea for a while. I'll be submitting my resignation today."

"What?" Buckner replied in shocked surprise. "You can't be serious! Mr. Shardeen, this is the opportunity of a lifetime. How can you possibly pass it up?"

"Simple. Until today, I had no anchor. But now"—Luke held up his letter—"now I am a man of property, and I can no longer afford to sail all over the world."

"Are you absolutely positive of that? Because if you are, then we will have to promote someone else to captain."

"I am positive."

"Very well. The company will hate to lose you, Mr. Shardeen. You have been a good officer. If ever you wish to return to the sea, please, come see us first."

"I will do so," Luke promised.